FINDING A MIRACLE

Deborah Flitcroft

This is a work of fiction. Names, characters, places, and incidents either are the product of the author's imagination or are used fictitiously. Any resemblance to actual persons, living or dead, events, or locales is entirely coincidental.

Copyright © Deborah Flitcroft 2024

The moral right of Deborah Flitcroft to be identified as the creator of this work has been asserted in accordance with the Copyright, Designs and Patents Act, 1988.

All rights reserved. No part of this book may be reproduced or used in any manner without written permission of the copyright owner except for the use of quotations in a book review. For more information, address: dcflitcroft@gmail.com

First paperback edition April 2024

ISBN (paperback): 979-8-880234-29-5

X @dcflitcroft
Instagram @debflitcroft
Facebook Deborah Flitcroft Writer

For Stu, my North Star.

Chapter One

It had felt like a long week, and Melissa Jones was rather pleased it was Friday. Not because she had any wildly exciting plans but because she fully intended to relax, unwind and do as little as possible this weekend. As she slowly massaged her temples, she let out a weary sigh. Right now, a couple of days spent at home, mainly in her pyjamas, taking extra-long bubble baths and binge-watching a box set, sounded ideal. The addition of a few G&Ts and some chocolate would make it even better. Mel's week had dragged because she'd had late evenings at work every night catching up on admin tasks and outcome reports. She had put them off to the point where she was out of time and excuses. Her role as the lead training facilitator of a charity that supported carers meant that most of her time at work was spent in her group room, where she delivered her workshops. Mel was, however, obliged to provide feedback to show their effectiveness to satisfy the funders and ensure the long-term survival of the charity. That was the only part of the job she resented, and it was because it took her away from doing the work that mattered and was closest to her heart.

With the paperwork finally complete, Mel was tidying her desk and packing up for the week when her friend Cat appeared at her office door. Catherine 'Cat' Richards was the Children and Young Persons' lead of the organization. Cat joined the charity a few years previously, and the two had quickly become firm friends, even though Mel was old enough to be her mother.

'What are you up to at the weekend, Mel? Got anything nice planned, pet?' Cat asked in her soft Geordie lilt. She plonked herself down on the chair near Mel's desk.

'Not really. I'll be doing a whole lot of sod all tonight, and I can't bloody wait, love! I might venture beyond my front door and go for a walk on Sunday though, if it's nice out. I'm just looking forward to having a quiet weekend to recharge my batteries after this week.'

'Is "go for a walk on Sunday" code for popping to the Red Lion for a few drinks by any chance?' Cat winked.

Mel laughed. 'I will neither confirm nor deny, my darling! What about you? Doing anything nice?'

'Thought as much! I'm having a quiet one tonight, too. I think we'll probably get a takeaway and maybe have a few drinks. Not sure about the rest of the weekend yet. I'm waiting for Mike to tell me what he's doing. He mentioned going to the gym and watching football.' Cat rolled her eyes and sighed. 'He's never away from the bloody gym lately, but I'm still waiting for the Jason Momoa transformation! I'm beginning to think he's wasting his time; He's not even close, but don't tell him I said that!'

'Well, Cat, why not make your own plans for tomorrow and arrange to go for Sunday lunch with Mike

CHAPTER ONE

the following day? It's not fair to put your life on hold for a Jason Momoa wannabe or anyone else, for that matter! You've got to make the most of the weekend, especially at your age. Ha! Says the old fart that has a date with her dressing gown and sofa!' said Mel with a big smile. She hated to see the look of disappointed resignation on Cat's face. At thirty-two, she was *way* too young to settle, so Mel had felt the urge to encourage her not to wait around for a man. She had done that herself in the past and knew how miserable it felt. *If it's like this now, what will it be like when she's fifty-two like I am*, Mel wondered. She felt like her friend deserved a lot better than how Mike seemed to treat her lately.

'*You* are far from an old fart, Mel! Old farts don't wear bright red lippy or Alexander McQueen skull scarves! You're right about one thing, though. I shouldn't sit around waiting for Mike all day, so I'll make my own plans. Thanks for the pep talk. Now, give me a cwtch before I go, pet!' she demanded.

After gathering her things, Mel too, headed for home. She felt at least half of the week's stresses leave her as her faithful Nissan Micra turned down the high street of her small Welsh village, past the Red Lion, then took a sharp left down a blink-and-you'd-miss-it single-track lane. At the end was a cul-de-sac of seven Victorian houses laid out in a horseshoe formation. The houses on Harlech Close all looked over a grassy area that had an ornate wrought iron fence around it. 'The Green', as it was known to the occupants of the seven households surrounding it, contained three benches and a rather beautiful holly tree. Just to the right of the gate outside the Green was a post box. Between them, Andrea, in number five, and Suzanne, in number six, kept the post box decorated for most of the year with a variety of creative displays. Last Christmas, it was decorated within an inch of its life, transformed into a Mrs Claus with a variety of crochet, knitting, felt, and tinsel. It wouldn't be long before they would be decorating it for Christmas again, thought Mel. Buying number one Harlech Close was one of the best decisions Mel had ever made, and today was one of those days she appreciated it just that little bit more. She parked her little red car outside her house and then dashed up the three steps to her front door to get out of the rain that had just begun to fall.

Once inside, she felt the warmth of home greet her instantly like the arms of a loved one. It was a bleakly cold late November evening, and Mel was relieved to be able to shed her thick coat, hand-knitted scarf (courtesy of the lovely Suzanne from number six), her beloved Doc Martens, and cosy up for the night. She padded down the hallway in her socked feet and into the kitchen. It was time for a big mug of tea before she thought about what she would eat for dinner. After filling the kettle and switching it on, Mel took a seat at the kitchen table that overlooked her back garden. The rain was heavy now, and Mel was almost hypnotised watching it stream down the window in little waterfalls. The spell was broken by the rumbling sound of the kettle switching itself off after it had boiled. Just as it did, Mel's mobile started ringing. Her phone was still in her bag, so she rooted around and retrieved it. She really *must* sort her bag out, she thought for about the third time that week. She saw her dad's name on the screen as she answered the call.

CHAPTER ONE

'Hiya,' said Mel, trying to sound brighter and more awake than she felt.

'Hiya, love. It's your dad, it is.' Mel smiled. He said the same thing *every* time he rang her. She had told him several times that his name came up on the screen when he phoned and that he didn't need to announce himself. At seventy-seven, her dad, John, was unlikely to break this habit, and Mel had long since given up explaining it to him. Instead, she just accepted this was one of his many dad-isms.

'I just thought I'd give you a ring to find out what time you're coming round tomorrow, love.'

'Tomorrow?'

'Yeah, do you remember we planned to go through your nan's things we've had stored in your old bedroom? Judging by the sound of things it slipped your mind.'

'Guilty as charged, Pops. I've had a bit of a tiring week, and it absolutely had slipped my mind, sorry.'

'Good job I phoned then! How does ten o'clock sound?'

Mel took a couple of seconds to reply. She badly wanted a lie-in the following morning and to just have a rest day. John sensed his daughter's hesitation.

'What's up, Mellie Adelie? Everything okay?' John had adopted several pet names for his daughter over the years, and this was just one of them. It was also one that had firmly stuck. He called her 'Adelie' after watching a documentary about penguins of the same name. They were deemed to be the feistiest of all penguins despite their diminutive stature. John figured if his only child had a spirit animal, it would, without any doubt, be an Adelie! At a mere five foot two and a bit, her height did not reflect the spark contained within. Besides, it rhymed nicely.

'Oh, I'm fine, Dad, just a bit tired, that's all.'

'Ah, bless you. Tell you what, how about I make you breakfast in the morning before we get started, eh? We really *do* need to deal with the last of your nan's stuff, love. Let's at least make a bit of a start tomorrow, shall we? It's been a couple of years, and we can't avoid it forever.'

Avoiding it forever was exactly what Mel had been subconsciously hoping to do. Her nan, Lizzie Roberts, had been a *huge* part of her life, and going through the last of her belongings was going to be emotional. She'd had enough trouble bagging up her nan's clothes after she passed away, and the things that were left to sort out were likely to be way more of a challenge. She knew her dad was right; she had been avoiding it and had changed the subject a few times over the past year or so when he had suggested they sort things out. She also realised that it wasn't fair to her dad to use her old bedroom in his house as a storage facility for his late mother-in-law's possessions. Thinking about it made her feel suitably guilty. She felt her cheeks sting and redden slightly.

'Ten o'clock it is, Dad. Only on the condition you make me poached eggs on toast, though,' Mel insisted playfully. Nobody made poached eggs on toast like her dad.

CHAPTER ONE

'Course I will. It's the breakfast of champions! Now, have yourself an early night, you sound shattered. See you in the morning, love.'

Mel decided to scrap the idea of tea as its appeal had vanished about as quickly as her Saturday morning lie-in. It now felt like more of a gin and tonic moment. She poured herself what could only be described as a generous measure of Hernö with plenty of tonic water and ice. As she carried her drink through to the lounge, she felt comforted by the familiar fizzing sound coming from her glass and felt a tiny explosion of bubbles tickle her hand. She switched on her table lamp, sat down on her tall-backed reading chair, and took a thirsty gulp. Thinking about sorting out the remainder of her nan's things brought back memories of when she and Lizzie had helped sort out Mel's mother's belongings after she'd passed away more than thirty years ago. Mel's mother, Anne, died when Mel had just turned seventeen. She'd had a short battle with cancer, which was already in advanced stages when it was diagnosed. It came as a huge shock to their little family and was a truly terrible time. Lizzie had come to stay at their house for a while. Looking after them had helped her to deal with the death of her only child. It had given Lizzie a sense of purpose, knowing that it was just what Anne would have wanted. It may have been over thirty years ago, but it was still fresh in Mel's mind, nonetheless. She had been very close to her mother and her passing at such a young age had made Mel grow up quickly. She'd often hid her own grief because she wanted to protect her dad and nan, as they were also naturally devastated at the loss of her mother. Losing Lizzie was like losing a second mother because, effectively, that was exactly what she had been. She and Mel were like two peas in a pod and as thick as thieves before Anne died, but this only intensified afterwards. Lizzie had left everything to Mel in her Will, including her home. With help from her dad and a few friends, they'd removed all the furniture and taken most of Lizzie's clothes to a charity shop in preparation for the sale of the house. The remaining personal effects were taken to Mel's dad's house because Mel had been having some renovation work done at the time.

Just as Mel drained the last of the gin in her glass and was about to get up and pour another, the doorbell rang insistently. Neither expecting nor wanting visitors, Mel muttered to herself as she walked down the passageway. As soon as she opened the door, Olivia, her neighbour from number four, barged her way in, her arms full carrying a box in front of her.

'Hurry up, woman, out of the way, it's pissing down out in case you hadn't noticed.'

'And good evening to you too, Liv; please do come in!' Mel said playfully as she stood aside to let her pass and watched her walk straight to the kitchen. Olivia, or Liv as she was more commonly known, was one of Mel's favourite people on the planet. It was never the wrong time to see her face, even tonight. At nearly six feet tall in heels, she never failed to turn heads but was often the centre of attention due to her vibrant personality. That, and her inability to do anything quietly.

Liv clocked the empty glass in Mel's hand. 'Looks like I called at the right time. I made some curry and rice, too much for me, so I brought it over so we can eat together.

CHAPTER ONE

We haven't done a Friday night supper in a little while, so ta-da, here I am!' she said with a flounce.

'I couldn't be happier to see you, Liv, but only because you cooked, obviously,' Mel said with a smile.

'Obviously!' said Liv, pulling a fake scornful expression that morphed into a laugh. She instructed Mel to pour some drinks and set the table while she served up the food.

Over drinks and a delicious meal, Mel updated Liv on her newly changed weekend plans. Liv was particularly understanding of Mel's situation, as it was one she came across fairly frequently. In her work as a medium and tarot card reader, the subject of letting go of loved ones' possessions often came up.

'Your dad's right, darling. It's time. Having it hanging over you is no good, and you can't avoid it forever. It might even bring you some comfort. Spending time going through the things your nan loved could bring back some great memories, and she would want you to focus on your happy times together and not be sad; we both know that,' said Liv gently.

'That's true. I think I've just delayed it because it's so hard to accept that she's really gone. I realise that probably sounds daft, as I'm well aware of how lucky I was to have her for as long as I did. She was clearly determined to stick around to look after me well after I needed looking after! But I don't half miss her.'

'Your nan will never *truly* leave you, darling. She lives on in your memories and your heart. She was an absolute treasure, and you are just like her.'

After clearing the dishes, Mel and Liv went into the lounge, grabbed a blanket each from the basket next to the fireplace, and made themselves comfortable on the sofa. As was usual for them, they chatted about all sorts, interspersed with laughter and the refilling of their glasses.

'Right, it's nearly midnight, so I'd best be off, darling,' said Liv a couple of hours later, getting up from the sofa.

'Thanks so much for coming over, Liv. I thought I needed cheese on toast and an early night, but it turns out what I really needed was a night with you instead,' said Mel with a chuckle.

'Well, I clearly know you better than you know yourself then, don't I? Besides, you cheeky wench, I'm *always* a better option than cheese on bloody toast!'

Mel walked her friend to the front door, kissed her on the cheek, and said goodnight. She stood keeping watch to check Liv was safely down the street, as was their usual routine. Liv turned and waved before disappearing into her house. *So much for an early night,* thought Mel as she closed the door with a contented smile on her face. Tonight had been *exactly* what she'd needed, and strangely, she now felt ready for what the coming day would bring. It was uncanny how Liv always turned up at the right time, and Mel never failed to feel better for having spent time with her. Friends like Liv were worth their weight in gold. Friends like Liv were family.

Chapter Two

The next morning, Mel woke up feeling a lot livelier than she had expected. A combination of being exhausted from work and a few drinks the night before ensured she'd slept like a log. She had even woken up a few minutes before her alarm went off, which rarely happened. After she picked out what she planned to wear and then had a large mug of tea, Mel took a long, hot, steamy shower. She emerged feeling better still, and after applying some light makeup and drying her ash-brown hair, she was ready to face the day.

John, Mel's dad, lived a ten-minute walk from Mel's house, and she decided that as it looked like such a lovely morning, she would walk over. The rain of the previous night had cleared the air, and today the sky was bright blue with a few white fluffy clouds dotted here and there. She'd shivered as she stepped outside. Although it had looked like a summer's day from the warmth of her home, it certainly didn't feel like it. Autumn was done, and winter was fast on its heels, decided Mel, as she noticed the vast number of red and golden leaves that lay on the ground, victims of the wind and heavy rain of the previous evening. All yesterday's feelings of dread were behind her, and she realised on her walk that she might even be looking forward to going through her nan's belongings. Liv had managed to change how she felt about today when she spoke about looking back with appreciation and not focussing on the sadness of her loss.

Mel knocked firmly on her dad's front door before letting herself in so as not to scare him.

'Morning, Dad,' she shouted. John's hearing was what could be described as hit-and-miss.

'Who's that? I don't want anything, so whatever you're selling, you can bugger off and take it elsewhere!'

Mel rolled her eyes and chuckled. Of course, John knew exactly who had walked into his house, and this was just one of his typical 'welcome' greetings. Just then, he appeared from the kitchen with a big grin on his face.

'There she is! Come and give your old man a cwtch, little one.'

'Little one' was another of John's regular names for his daughter. She had been called that for as long as she could remember. As a toddler it was cute, as a teenager it was mortifying, and as life tends to go full circle it was back to being cute again. Mel had often found herself calling all her favourite people the same thing, so much so that it was one of her many Mel-isms. She was more like her dad than she realised or was prepared to admit.

Mel did as he asked, not needing to be told twice. She loved the bones of her dad. The pair went into the kitchen, and while John took charge of cooking the poached eggs, Mel made a pot of tea and popped some bread in the

CHAPTER TWO

toaster. Five minutes later, they sat comfortably at the kitchen table, drinking tea and making a start on John's perfect poached eggs.

'Are you feeling better after an early night then, Mel?' asked John, taking a big slurp from his favourite mug.

'Well, as it turns out, I do feel a lot better, but not because I had an early night. Liv called around about ten minutes after we spoke and didn't leave until almost midnight. It was just what the doctor ordered, though, and I feel so much brighter today.'

'Well, I'm glad to hear that Liv worked her magic; she's a little star, that one. Obviously, she's as mad as a box of frogs, but you've got to love her.'

There was no avoiding the fact that Mel marched to the beat of her own drum, just like most of her friends. She chose them well and wisely, though, in John's opinion. With Mel being single for the last few years, it brought John a great deal of comfort knowing that Mel had some great people around her.

'No need to worry, Dad, I'm good. After your poached eggs, I'm fabulous, actually!' Mel flounced an arm dramatically. She gave her dad a wink. 'Come on then, old-timer, let's get the show on the road, shall we?'

Mel led the way upstairs, noticing the familiar creak on the fourth step from the bottom that had always been there, and turned right at the top towards her old bedroom. It had been a long while since she had been in there, and it felt like it. They had replaced her old bed a year or so ago in case she ever wanted to stay over. She felt a heavy pang of guilt in her heart, realising she had never slept in that bed. Not once. The room being the storage spot for her nan's things didn't exactly make her feel comfortable because it was a stark reminder of her unwillingness to deal with them. She looked at her patient, kind dad and knew that it was time for that to be rectified.

John sat with Mel after she looked over the array of boxes and containers that held her nan's precious things. He reached for his daughter's hand and squeezed it. They shared a look between them that needed no words. They both knew their grief would always be with them. It never leaves when you truly love someone, Mel thought, no matter how long it's been.

Mel took a deep breath and decided to get straight into the sorting. First, she tackled the remainder of her nan's clothes. She had kept more than she remembered. At the time, some were just too painful to part with, and so she didn't. Now that time had passed, she felt more able to donate the majority to charity. Just as that realisation landed, out of the corner of her eye, Mel spotted something that brought her to an absolute standstill. It was as if she froze in time for a few seconds, unable to move. Eventually, she reached out, picked it up, and held it close to her. It brought a cascade of memories flooding back, tripping over themselves, fighting for her attention. It was her nan's favourite coat. She'd had loads of coats, but this was the one she wore most often because it was by far the warmest. Lizzie's anaemia meant she was always cold. Even in the glorious summer of 1976, she'd worn a cardigan at night because it got a bit 'chilly'. Mel's grandad

CHAPTER TWO

often commented on her having a wardrobe full of coats but that he had only ever seen them the day he bought them for her. Of course, Lizzie had taken absolutely no notice of him, but he hadn't expected for a second that she would!

'It's Nan's coat, Dad. What do I do about this? I can't give it to charity. It looks like it's been worn a million times, and even if it didn't, there's no way I could let someone else wear it. Not *this*.'

John contemplated for a moment as his daughter searched his face in earnest for an answer, almost childlike. 'So, I was watching this documentary about hoarders the other week, Mel. One of the suggestions the TV expert made was to take photos of items rather than keep them. How does that sound?'

Mel hugged her nan's prized coat tightly to her chest as she considered the prospect of letting it go. In her heart of hearts, she knew she needed to.

'That sounds like a good idea, Dad. But after the photo, I'm going to take off a few buttons to keep. That way, I'll still have a piece of it without keeping the whole coat.'

Seeing the sad look on Mel's face as she held her nan's coat close to her, John felt the years slip away. For a brief moment in time, he saw Mel as a little girl again. He felt a stab of emotion for his daughter but managed to smile at her and tell her what a good idea that sounded before he turned away to compose himself for a moment. He felt some tears well up in his eyes and willed them away. His daughter's sadness hurt him more than anything else ever could in this world, but he would never let her see that. He was her dad, and that meant he had to be the strong one.

After a couple of hours, the place looked a lot more like a bedroom than a storage unit. Mel had managed to let go of a lot, and she felt proud of her achievement. She had taken a few photos of some of her nan's things, including her favourite brown winter coat that she'd also snipped a couple of buttons from. She took the bags destined for the charity shop and recycling downstairs and put them into the boot of her dad's car. He went straight to the local Cancer Research shop and recycling centre and dropped them off. He'd said he'd better do it before Mel changed her mind, but she knew it was because he realised it would be harder for his daughter to hand over her beloved nan's things to a shop assistant and harder still taking them to be recycled. She might be in her fifties, but her dad would still protect her in any and every way he could.

Mel decided to keep going, and after looking through what was left, she felt it would be best to take it all to her house and sort it out there. That way, she could do it a bit at a time without inconveniencing her dad. There seemed to be a few boxes of miscellaneous items: old greeting cards, her jewellery box, scarves and hats, and some photo albums. After having taken the last of the boxes downstairs, Mel looked around her old bedroom and felt a sense of achievement for doing something she had been avoiding for so long. She also resolved to have an overnight stay now the room was cleared. As she got to the bottom of the stairs, her dad walked back in and suggested

CHAPTER TWO

a cup of tea. He put the kettle on whilst Mel loaded the last of the boxes into the boot of his car. He would take her back home after a cuppa.

'So, what's the rest of the weekend got in store for you, love?' asked John as they sat down with steaming mugs of their new favourite Yorkshire Biscuit tea.

'Well, I was planning a quiet one, but I've changed my mind. I think I'll pop to the shops to get what I need to make a Sunday roast for tomorrow if you want to join me. Then I might make a start on Nan's boxes. I'll probably go to the Red Lion at some point to see Jeff and Tony. I've not seen them for a little while, and I'm *bound* to see them there at the weekend.'

Jeff and Tony lived in number seven, the house directly opposite Mel's on the other side of the Green. They'd moved in shortly before Mel, and they had become great friends over the years.

'Those boys spend almost as much time there as they did when they ran the place, and I can't say I blame them.'

The two chatted until their cups were empty and could have easily carried on for an hour or two, as they often did.

'Right then, let's get going. Sounds like you've got a lot to do. Last one to the car is washing it!' said John as he made a dart for the door.

A few minutes later, John pulled up outside his daughter's house, and she got out to grab some boxes from the boot.

FINDING A MIRACLE

'Oi, you old bugger!' The voice seemed to come from nowhere. Mel, of course, instantly recognised it. The familiar broad Scottish accent was that of her next-door neighbour Dougie McLaren. She hadn't noticed him, but her dad had, and that comment was directed at him. Dougie had lived in number two for more of his life than he had ever spent in Scotland. He and his wife had been so kind and welcoming to Mel when she moved in. Sadly, Joanie had passed away from dementia some years ago, leaving just Dougie and his cat living there now.

'Alright, Dougie? What's going on with you, young man?' John shouted down to his mate. The two had become firm friends over the years. John knew how well Dougie and Mel got along. Dougie did what he could for Mel and vice versa. Now, that mainly consisted of Dougie taking in parcels for Mel whilst she was at work. Mel, on the other hand, had gradually increased the help she gave as Dougie's mobility and health began to decrease. He was a proud man, so there had been a bit of a battle to get his consent when it came to putting out his bins for him. There had been a bigger battle still when it came to convincing him to get some help with the garden.

'Not a lot, pal. This dodgy hip of mine stops most of my fun. I had planned a bank job, but I think I'm a yard too slow these days,' Dougie said with a wry smile. 'Oh, I do have a bit of news, though, now I think of it. My Kev's coming home from Australia for good! He'll be back sometime next week. He's staying with me for a bit. He says it's because he needs a base and doesn't want to rent a house until he's got himself a job. Allegedly, it's to save money, but I know what he's up to; he can't pull the wool

CHAPTER THREE

over my eyes. He wants to check on me to make sure I'm not a danger to myself or anyone else.'

'Oh, Dougie, you've always been dangerous! A proper terror down the Legion you are, especially on bingo nights if you don't win.' John chuckled. 'That will be nice, though, having Kev back home. Hey, our Mel's doing a roast tomorrow, so get your order in now if you want in on it.'

'Err, I am listening, you know, Dad! Come in at two o'clock and bring your rubber gloves, my love; you and my dad are on washing-up duty,' joked Mel.

Dougie happily accepted the invite not only because Mel made a cracking roast dinner, but he loved spending time with them both. He felt so blessed to have Mel living next door to him. He said his goodbyes to both and went back to the warmth of his lounge and Mrs C, his beloved cat.

Three trips later, Mel had emptied her dad's boot, and he had left her with a kiss and a request for pigs in blankets, apple sauce, stuffing, and Yorkshire puddings. She loved how much he enjoyed her cooking, especially her Sunday roasts. Her small way of looking after him pleased her no end. As her nan always used to say, 'Cooking for people you love fills *your* heart as much as *their* stomachs.' The older she got, the more she realised her nan had been right about nearly everything.

CHAPTER THREE

Just as Mel had finished putting the last of her shopping away, her phone rang. *Good timing,* she thought as she retrieved her phone from the pocket of her cardigan. She looked at the screen and saw that it was Cat.

'Hiya, Cat, how are you, my lovely?'

'Had better mornings, pet. I'm not disturbing you, am I? I wasn't sure whether I should call or not,' Cat muttered quietly.

'Don't be daft; of course you're not disturbing me. What's wrong, love, you don't sound yourself?' Mel asked, worried about how faint Cat sounded.

'It's Mike. I think he's having an affair.'

The comment stopped Mel dead in her tracks. She had *not* expected to hear that.

'Do you want me to come over?' she asked.

'Would it be okay if I came to you? I feel like I need to get away from the flat for a bit,' said Cat, a slight tremor in her voice.

'Course it's okay. I'll get the kettle on, love.'

CHAPTER THREE

Fifteen minutes later, the doorbell rang, and Mel hurried to let Cat in. Cat's face was ghostly pale. She trod the familiar path into Mel's kitchen, dumped her bag on the floor, and immediately walked into Mel's waiting arms for a much-needed cwtch. Tears pricked her eyes, and she couldn't stop them from falling. She felt safe and able to just let out the emotion she had been straining to keep locked up for the short journey to Mel's place.

Cat slowly pulled away from her friend's embrace and squeezed her hand. She retrieved a tissue from her pocket and dabbed at her puffy eyes, blew her nose, and then sat down at the kitchen table. Mel brought over two mugs of tea and took a seat opposite Cat. She had seen her in tears before but never *this* upset. Cat took a deep breath and then blew on her tea before taking a big sip. She felt a little steadier and was now able to tell Mel what had happened the previous night and that morning.

'We had a takeaway last night and ate it in the lounge because we were in the middle of watching something on TV. A little while after we finished, Mike got a text, so he picked up his phone, read the message, and put the phone on the arm of the sofa, face down. A few seconds later, he stood up, put his mobile in the pocket of his tracksuit bottoms, and took the plates to the kitchen. This was odd because the programme didn't have long left. He had been gone a few minutes, so I thought I'd pause the TV and go and get a drink. When I walked into the kitchen, Mike was on the phone. He looked like he'd seen a ghost when he saw me, then he quickly ended his call with a very firm "Yeah, see you tomorrow, mate."' Cat paused to take another sip of her tea before continuing.

'I knew he must have been whispering because I'd have heard him speak from the lounge, even with the TV on. You know our flat. It's hardly huge, and the walls aren't exactly thick. The look on his face gave him away, too. His cheeks were crimson, Mel. I realised straight away that there was something going on. He tried to cover it up and said it was his brother and that he wanted some help building a shed today. He looked so bloody shifty, though, love. It was obvious he was lying. I could tell he was looking at me closely to see if I believed his bullshit excuse. I think he feels he got away with it.'

'That must have been really hard, Cat. How did you manage to sit with him for the rest of the night with that happening?'

'We pretty much sat in silence with the telly on until I faked a headache and went to bed. Mike stayed up watching football highlights, and I didn't hear him come to bed, so it must have been late. It took me ages to drop off, obviously. I know he's been going out a lot more lately, but I never dreamt he would do this. I didn't think he could. He's always one for doing the right thing. He's a decent bloke, or so I thought. Maybe I got that wrong.'

'I'm not saying you're wrong, but this has blindsided me too. I would *never* have expected Mike to be keeping secrets or to cheat. I'm a bit lost for words, to be honest, love.'

'Well, there's a bit more. When Mike went for a shower this morning, I checked his phone. You know, that's something I would *never* dream of doing usually, but I just wanted answers. When I typed in his password, it came up as "incorrect PIN". I tried again in case I mistyped it, and the same message came up. He's changed it, Mel. We both had each other's passwords, so this is strange. Anyway, when he came out from his shower, I told him I was late for a breakfast date with you and jumped in the shower myself. I didn't know how to be around him; my head was all over the place. I stayed in there a bit longer than usual to try to calm myself. Just as I got out, he stuck his head around the door and said, "I'm off out now. Have a good day. Love you." He had closed the door before I had the chance to reply.'

Cat picked up her mug and finished off her tea. It felt comforting as it warmed her insides, which ached with emptiness. She also felt better for having gotten all that off her chest. They were both silent for a few moments while Mel tried to take in the details of what she had just been told. Immediately she realised they were short on facts but from what she had heard this didn't sound good at all. Mel was a great believer in intuition and gut instinct, and she sadly conceded that Cat was right to follow hers on this. She reached across the table to hold Cat's hand. A solitary tear fell from Cat's eye, which she didn't have the energy, motivation, or strength to wipe away. She had thought there were none left bottled up inside her, but it seemed she was wrong.

'Okay, love, from what you've told me, Mike does seem to be acting out of character, no question. Whispered conversations, changing his PIN, and being out a lot doesn't prove he's playing away, but I can see why you've come to that conclusion. So, right now, he doesn't know you suspect anything. He probably thinks he got away with the phone call because you didn't quiz him about it. The question is, what do you want to do now?'

'Oh God, I don't know, Mel. Deep down, I know what's going on, and if he's seeing someone else, then it's over. Trust is everything, and if he's betrayed that, then I'd be done with him for my sanity and my self-respect. I could forgive, maybe, but it would always be there, like a great big elephant-sized gulf between us. There could be another, more innocent, explanation for all this, of course. So, do I throw away a three-year relationship on something I might be wrong about? If I ask him and it turns out I'm mistaken, he could think I've lost the plot. Then again, if he is guilty, he could lie about it and just try to be more careful going forward. Neither of those is a good outcome.'

'There is another potential outcome, darling. He could admit he's up to no good,' said Mel gently.

'Shit, I'd not even considered that.' Cat fell silent as she thought about how that might feel, the practicalities of it all. She had given up her flat over two years ago to move in with Mike only about six months after they became a couple. His place was bigger, so it made sense to do it that way, as her place barely contained her with all her things. She felt her stomach churn and become knotted as she remembered the excitement, she had felt moving in with him. She'd truly believed he was going to be her forever. The anxiety of this was already unbearable; she needed to know what the hell was going on.

'Clearly, I need to form a plan in case he either A) admits it or B) I somehow catch him out. I have some

CHAPTER THREE

savings, so I could get a flat, but how quickly? If he is with someone, I will want out of his place pronto.' *His* place. How quickly it had become *his* place, thought Cat. It was like the decision to leave had already been made in her mind, but her heart hurt at the very thought of it. It felt to Cat like she had already vacated Mike's home and his life.

'Well, there's no point in looking for a flat and paying out lots of money right now. There's still a chance this is a misunderstanding, love. I know that if you were to find out he's cheating, you'd want to leave his place ASAP so you could always come to stay with me until you're ready to find somewhere. I could move my dusty exercise bike out of the spare room, no problem! Now we have that covered, what do you want to do about Mike?'

Cat knew it would eat her alive, living in a state of suspicion, and that she had to find out. Coming straight out with it and asking Mike directly probably wasn't the best option. Going by how red-faced and sheepish he'd looked the night before, Cat felt sure he would deny it. That would make the situation even worse than it was now. It sickened her to think that there was only one option remaining, and it wasn't a pleasant one.

'We need to catch him, don't we? It's the only way. How the hell we manage to do that is totally beyond me, though. It's not something I've done before. Checking his phone this morning made me feel like some kind of master criminal. I wouldn't have a clue where to start.' Cat looked to the heavens in a silent, desperate plea for inspiration or guidance and then jumped a country mile as Mel banged her small fist on the table and shouted,

'Catfish! Have you seen that programme on MTV, where people set up fake social media profiles to land themselves a hot partner, sugar daddy or mamma, or if they're lucky, both?'

Cat had seen the programme and nodded slowly. She considered the prospect of setting up a honey trap for the man she lived with, the man she loved, and it floored her. As sad as this made her, she knew it was a good idea. If she was wrong, she'd have peace of mind and could put all this behind them, and he wouldn't have to know a thing about it.

'Catfish! That's how we catch the little bastard if he's up to something. He's made a big mistake if he thinks he's getting away with it. And if he isn't, then sorry for calling you a bastard, Mike!' Mel's green eyes flashed with fiery anger. If Mike was having an affair, she was determined to find out. Seeing her friend look sad and lost broke Mel's heart. She didn't deserve to be treated that way, and Mel would do whatever it took to support her through all of this. Fiercely protective of her loved ones, Mel was a little lioness, and she had her sights firmly fixed on her prey: Mike Wood.

Chapter Four

When Mel got downstairs the next morning, she was surprised to see Cat already up and dressed, making them a pot of tea.

'Morning, darling. Daft question, but how did you sleep?' asked Mel.

'Not the best, but I'm sure I slept better here than I would have if I'd gone home. Thanks for letting me stay, pet. I sent Mike a text earlier saying I'm coming down with a cold. It will explain my pasty face and dark circles. It also gives me an excuse to go to bed and be alone if I need to get away from him for the next few days.'

'Wise move that, love,' said Mel as she popped some bread in the toaster. Cat would be having breakfast whether she wanted it or not; it was not up for debate. 'Do you want to stay for lunch? I'm making a roast.'

'Staying here for the day sounds great, it really does. I can't avoid going home forever, though.' Here, Cat didn't have to pretend to be anything other than herself. No act, no brave face needed at Mel's.

After a couple of mugs of tea and a breakfast of toast with honey, Mel started preparing the vegetables for the roast she would be making later that day. Cat rolled up her sleeves and started to peel potatoes.

'How many have you got coming round for lunch exactly?'

'Oh, you know me, I always make too much! My dad's coming over at 2 o'clock, Dougie too. Looking at all this, I may need Liv to help us out too!'

With all the vegetables peeled and prepared, Cat announced it was time to go back home. Mike would probably be starting to wonder why she wasn't home, especially as he was under the impression she wasn't feeling well.

'Okay. Well, if you need anything, and I do mean *anything*, ring me. My spare room is yours if you need it, my lovely. You are more than welcome here anytime, so keep that in mind.'

Cat had always loved and appreciated Mel, but she could never love and appreciate her more than she did right now. *It's always when you're at your lowest point you discover who your true friends are*, she thought. They arranged to have lunch together the following day at work, where they would investigate setting up a fake profile on Facebook. It was the only social media platform Mel used, and luckily, Mike used it too. As she walked to her car, Cat reassured Mel that if there was a problem, she would ring her. With final thanks given and kisses blown, Cat jumped into her car and headed off down the little cobbled lane to a place that, for the first time, didn't feel like home to her.

CHAPTER FOUR

Mel came in from the cold outside and shivered. She decided to fire up the log burner. Her dad was often chilly, and she wanted the house to be warm and cosy for him when he arrived. She put the pork and chicken in the oven and decided she would make another cuppa before starting to look through some of the boxes she had brought over from her dad's. As the kettle boiled, she texted Liv.

2 o'clock, roast dinner. Chicken and pork with all the trimmings. Dress to impress – we have two gorgeous men joining us. xxx

Sounds good. I will bring wine and dessert. Looking forward to seeing John and Dougie xxx

How did you know it's my dad and Dougie? Are you psychic or something?! Lol. See you at 2, love. xxx

Mel wandered into the lounge and felt her spirits lift at the sight of the logs starting to flicker with an orange glow. She set her tea down on the little table to the right of her reading chair and went to light her favourite Woodwick candle. As she got settled in her chair, she loudly exhaled. *What a day yesterday was*, thought Mel. She sat for a few moments enjoying her tea in peace before her mind drifted back to Cat and how they would manage to catch Mike. They were hardly Cagney and Lacey, and thankfully, this situation was new territory for them both. Mel had been single for a few years now, and with what was happening with Cat, she wondered if she was better off staying that way. Her last serious relationship ended just after her nan passed away. Losing her nan had made Mel take stock of her own life. She realised her relationship had been treading water for a long time and that she wasn't even close to getting her needs met. He had long since stopped making any effort, and when she'd reflected on it, she knew she wanted more. She *deserved* more. They had become a habit long past its sell-by date, and so Mel had decided to end it between them. As she had great friends, her dad, and a job she loved, it wasn't like she felt she missed out on much. In fact, she felt happier alone. It was far better being single than in a loveless relationship. Mel had several serious relationships in her life which had simply just run their course or overstayed their welcome. Life was less complicated now, and Mel was pretty content with her lot.

Her mug drained of tea, Mel popped it down on the table next to her. Checking the time, she figured she had about an hour to go through one of the boxes of her nan's belongings that she had stored under the bay window of her lounge. Now they were here, she wanted to make a start on them.

She took the top box, which was one of several called 'Photographs'. The word was barely visible as the marker pen ink was badly faded. Unsurprisingly, an old smell came up from the box as she opened it. She had wiped most of the dust off the day before, but the box felt like it had been left suspended in time, untouched for many years. Gently, she took out the top photo album. She had seen it many times before, and one she knew she would never part with. There were just a few photographs of her grandparents, Lizzie and Bill when they were babies, toddlers, children, and teenagers. Money had been tight for both her grandparents' families, which was why there weren't many photographs of them when they were young. There was

CHAPTER FOUR

just one photo of them on their wedding day: Bill, with his black hair slicked back, shoes shined to within an inch of their life and dressed in a smart charcoal three-piece suit, and Lizzie in a simple cream lace dress with pearl earrings and a matching clutch bag. She looked beautiful and so elegant. Her face beamed with love and happiness as she stood next to her husband. *Her* Bill. There must have been at least a one-foot difference in height between them, yet they were the perfect fit. A perfect match. Remembering what a happy couple they had been and what a wonderful marriage they had shared made Mel smile. She closed the album, and instead of feeling sad as she had expected, she felt happy. Knowing how much they loved and cared for each other and made each other laugh every day of their lives together was priceless. Liz always said that Bill was the missing piece of her jigsaw, and without question, he'd felt the same about her. *Some love stories do have a happy ever after*, Mel thought.

The next album was full of photographs of the couple after Mel's mother, Anne, had come along. Lots of captured images of day trips to the beach, Anne's little hand clutching an ice cream and wearing a lot of it on her face. Anne having a donkey ride on the beach at Barry Island. Picnics in the park. Bill proudly sat behind the wheel of his first car, a Morris Oxford. How Mel wished her mother could be sitting there leafing through these memories with her. To lose her at such a young age had always felt *so* unfair. There were so many things she had missed out on. Mel's eighteenth birthday, getting her first job, passing her driving test, and buying her house. Her mother hadn't seen any of those milestones. Mel closed the album and sighed. It had been so hard losing her mother, and she still felt her loss as much today as the day she died. Time didn't heal; it just gave you longer to miss the people you loved, she had always thought. Trying to shake the empty feeling, she decided there was time for one more album before she needed to play Nigella in the kitchen.

When she opened it, Mel realised this was more of a scrapbook than a photo album. She couldn't remember ever having seen it before. As she slowly turned the brittle pages, she noticed postcards, ticket stubs, and adverts for performances. They looked so old, almost like museum pieces. The colours had faded on some items, and on others, the printing was so aged it was difficult to read. Most of the adverts were for somewhere called The Metropole Hotel, London. *Why the bloody hell has my nan got so many promo leaflets for a hotel in London,* wondered Mel. It made no sense to her. Her nan had been born in a little cottage called Hen Bandy in a village called Llanllyfni in rural Caernarvonshire. From there, she moved to the outskirts of Cardiff, where she remained until her passing. Feeling confused and intrigued, Mel took a closer look at the adverts.

Reginald Newman

Proudly presents

The Maurice Newman Band

With special guest

The Enchanting Miss Alice Miracle

CHAPTER FOUR

Reginald Newman

Proudly presents

The Maurice Newman Band

With resident vocalist

The Enchanting Miss Alice Miracle

There were several more similar adverts. Mel paused to think about what she had been looking at. Why would her nan have kept these? Had she been to London and attended one of these shows? She must have bloody loved them to keep all these leaflets. *Nan, you dark horse. You never mentioned nights out in London*, thought a bemused Mel. In fact, she'd never mentioned visiting London at all, never mind seeing bands in a hotel. Mel quickly leafed through a few more pages, aware she needed to check on the meat and get the veg on to cook. A couple of pages before the end, there was a black-and-white photograph of a group that looked like a promo shot. Three male musicians and a female vocalist. They were on a stage in what looked very much like an Art Deco–style venue. There were a couple more images of the group taken from different angles and positions. One had captured an audience that had gone to see a show, all dressed in their finery, looking opulent, glamorous, and happy. Above the stage was the letter *M* encased in a diamond shape. *M for Metropole?* Mel mused. The final group photograph she looked at was a close-up of the band standing together and posing for the camera. Underneath the photo were the names of the band members from left to right.

FINDING A MIRACLE

Maurice Newman on piano, Miss Alice Miracle vocalist, Pete Dewhurst on bass, and Jeff Morrow on drums. Mel was about to put the scrapbook away to continue looking at it later when she took a sharp intake of breath. She looked more closely at the photo. Miss Alice Miracle bore a striking resemblance to her nan when she was a young woman. She looked again, searching for answers from this picture taken many years ago. Mel rubbed her eyes, which felt slightly strained from poring over the photos, and laughed at herself for being so daft. Her nan didn't work in a hotel in London as a singer. She and Mel's grandad led a very ordinary life. Mel didn't remember them ever going to London and was sure they'd have talked about it if they had. They saw shows in the New Theatre in Cardiff or St David's Hall in later years, but never in London. Time to hit the kitchen, thought Mel as she stood up and closed the scrapbook. She must have shut it more forcefully than she intended because something fell out and fluttered to the floor. 'Shit,' she muttered under her breath as she bent to pick it up. There was some faded writing on the thick piece of paper in Mel's hand. It read, *From your Alice with much love xxx*. The handwriting looked familiar. As Mel turned the paper over, she saw it was a photograph. As she looked at it, she felt her legs fold and knees buckle and almost fell back into her chair. Her trembling hand gently held a photograph that had the familiar *M* logo at the bottom together with the title 'Miss Alice Miracle' and showed a close-up of a beautiful young woman's face. There was no mistaking it. It was the face of her beloved nan, Lizzie Roberts.

Chapter Five

The kitchen was a feast for the senses, with steaming pans of vegetables bubbling away on the stove, but Mel's appetite had waned a little since finding the photo of her nan. She couldn't take her mind off it for more than a few seconds at a time. The possibility that Lizzie had been a singer in London and not told her about it was almost unthinkable. They were incredibly close, and Mel had always felt she knew everything there was to know about her nan. This made no sense.

Her phone buzzed with a message from her dad after she'd asked him to come over as soon as he was ready.

No problem, love, I'm on my way. Is everything ok? xx

Yeah, I'm fine, Dad. See you soon. xx

This wasn't a conversation to start having via text. Mel's mind was spinning with questions. Did her dad know about Lizzie being a singer in a fancy-looking hotel in London? She couldn't quite believe it. Her little nan. A singer. In *London*. She put her hand to her mouth to stifle a nervous laugh. The thought tickled her because it just seemed so utterly ridiculous! Her nan was a *proper* nana. She knitted and sewed buttons back on shirts, told Mel bedtime stories, and made soup, apple and blackberry tarts, and Welsh cakes. In fact, she made the *best* Welsh cakes. She was everything you could want in a grandmother: the perfect nurturer. The notion that she was a resident singer with a band in London was *way* too far-fetched to be real.

Her thoughts were interrupted by the arrival of her dad. Mel quickly ushered him into the lounge. He barely had the chance to get settled on the sofa before Mel put the scrapbook in his hand.

'What's this, love?' asked John, looking up.

'I started going through one of Nan's boxes, and I found that,' said Mel, nodding towards the scrapbook in her dad's hands. 'Look through it and tell me what you think.'

Mel's eyes didn't leave his face as he did so, scanning, searching, and looking for a sign that he already knew about all of this.

'I'm waiting for the punchline, Mel. You almost got me with a good one there, love. For a split second there, I thought that was your nan,' John said tentatively with eyes as wide as bin lids and an uncertain half-smile.

'No punchline, Dad. Not this time. I think I can assume that you had no idea about this either then, going by your reaction. Unless you've been taking acting lessons from Michael Sheen or Christopher Walken without telling me.' Mel paused, taking in her dad's bemused expression. 'I wonder if my mother knew about any of this. I'm *sure* she would have said something if she did. Got to say, Pops, for once I'm lost for words.'

CHAPTER FIVE

John sat quietly for a moment, trying to take all this in, slowly re-examining the contents of the aged scrapbook. He thought about his mother-in-law. She had been more like a second mother to him and could do no wrong in his eyes. His parents, Bessie and Albert, had loved Lizzie too. She was so full of fun, so kind and thoughtful, it would be impossible not to love her. The phrase *good things come in small packages* could have been written especially for her. What she lacked in height, she more than made up for in character. If she was ever asked how tall she was, her stock response was, 'Five feet on a good day, love.' *If that had actually been true, then she wouldn't have been blessed with too many good days,* John thought with a smile. A smile because it wasn't true; Lizzie had had a good life other than losing the husband and daughter she adored. How John loved her and how he missed her.

'Honestly, Mel, I can't quite get my head around this. It's a lot to take in, isn't it? How is it even possible? Lizzie, a singer and in *London* of all places? Why didn't she ever talk about it? Bloody hell, what else is in those boxes, I wonder? What *else* will we find out about your nan, love?'

'No idea, Dad, but I think I – *we* – need to just let *this* sink in first. It *could* be possible that Alice Miracle is just someone who looks a lot like Nan. But then it makes no sense that she would keep all those things unless it *was* her.'

'No doubt in my mind that's your nan, Mellie Adelie, and the writing on the back of that photo looks a *lot* like hers too. It's just so surprising that it's hard to make any sense of it. She led such an ordinary life it's hard to believe this is something she kept to herself. For most people, this would be a highlight they'd want to talk about, surely? It probably would be easier if it *weren't* your nan. There'd be no mystery if that were the case!'

The sound of the doorbell interrupted them, and John announced he would answer the door. Mel went to the kitchen to check the vegetables as she shouted her hellos to Dougie. She brought the chicken and pork out of the oven and set them to one side to rest before checking on the stuffing and pigs in blankets. In the background, she heard the typically exuberant exchange between her dad and Dougie, the pair trading good-natured jibes mainly focused on their age. This was interrupted fleetingly as John once again played doorman and went to let Liv in. The volume and energy levels got turned up more than a couple of notches as Liv shrieked, giggled, and flirted with the two old-timers sitting in the lounge. She complimented both on their dashing good looks, and they competed for her attention, which she lapped up, of course.

Liv eventually left the 'boys' to it and click-clacked her way down the hallway. 'Lunch smells *amazing*, Mel. I didn't have breakfast, so no pressure for it to taste good, too! Need a hand, darling?' Liv appeared at the kitchen door. She popped the wine, a cheesecake, and a chocolate cake on the worktop next to her.

'So good to see you, Liv! Pour the wine, will you, love, and get that pair to the table while I get this lot served up.'

Five minutes later, John had carved the meat, and all the veg and trimmings were in serving bowls on the table as Mel brought the pièce de résistance, a steaming

CHAPTER FIVE

jug of homemade gravy, to the table. She plonked a kiss on Dougie's cheek before sitting down next to him. Without invitation, they all started helping themselves, passing around bowls of food and filling their plates with the bounty Mel had prepared. Listening to her lot chatting, laughing, and arguing over who wasn't going to be clearing the table after dinner and who had grabbed the biggest Yorkshire pudding warmed Mel's heart. She cherished nothing more than having her loved ones around for times like this. *Who needs a man when you're this happy? Single doesn't have to mean lonely,* thought Mel. Deciding to park any thoughts of a certain Miss Alice Miracle for the time being meant she could enjoy the time with the family sitting at her table. Liv and Dougie might not be linked via DNA, but they were family in her heart, where it mattered most. Her nan would approve if she were able to see Mel enjoying a meal with these three. In fact, Lizzie would have loved every second of this, Mel thought.

With happy stomachs that were full to bursting, they all decided that moving into the lounge felt like too much effort at that moment in time, so they sat chatting and topping up each other's wine glasses. The cheesecake was likely to be a takeaway dessert after that lunch. Mel went to retrieve another bottle of red from the wine rack, and before sitting down, she popped some chicken into a container for Dougie to take back for Mrs C, his beloved cat. She was no stranger in Mel's house. She often visited if the back door or kitchen window was open. She was a beautiful black cat with white socks and mittens, and she had a wonderful temperament. She made herself very much at home, stretching out in front of the log burner when it was cold out and periodically going to Mel for a fuss. Mel loved her visits, too. There were a few occasions when Mel had to pick her up and return her to Dougie. He always joked that Mel's house was Mrs C's holiday home.

Liv stood and started clearing the table, leaving the 'boys' to their conversation about Dougie's son, Kev, returning from Australia. She and Mel set about scraping plates, rinsing pans, loading the dishwasher, and cleaning the worktops. Before too long, the kitchen was back to an orderly state.

'Fancy popping to the Red Lion later, Liv? I've not seen Jeff and Tony in a couple of weeks, and it would be great to spend some time with them.'

'Well, we do stand a good chance of seeing them at the Lion on a Sunday evening! Sounds good to me, but I may need to have a coffee instead of more wine,' said Liv, only half believing it.

An hour or so later, Dougie decided it was time for a nap in front of the telly, and John thought that seemed like a good idea, too, so they headed home. After seeing them out, Mel joined Liv in the lounge and flopped down on the settee next to her. The scrapbook's contents had been on Mel's mind since she found it, so she decided to tell Liv all about it to get her take on it. Liv sat in silence, totally absorbed by what Mel told her.

'How fabulous is that? Let me see the scrapbook!' declared Liv enthusiastically after Mel had finished.

'Is it?' asked Mel, genuinely surprised by Liv's reaction. She felt it was more confusing or even unsettling

CHAPTER FIVE

than fabulous. She handed the scrapbook to Liv, who started leafing through it immediately.

'Course it bloody is! Your little nan had this whole other life before you were even born, and now you have the pleasure of finding out about it. I'd be so excited to find something like this out about my relatives. If you want help researching, I'm in!'

'I might take you up on that, love. I've still got a few boxes to go through first. I'm wondering what else I'll find. What else did she get up to, I wonder? I'm almost afraid to say that out loud!'

'I have to say that I'm sold on the fact this is your nan from these photos. I'm in no doubt whatsoever, darling. Well, I think this is super exciting, and I'm looking forward to hearing what you find next. Ooh, maybe you could write a book about it. I can picture the cover now. *Adventures at the Metropole Hotel* by Melissa Jones.' Liv swept her arm in the air in front of her as though imagining Mel's name up in lights.

With a laugh, Mel threw a cushion at her friend and told her not to be so bloody daft. The pair decided that if they didn't get up and go to the pub now, there was every chance it wouldn't happen. In less than two minutes, they were closing the door behind them and setting off on the short walk to the Red Lion.

The pub was lively but not packed, and they quickly spotted Jeff and Tony sitting in the corner of the lounge. Mel went to the bar and ordered a round of gin and tonics with Liv behind her, waiting to help carry them to the table.

FINDING A MIRACLE

'Aren't you two looking bloody *gorgeous*?' declared Tony, delighted to see them both. His London accent was more in keeping with the set of *EastEnders* than a little village in South Wales. He and Jeff had met at a conference held by the brewery they were connected to. Both had been landlords of their own pubs back then. When they met, it was love at first sight. Within a year, Tony had sold his London boozer and moved in with Jeff. They ran the Red Lion together for many years before deciding to retire and enjoy being customers instead.

After lots of cwtches and kisses, the four settled down for a good catch-up. Jeff told the girls about a holiday to Mexico they had booked, recommended a series they'd been watching on Netflix, and updated them on the work they planned for their garden next spring. Icy gin and tonics slipped down nicely as the four friends talked and laughed. Mel loved Sunday evenings with this bunch.

'So then, our Mel, what's new with you, love?' asked Jeff.

Mel filled the boys in on clearing her old bedroom at her dad's. She mentioned that Dougie's son, Kev, was coming home from Australia next week and would be moving in with his dad for a while.

'Er, aren't you forgetting the most important part of your news, madam?' asked Liv, flicking her long blonde hair in her typically dramatic Liv way. 'Mel's found some photographs of her lovely nan from when she was young. It seems that she was a singer, and at a hotel in London, no less. And nobody knew a thing about it! She was the resident artiste at The Metrodome Hotel.' Liv's wide-eyed

CHAPTER FIVE

expression displayed an air of being utterly impressed by this despite never having set foot in the place or knowing the first thing about it.

Mel rolled her eyes playfully and corrected Liv. 'It's the *Metropole,* you daft bugger, not the Metrodome.'

'The Metropole!' said Tony, almost falling off his chair. 'Do you mean *The Metropole*? As in The Metropole in the West End?'

'No idea where it is, Tony, my love. The photograph only had London written on it.'

'If it's the place I think it is, then it doesn't need a lot more of an address than that. After all, a lion never needs to tell you it's a lion, my darling! Your nan must have been something *very* special, Mel. That place was the playground of the rich and famous years ago, so your nan would have rubbed shoulders with plenty of celebrities from yesteryear.'

'See! I *told* you this was fabulous!' shrieked Liv. 'I am *very* excited about this!' she proclaimed loudly. Several heads turned towards their table, and Mel was embarrassed and amused in equal measure by the reaction of her friends.

'I think we're all excited!' said Jeff. 'This kind of thing doesn't exactly happen every day now, does it? Imagine finding out your nan had this whole other life, and a pretty bloody fabulous life it must have been, too. If you want to text us copies of the photos, I'm sure we could do a bit of digging on The Metropole for you. Tony still has plenty of friends and contacts back in London who might be able to help you find out a bit more.'

'Thanks, boys, I'd really appreciate that. It's starting to feel like a bit of an adventure, isn't it?'

'Can I have copies of everything too, in case there's something I pick up from them psychically?' asked Liv, who could never bear to be left out of anything.

'Course you can. As if you'd be left out! I wouldn't dare,' teased Mel.

Jeff got to his feet, declaring this called for another drink, and headed off towards the bar. Mel hadn't really considered there being any more surprises, but she had just been landed with another. It seemed like her nan was singing at *quite* the venue, not just any old place. Hearing this news only made her question why her nan had kept it to herself even more. This should have been something she was proud of and happy to tell her family about, so what stopped her? Why was it a secret, what else could she have kept from them, and why the hell was she called Alice Miracle?

Chapter Six

Mel arrived at work early to catch up on emails and prepare for her group session later. She also hoped to have a chat with Cat and find out what had happened the previous day. Despite having had quite a busy and boozy weekend, Mel felt fresh and energised, which surprised her. *There's life in the old dog yet*, she thought with a satisfied smile. She had even been early enough to call into the little bakery a few doors down from the Centre to pick up some of Cat's favourite biscuits as a treat.

Having completed the tasks she had wanted to get done first thing, Mel went to the staffroom to put the kettle on. Someone had already beaten her to it, though: Janet Jervis, the accounts and HR manager. Janet was originally from Slovakia and had an accent reminiscent of a seductress from a Bond movie. She almost purred as she spoke.

'Janet, I didn't know you were in already. How are you? Good weekend?'

Janet beamed her beautiful smile and gave Mel an edited highlights overview of her weekend. She had spent the previous day in IKEA with her husband, Simon. Her idea of heaven was organising things and people (or watching programmes about home organisers on TV) and she went on at least one trip per month to stock up on things that kept her home just as she liked it. She had recently bought a labelling machine so that her whole family knew exactly what to put where. There was so much more to her than that, though.

After a little chat, Mel put some biscuits on a plate and handed them to Janet.

'Well, of course I should say no, but of course I won't. Ha! Thank you, Mel. I will pop the plate into the main office. Want to wager they will be gone by half ten?' she said with a laugh and one eyebrow raised as she peered over her funky crimson glasses.

Cat walked in as Janet opened the door to head to her office. Both exchanged a 'Good morning' and 'How are you?' as Mel started making Cat a cup of tea on autopilot.

'Want to have this in my office, little one? I bought you some of those posh biscuits you like from the bakery for breakfast.'

'Yes, please, Mel.'

There was a catch in Cat's voice that confirmed to Mel that things hadn't improved since the previous morning. Her face was ashen and drawn, and it looked very much to Mel as though Cat hadn't long stopped crying.

Cat took off her coat and settled in the chair, then proceeded to tell Mel how the following day had gone.

CHAPTER SIX

'I pretty much went to bed as soon as I got home. I'm not exactly looking my best, so Mike completely bought my faking being ill. He was in all day, which is why I didn't text. There was nothing new to report anyway. I think I'm just bracing myself now for the end of my relationship, Mel. I feel like I've already lost him, and I miss him. I miss *us*.' Cat stopped to wipe a tear from her cheek.

'Oh, Cat, I'm so sorry, my love. I wish there was something I could do to make it better, I really do,' said Mel with a heavy heart.

'I'd drifted to sleep on the sofa in the evening after we'd had our tea, and when I woke up, I saw Mike engrossed on his phone, smiling at the screen. He hadn't noticed I was awake, so I just lay there watching him. He was typing so quickly and just sat glued to the phone, waiting for a reply. His phone made a buzz, and his face lit up. His smile let me know that whatever he had just read pleased him no end. Once again, he was texting back as though his life depended on it. I closed my eyes to buy a little time to compose myself. Then I made an obvious show of waking up, and as soon as Mike spotted this, he quickly slipped his phone into the pocket of his hoodie, hiding it like a dirty secret. After that, he seemed agitated and restless. It seemed like not being able to use his phone was tearing him up inside, and I knew it.'

Mel sat quietly, listening to her heartbroken friend. It took her a moment to think about what to say. Clearly, the situation sounded troubling, and she knew it wouldn't do any good to try to find some random excuse for Mike's behaviour. Cat was picking up on enough red flags to cause her to fear for her relationship. Mel was, too. Something was off; they just needed to work out what it was. Mel reached across the desk and put her hand on Cat's.

'So, what's your plan, my love? All this will make you ill the longer it goes on, so what do you want to do about it? Mike has no idea you suspect him, so the ball is very much in your court.'

'Good question, Mel, and one I spent most of last night lying awake thinking about. I gave more thought to some of the things we've already talked about, plus a few more. Things that I would have never dreamt of doing before.' Cat grimaced and felt her face redden.

'Such as...?' asked Mel.

'Well, such as having him followed, putting a tracker on his car, putting a voice recorder in the house and in his car, and the fake Facebook profile. God, listen to me. I sound like a professional bloody stalker, or like I'm some insecure, needy little weirdo. I'm embarrassed even thinking like that, never mind saying it out loud.'

Cat looked at her friend and searched her face for a sign of disapproval but found nothing but love. She exhaled a long, deep breath, knowing in her heart that she hadn't been judged. Maybe that meant her suggestions *weren't* so terrible after all, she hoped.

'Okay, well, from what you've said, I'm guessing that confronting him isn't something you're ready to do just yet. You're more looking to get a bit of actual evidence before you decide on what to do next, right?'

CHAPTER SIX

'Exactly that. As he changed the PIN on his mobile, I can't check his messages or install spyware. Not that I'd have the first clue how to do that, but I'm sure Colin in IT would have been able to talk me through it. That leaves setting up a fake profile on social media, putting a tracker on his car, voice recorders, and having him followed.'

The two discussed the pros and cons of each option and decided that a voice recorder seemed the least popular choice in case it was discovered. That would be a last resort. Neither Cat nor Mel would be able to carry out any surveillance because Mike would, of course, recognise their cars instantly. As Cat needed to keep her money in case she had to move out quickly, paying a private investigator was totally out of the question.

'Who do we know that goes to the gym? Or more to the point, who do we know that would be prepared to go to the gym one night to look for Mike? Would you be okay with us drafting in some help on this, love, because clearly, I can't do it,' asked Mel.

'At this point, I'm desperate for answers and will do what I need to. Obviously, it can't be someone that Mike knows, and I'd prefer it to be someone we can trust to not go and tell the world what we're doing. If this got back to Mike and he's not doing anything wrong, it would be the end of us, I'm sure.'

'I'm sure Liv would do it for us, but she wouldn't exactly blend in. We need someone who wouldn't be noticed, and with her glamorous looks, that's never going to happen. You mentioned Colin from IT earlier. I know he likes to keep fit; he often goes for a run after work in the evenings. I'm not sure he goes to the gym, though. There's only one way to find out. Let's ask him.'

A few minutes after getting Mel's call, Colin joined them, closing the door behind him. A self-confessed nerd that Mel had a huge soft spot for, Colin was the kind of man she would be proud to call her son had she chosen to have kids. She filled him in on everything that had been happening to make it easier for Cat.

'So how do you think Cat can best move forward, Col?'

'I'm a bit worried about what might happen if you don't get the answer you're hoping for, to be honest,' said Col, looking at Cat's face for a reaction.

'Honestly, I think I'm prepared for the worst, and if Mike is up to something, then it will only confirm what I already suspect. Getting confirmation is what I need, no matter what the outcome is.' Cat's tone was weary and flat.

'Okay, well, if you're sure about that, I'll pop along to the gym to see if Mike's there. I'll need a photo of him and maybe even the number plate and a description of his car. If you're 100% sure about the fake Facebook profile, I can set one up for you. I'll be able to source a photo that he wouldn't be able to find if he decided to do a reverse image check.'

'That's brilliant, thanks so much, Col. I can give you a hand with additional information too. We'll need our profile to have a bit of a back story for it to be believable. We don't want Mike to smell a rat or think it's some kind of scam.'

CHAPTER SIX

It was that simple. Cat realised that she had a formidable set of friends she could trust and rely on, and she had never been more aware or grateful for that fact until that very moment. She stood, grabbed her things, thanked them both, and went to her desk in a bit of a daze.

'If he's up to something and we find out, I'm going to feel terrible.' Col's eyes were fixed on Mel's as he spoke.

'I know, Col. It won't be easy, and I worry about that too. But if he is up to no good, then Cat deserves to know. She *needs* to know. It can't go on, and if the worst turns out to be true, then at least we'll be there to help pick up the pieces.'

Chapter Seven

Before going home, Mel decided to take a quick detour next door to Dougie's. She had lots of leftovers from Sunday lunch, so she thought she'd make some vegetable soup and wanted to check if Dougie might like some. She rang his doorbell and was shocked to find that it wasn't Dougie who answered the door, but a tall, tanned man.

'Kev! Well, this is a shock! I thought you weren't coming back for another week or so!'

Kev's face lit up, seeing Mel standing there. His smile was broad, and his twinkly blue eyes seemed to sparkle.

'Mel, how great to see you! How *are* you?'

Without waiting for an answer, he reached out and enveloped her in the biggest cwtch. At six foot three, he towered over Mel and swamped her in his big arms. Kev was built like a barn door but the very definition of a gentle giant who gave the best cwtches.

'Sorry, what am I thinking, keeping you on the door? Come in, it's freezing!' Kev raised his eyes and tutted at himself with a laugh.

CHAPTER SEVEN

'Actually, it was just a flying visit, Kev. I called to see if your dad wanted some soup for his tea. I've just got home from work and was about to make some.'

'Knowing my dad, that's a yes!'

'What about you, Kev? I'm sure you must be used to more fine dining these days, but of course, you're welcome to some of my humble home cooking, too.'

'You don't need to ask me twice, Mel. Can't beat home cooking. What time shall we come around?'

This caught Mel completely off guard as she hadn't intended for them to eat with her. She had only planned to drop the soup at the door as she had done countless times before.

'Er, give me an hour or so? Right, I'd better get cracking,' said Mel, and after a wave goodbye she walked down her neighbours' front path, wondering how she'd managed to accidentally invite them to hers. She'd been planning a quiet weekend, which hadn't happened, and suddenly her Monday in front of the telly with her feet up was out of the window, too.

'Perfect, see you in an hour, Mel. Thanks so much. Looking forward to catching up.'

Mel quickly trotted up the few steps to her front door. She went inside, shed her coat, bag, and boots in the hallway and headed for the kitchen. She quickly blended down the vegetables from yesterday with some stock and popped it on the stove to boil before turning down the heat to simmer. She sliced the crusty loaf she had bought from the bakery at lunchtime and cut an extra slice to fry up as croutons. Mel didn't usually do that but thought it might be nice to make a bit of an effort for her unexpected guests.

With half an hour left, she decided to pop upstairs to freshen up a bit and get out of her work clothes. She looked in the mirror and chuckled at the state of her hair, which was looking more than a bit windswept from the icy late November chill. She tamed it into less of a bird's nest and quickly changed into some black leggings and an off-the-shoulder top. Next, she applied a little bronzer, an extra coat of mascara, and some tinted lip balm. Enough to look polished but not too made up. Why was it often easier to do a full face of 'going out' makeup than achieve the so-called natural look? A quick squirt of Baccarat Rouge 540, her signature scent, and she was done.

With five minutes to spare before her guests were due to arrive, Mel laid the table, deciding to light a few candles to make the kitchen look cosy. After sampling the soup, she added some extra seasoning and a splash of cream to make it a little more indulgent. She tried it again and was happy.

The sound of knocking at the door brought Mel back from her thoughts. She ushered in Dougie and Kev and sent them through to the kitchen after both had kissed her on the cheek on their way past. Mel couldn't help but notice how good Kev smelled.

'Gin and tonic, beer, wine or a soft drink?' Mel asked brightly, hoping that she wasn't going to be drinking alone.

CHAPTER SEVEN

Both men opted for a beer while she went for her usual gin and tonic.

'Can I help with anything, Mel?' asked Kev after taking a long drink from his ice-cold pint of beer.

'No, it's all done, thanks, Kev. Just pop this bread and butter on the table for me, then make yourself comfy.'

'This food smells lovely, Mel. I should still be full after yesterday's dinner, though, but I wasn't about to say no to another of your meals now, was I? I was that full I didn't eat my cheesecake until suppertime last night! Twice in two days, my wee darling, the rumours will be starting about us two.'

'Well, Dougie, I don't mind if you don't, my love,' whispered Mel. She gave Dougie a playful wink as she set a big bowl of soup down on the table before him. She loved his wicked sense of humour, which was very similar to that of her dad. No wonder they got on so well.

'Is there a boyfriend that'll be getting jealous of you two, Mel? I don't want my dad getting into trouble if there is,' joked Kev.

'No boyfriend, Kev. Your dad is safe as houses. But I'm keeping my options open, Dougie, so don't you go getting complacent on me! I'm expecting flowers and chocolates every week now!'

The three dinner companions tucked into their meal, laughing and talking about old times as they ate. Mel was pleased that Dougie hadn't brought up the subject of her nan and the recent discovery. She was happy to talk about something other than that tonight.

'So, Kev, how come you're back?' asked Mel.

'I was meant to come home next June when my contract was due to end, but I got an offer recently to cut it short. The company I was with gave me the option to extend by two years to work in a different department or to leave early. I knew I didn't want another two years in Australia, so it was a reasonably easy decision.'

'I can't imagine it was *that* easy with our bloody weather!'

'You make a good point. I thought I'd landed in the Antarctic when I got off the plane, it's summer down under! No place like home, though, is there? How long is it since we saw each other last? I was home about eighteen months ago but didn't see you.'

'That sounds about right. I was on holiday in Menorca with Liv.'

'Ah, Liv! How is she?'

'She's great. Still the same, isn't she, Dougie?'

'Aye, she's not going to change now. As full of life as she's always been. You lot need to have a get-together. Jeff and Tony, too.'

'I'm here for good now, Dad, so I'm sure we will.'

With the meal all finished, Mel stood to clear the table and asked if anyone wanted another drink or some dessert. Both went for some tea and a piece of the chocolate cake that Liv had brought around the day before. Shortly after

CHAPTER SEVEN

finishing their dessert and tea, Mel's dinner guests decided to call it a night. Dougie had a TV programme he wanted to watch at nine o'clock, and Kev was starting to feel the effects of his long-distance flight.

'Thanks, Mel. That was delicious as always, my wee darling. Same time tomorrow, is it?' said Dougie, chancing his arm.

'Oi you, I'll be charging you rent if you're not careful!' Mel gave Dougie a cwtch, wished him a good night, and he started off down her steps.

'Mel, that soup was great, as was the company. Thanks so much for making my first night back feel like home. Of course, to thank you properly, I'll have to return the favour. My cooking's not a patch on yours, though, so it will have to be dinner out, sorry.'

'Don't be daft; there's no need to do that. It was just some soup. It was lovely to see you and catch up.' Sensing a fleeting look of disappointment flash across Kev's face, Mel added softly, 'But if you insist, I'd love to go out for dinner with you and hear more about what you've been up to.'

Any trace of disappointment that Mel had noticed disappeared in an instant. Kev bent to kiss her goodnight on the cheek.

'Great! That's a date then!' he said.

Chapter Eight

Once at the centre, Mel sat at her desk and turned her PC on. After shrugging off her coat and bag, she went to grab her mug to find it was missing from its usual place on her desk. She wandered off to the kitchen to find it was more densely populated than she had expected. Cat was stood to one side, deep in conversation with Colin. When Cat saw her come in, she raised her left hand, which was clutching Mel's mug, minus tea. Mel smiled and winked at her as she went to put the kettle on. Knowing that Cat would come over when she was finished talking to Colin and not wanting to disturb them, Mel took a detour into Janet's office to offer her a drink.

'Good morning, darling,' purred Janet. 'You are looking fabulous as always. How are you?'

'I'm okay, thanks, Janet. I came in to offer you a cuppa, and I'm glad I did now,' said Mel with a chuckle. She went to pick up Janet's mug from her perfectly organised desk and noticed that she was too late, and that Janet had already beaten her to it. Janet's mug was full to the brim of terrible-looking tea that appeared lukewarm and approximately two shades darker than milk, just how she liked it.

CHAPTER EIGHT

After a brief chat with Janet, Mel returned to the kitchen and joined Cat and Colin.

'Morning, you two. Any news?' asked Mel, her focus switching between Colin and Cat.

'Not too much,' replied Colin. 'I found some suitable profile photographs last night that I'll send you both on WhatsApp.'

'Mike said he's going to the gym straight from work this evening, so Col has kindly agreed to go along tonight, too. Mel, will you give me a hand later with the background for this Facebook profile, please, pet?'

'Course, my love. What about going for a coffee straight after work while Mike's at the gym?'

'That's perfect. Thank you, both. I'm so grateful to you; I'd be a mess without your help. Make that a bigger mess!' Cat said with an ironic laugh.

'Don't be daft, Cat,' said Colin. 'We're mates and that's what mates do. I'm sorry, but I've got to shoot off now, though. I've got an extremely dull meeting with some contractors in five minutes.'

'Isn't he canny, Mel?' said Cat as Colin walked down the corridor to his office.

'He's an absolute star, love. I can tell he's worried about you. We both are.'

'I know, and I'm sorry. I am feeling a bit better today, though. Things have had a chance to settle in my mind.

I do realise this might be the calm before the potential storm to end all storms, but I accept that. I'm hoping for the best and braced for the worst,' said Cat, placing her hand on Mel's arm as though to reassure her. If the worst did happen, then while it would hurt like hell, she would cope. Cat knew she would survive. And at some point in the future, with Mel's support, she might even thrive.

As Mel welcomed her carers into the group room, she realised just how much she needed to take her mind off the torrid time Cat was having. Today, her session would be a welcome respite for her as well as her carers. She loved being in her group room and was blessed to have it as a space for just her and the various teams she worked with. It was a colourful space, full of character and easily the most decadent room in the building. All her colleagues felt it was quintessentially Mel. She'd had a crystal-clear idea of how she wanted the room to look and feel. It was primarily a place of learning, of course, but Mel felt it was important that it was a safe, welcoming, comfortable, and almost therapeutic space. Her unique style was evident throughout, from the choice of tones and fabrics for the soft furnishings and room layout to the gentle music she played in the background and the choice of essential oils she used in the diffuser to scent the air. It had a calm yet energising feel that, for the various groups she worked with, was a sanctuary away from their daily responsibilities. Here, they could just be *themselves* and become immersed in the empowering, uplifting workshops that Mel created and facilitated. She felt it was crucial to offer her attendees an opportunity to just focus on themselves, if only for a short time. Mel had such admiration for the dedication, love and care they gave to their loved ones. Supporting

CHAPTER EIGHT

these unsung and overlooked heroes who did so much for others meant the world to Mel. For the time they spent here, they were not only given permission to put themselves first but it was actively encouraged.

Gratitude was today's topic. This session was one of Mel's favourites because it was inspired by her amazing mother. Anne had been such a positive soul who had always been grateful for the most insignificant things. Things that most people wouldn't even notice. The session always seemed to go down well with the group members, too. Many were so heavily laden with their duties as carers they struggled to think of something to be grateful for at the start of the session. By the end of the two-hour workshop, Mel never failed to work her magic and turn their thinking around. She was always so happy to see her attendees leave the session, feeling that, in fact, they had much more to be grateful for than they had realised. Seeing this kind of change was incredibly rewarding, and it motivated Mel to keep writing workshops and finding new ways to uplift and inspire her carers.

The group was given an exercise where they had to think of the people and things, they were most grateful for. One of the more playful members joked that they would only do it if Mel did and that they also wanted feedback. The whole group laughed and joined in with the request. Mel put her hands up in mock surrender and agreed that on this occasion only, she would complete the exercise with them. Usually, of course, she wouldn't take part, as her role was to monitor the group and be on hand and notice if anyone was struggling with an exercise. Having facilitated several workshops with this particular group, she made the judgement that she could do a reasonable job of the exercise whilst still being able to spot any issues any of them may have.

Mel sat at the end of one of the tables and began giving some thought about who and what she was most grateful for. She was able to name more people than things and felt that was something to be grateful for in itself. Other than her health, the things she valued seemed to come back to people too. A perfect example was her home. Her kitchen was something she particularly valued. It gave her the opportunity to cook for and enjoy time with the people who meant the most to her. Just thinking of that room made her feel warm inside. She was lucky enough to have spent many happy hours around her kitchen table with those she loved. When it came to gratitude, Mel valued the people in her life above everything. She felt extremely blessed at that moment. Whilst she loved her house, it faded into complete unimportance when compared to how she felt about her mother, nan and grandad. She would trade her home in half a heartbeat if it meant she could have them back.

Thinking about her nan reminded Mel about Liv, Jeff, and Tony and how quick they had been to offer help in finding out more about her nan's other self, Alice Miracle. She really was blessed to have such supportive friends. At the end of the exercise, the group provided feedback. Some mentioned that they found it tricky to think of things to write at the start. Mel expected a few people to say that because that happened every single time she ran this session. When life was busy and hard, as it nearly always was for carers, it could be all too easy to focus on

CHAPTER EIGHT

the more difficult or negative aspects of life. Every group member mentioned that they were surprised by just how many things and people they felt grateful for by the end of the exercise. Mel couldn't help but notice the difference in the energy in the room. The attendees seemed brighter, happier, and almost lighter than they had appeared at the start of today's session.

'Aren't you forgetting something, Mel?' one of the members piped up. 'You said you'd give us feedback, too!'

'Oh yes, so I did! Well, I found that to be an extremely powerful exercise, and it reminded me how lucky I am. Lucky because of the family I have and once had. Lucky because I have the most amazing friends and colleagues. And lucky because I get to come and work here with you lovely lot. So…my feedback is that I'm so very grateful for my wonderful dad, my gorgeous friends and all the other fabulous, inspirational people in my life. I'm very, very blessed.'

After she'd wrapped up the morning's workshop, Mel took a few moments to herself in her group room. She felt it had gone incredibly well and she was having a great day. She had loved every second of it. It lifted her heart to see the positive change in her group as they filed out of the building. It was incredible to see the difference that those two hours had made. The results she achieved always put a spring in her step, too, and inspired her in the role she loved so much. It felt great being able to do good things for good people. Almost instantly, she felt a pang of guilt jab at her heart as she thought about Cat. No doubt her day was about as far from great as you could get.

That afternoon, Mel decided that instead of going for a coffee that evening as planned, she would instead take Cat to Merola's, their favourite Italian restaurant. It was often busy at this time in the evening due to their tasty 'early bird' menu. It was a popular choice for a straight-from-work event as well as somewhere to go later on for a date. Mel decided it would be safer to book, so gave them a quick call to secure a table. She knew the manager, Spiro, well and so requested the corner table at the back so they could chat properly, away from the buzz of the restaurant.

Mel grabbed her things and went to Cat's office. She was in her coat, ready to leave, and was just ending a call with her mother.

'Merola's?' asked Mel. She didn't need to be psychic to know that Cat's answer would be a definite yes.

'Ooh, that'd be good, but I doubt we'd get in…'

'A table for two in the back corner is already booked!'

'Have I told you how much I love you lately, pet?' said Cat with a heavy sigh. A single tear fought to escape and tumbled down her face. Her fabulously thoughtful friend always seemed to know exactly what to say and do to make her feel better. *Always.*

Chapter Nine

As they walked into Merola's, they were hit by the delicious smells wafting out of the kitchen. Spiro dashed over to greet his regulars, and, in typical Spiro style, kissed them both on each cheek, then ushered them in like long-lost members of his family. No wonder it was their favourite place on the high street. Amazing food, great wine, and the warmest of welcomes.

With drink orders placed, they set about looking over the menu, not that they needed to as they knew it back to front and usually ordered the same thing. As a bottle of water and two small glasses of Barolo were brought over to them, Mel and Cat placed their food orders. Mel opted for margherita pizza with pesto and Cat chose the carbonara with a side of garlic bread. Whilst Cat hadn't eaten much these past few days, the gorgeous smells emanating from Merola's kitchen had certainly rejuvenated her appetite.

'I love this place so much. Thanks for booking us in, Mel. Being here makes me almost forget the shit that's been going on. It's a bit of normality, and I think I needed it.' Cat exhaled long and slow before taking a warming sip of wine.

'I love it here too, and it seemed like a much better option than going for a coffee. We've had some fun nights here over the years, eh? Do you remember last Christmas when we had our work party here after the carers' event? I dread to think how many bottles of wine we went through!'

'Ooh yes! I remember waking up under a blanket on your settee because I fell asleep while you went to fetch me some water. So many fab times, and I never imagined we'd ever be having a night here setting up a fake profile to trap Mike.'

'Shall we make a start before the food arrives?' asked Mel.

'Yeah, let's get it over and done with.'

As Mel reached into her large and chaotic handbag to retrieve her notepad and pen, a wave of sadness washed over her. What they were about to do felt so wrong and was so out of character for them both. Setting up fake accounts to try and catch a potential cheater was something they saw on television or read in a 'real-life' story in one of the trashy magazines that adorned coffee tables at a hair salon. Mel began to doubt herself. Was this *really* a good idea? Even if it was discovered that Mike hadn't been cheating, how would this leave Cat feeling about what she had done?

'Before we start on this, love, are you *sure* it's what you want to do?' asked Mel before taking a sip of her wine.

'It's not what I *want* to be doing tonight, Mel, but other than confronting Mike, I don't think I have many options. I'm hoping that Col discovers nothing suspicious

CHAPTER NINE

tonight and that we don't actually need to set up the profile on Facebook. I'm hoping this is no more than a backup plan.'

Mel reached across the table and placed her hand on top of Cat's. There was a look of resigned sadness in her eyes. Despite her saying that she hoped there was nothing untoward happening, her face told a different tale. The defeated look made it clear that whilst she did, of course, hope for the best outcome, she didn't believe it would happen. Not for one second.

'Right then, let's do it, my darling.'

They looked at the photos Colin had sent them and chose one that seemed perfect. A tall, striking brunette with big brown eyes whom they decided to call Lisa. Next, they set about listing her characteristics so she would appear to be more than just a pretty face. It was important she came across as friendly and approachable so he would not feel intimidated by her looks. They conjured up her likes and dislikes, ensuring there was common ground with Mike. He was a huge fan of *The Walking Dead*, so Lisa was too. Lisa also liked several of the bands Mike liked. As Mike's favourite food was Italian, surprise, surprise, so was Lisa's. There was a suitable number of things they had in common, but not too many. They didn't want to make Lisa a carbon copy of Mike, which might be too obvious and make him suspicious.

In no time at all they had conjured up a list for the profile that complemented the photo perfectly. Lisa was attractive, fun-loving, adventurous, independent, popular, and, most importantly, she was single. 'Right then, ladies,

I have a carbonara for you, Miss Cat, with the rather excellent choice of our legendary garlic bread on the side. And for you, Miss Mel, a finely crafted margherita with pesto. Can I get you anything else? Parmesan, black pepper, more wine?'

As Mel and Cat were both driving, they reluctantly refused more wine but happily accepted the offer of freshly grated parmesan.

'Enjoy, ladies,' said Spiro with a toothy smile.

As the two tucked into their delicious meal, Mel tried to lift the mood a little.

'This pizza is so bloody good, Cat. I've proposed marriage to Spiro a few times now, y'know. One of these days he'll say yes, won't he?' said Mel with a twinkle in her eye.

'I'd fight you for him for this carbonara!' said Cat.

Mel was pleased to see her tucking into her food and even happier to see her smile.

They discussed what might be happening at the gym tonight and how things were going. Colin had not texted Cat yet, which they took to be a good sign. Surely if Mike had not turned up, he would have been in touch by now, wouldn't he?

'I'm going to start doing a bit of a decluttering of my things at home. I bought a canny book about it last year, but it's just been sitting on the bookshelf gathering dust until now. The irony, eh? I left it on my bedside cabinet, so

CHAPTER NINE

it looks like I'm reading it. Not that I think Mike will even notice that I'm downsizing or question why. I just thought that if I end up moving out it'd be good to be travelling a little lighter in life. I didn't realise how much stuff I've accumulated over the past few years. It seems whilst I am excellent at buying things, I am well below average when it comes to getting rid of things I no longer wear, use, need, or want!'

'Oh, I think that's a fab idea, Cat. It's a win-win. Even if everything is fine and you decide to stay, you'll have less stuff and more space. But if you do decide to move out then it'll be easier for you on a practical level at least. Once I've finished going through my nan's boxes, I may well have a go at decluttering my things too. The beauty and I suppose the curse of living alone means you can fill your space with as much as you want. One of the minimalist YouTubers would have a bloody field day in my wardrobes alone!'

'With the amount of clothes you've got, I don't doubt it!' said Cat as she checked her watch. 'Would you mind if we skipped dessert, pet? I'm full to the rafters and ready for a hot bath and an early night. I'm absolutely knackered.'

'I couldn't eat another thing, either. I'm absolutely stuffed. I just need to pay a visit to the little girls' room before we head off.'

Instead of going to the loo, Mel went to pay the bill. Treating Cat to her meal felt like the least she could do. She went back to the table to collect Cat. As she put her coat on, she took a lip balm from one of the pockets and popped some on before pulling her gloves from the other pocket. After wrapping herself up in her scarf, she was ready to leave the warm amber glow of the restaurant and head out into the chilly night air. The pair linked arms as they walked down the high street before turning right and walking to the little car park behind the restaurant. Just as they arrived at their cars, Cat's phone rang, and Mel nodded encouragingly for her to answer it. It was Colin. She froze for a second before pressing accept.

'Hi, Col. I'm with Mel, so I'm going to put you on speaker phone. How did it go tonight?'

'Hiya, both. Hope you're doing okay. I'll cut to the chase. Mike was there and dressed in gym gear, but he wasn't on the machines a great deal. He went on the running machine for about fifteen minutes or so and did about five minutes on the weights. I didn't see him chatting with any female gym customers, but he did have brief conversations with a couple of the blokes. He spent a bit of time chatting with some members of staff, in particular the woman who works behind the desk. He looked as if he was doing a few little jobs there which seemed odd. I saw him empty the bins and he replaced an empty water bottle with a fresh one. I'm just wondering, is there any chance at all he might be working there, Cat?'

'Well, Col, of the various scenarios I've considered, him having a secret second job never entered my head!' said Cat, shocked by what she'd heard. Her whole body was trembling as her mind raced to process what Colin had just told her. She had been tense all day, fearing the worst possible outcome. Hearing this news had almost drained her of all energy, leaving her weak and emotional. Was all this worry for nothing?

CHAPTER NINE

'Just to make sure and put you at ease, I can go back to the gym again another couple of times, perhaps. I could try to get closer to Mike and see if he's wearing a staff badge. Maybe strike up a conversation with him. If you want me to, that is, Cat. So far though, I've not seen any obviously worrying behaviour. I hope it's a relief and a weight off your mind.'

'Okay, that sounds like a good idea to me. Thank you *so* much for what you've done tonight, Col. I am so grateful to you. Lunch is on me tomorrow, your choice where we go. Goodnight, Col, and thank you again.'

As Cat hung up the call she burst into tears. All the emotions she had bottled up that day erupted, and it felt good to set them free. She held on to Mel until the last tear fell. Mel felt around in her bag for a packet of tissues and passed one to Cat.

'Oh, Mel. How the hell could I get it so wrong? I was *convinced* he was up to no good.' Cat stopped to blow her nose. 'I feel like such an idiot. Why the hell did he get a second job without telling me? I just don't get it. It's not like he desperately needs more money. Well, not that I know of at least. I can't get my head around that. Him having an affair would make more sense!'

'You are *far* from an idiot, Cat. Look, it's great news that Mike really was at the gym like he said and not sloping off to meet a woman. It's definitely good that Colin didn't see anything dodgy going on tonight, but you're right that Mike is keeping some sort of secret. Your instincts *were* right. So don't you *dare* think of yourself as an idiot. There's still a mystery here and let's see if we can get to the bottom of it. Now, top up your makeup and get yourself home.'

'Mel, I can't thank you enough,' Cat said, exhaling deeply, sending a stream of misty breath up into the inky night sky. 'You're my rock, you know that? I'm blessed to have you.'

'No need to thank me, darling. I'm just as blessed to have you. If you need anything, text me. If not, I will see you in the morning.'

Mel and Cat got into their cars and gave a little wave to each other before driving off. A few minutes later, Mel pulled up outside her home and parked in her usual spot. She dashed up the steps to her house and hurriedly let herself in. It was cold enough to chill her bones to ice and she couldn't wait to be snuggled up on her sofa with a cup of tea.

Mel put the kettle on and then went to change into her cosiest pyjamas and warmest dressing gown. While she was relieved that Cat would rest more easily tonight and get a better night's sleep, a gut feeling told her there was something not quite right about Mike. She didn't mention it to Cat, but she hadn't forgotten that Mike had changed the PIN on his mobile. That in itself might well be nothing to worry about but there was an anxious feeling in the pit of her stomach that nagged at her. Mel was concerned about what her friend might discover in the coming days or weeks.

Just as she finished making her tea and putting a generous number of biscuits on a plate, she heard the alert

CHAPTER NINE

sound on her phone that let her know she had a text. She settled down in the lounge and blew on her tea, sending cooling ripples across the surface before taking a sip. Mel checked her phone to find a message from Tony. He and Jeff had set up a WhatsApp group with her and Liv.

Hey, gorgeous girl. Just to let you know, we have arranged to go to Liv's on Thursday at 6.30. Liv is cooking (thanks Liv, you're an angel), and Jeff is sorting the wine. All you need to bring are your nan's photos etc unless you fancy being naughty and want to bring pudding of course. I've made a few calls and started doing a bit of research and boy do I have some news for you! Not saying any more until I see you, so don't ask. My lips are well and truly sealed! Ha! I'm such a tease! Much love, T xxx

Chapter Ten

The morning had flown by for Mel. She had barely found time for a cuppa. Her stomach growled loudly in protest and reminded her it was lunchtime. She had skipped breakfast, which often happened throughout the week, so she was now more than ready for something to eat. It would have to be a quick sandwich at her desk as she still had her afternoon session on setting boundaries to prepare for. Just then her office door opened, and Cat walked in.

'Hey, Mel, how are you doing? Thanks again for last night, pet. I wondered if you fancied coming to the bakery. I'm taking Col for lunch if you're up for it. My treat. We're pushing the boat out and sitting in today, which as you well know means a cake after our soup and sandwich.'

A sit-in at the bakery sounded great and she toyed with the idea for half a second.

'Sorry, Cat, I've got a session to prep for, so I won't have time, sadly. I'll walk down with you though and pick up something to bring back. How are you feeling today? Do you feel better knowing that Mike was at the gym last night, where he said he'd be?' asked Mel, noticing how much brighter Cat looked today.

CHAPTER TEN

'It's like a huge weight has been lifted and I do feel a lot better, thanks, pet. I slept a lot better last night, that's for sure. I'm a bit pissed off if he has got a secret part-time job he's hiding from me, but it's nowhere near as awful as him cheating on me. So, all in all, it could be a lot worse. Small mercies!'

'I'm so pleased, Cat. Let's hope Colin got his wires crossed and it turns out that Mike's just after a six-pack,' Mel said with a chuckle. 'Right, I need to crack on so let's head to the bakery, shall we?'

***

The afternoon went just as quickly as the morning. Mel's group left with a spring in their step, feeling more assertive and ready to take on the world and .tackle anyone who overstepped their newly set boundaries. As she tidied up the group room, she considered what she would do that evening. Her mind drifted back to the text she had received from Tony the night before and she wondered what he could have possibly discovered about her nan. She felt a tinge of guilt that he and Jeff had been researching when she hadn't looked at anything since the weekend. Mel decided that she would have a quick snack later before going through more of her nan's belongings.

As soon as she got home, Mel kicked off her boots and hung up her coat in the cupboard under the stairs and gathered the post from the mat by the front door. She plonked the post on the kitchen table and went to put the kettle on. The house felt a bit chilly, so Mel decided to fire up the log burner. As she was going to be home all night, she wanted to make the lounge toasty warm. *Nothing beats a real fire,* thought Mel as she watched the flames start to dance in the hearth. She switched on her lamp and put her nan's boxes of photos on the coffee table before heading upstairs to shed her work clothes and change into something more comfortable.

Feeling snug and relaxed in her oversized jumper and leggings, hair tied up in a little red scarf, Mel set about making a pot of tea. She poured herself a large mug with plenty left for a second round. She had just placed her mug on the coffee table when the doorbell rang. There was no denying her heart sank at the sound. She felt that she hadn't had a night to herself in ages, probably because she hadn't. Reluctantly, she trudged down the hall and opened the front door.

'Hiya, Mel.'

'Kev. Hi,' said Mel, slightly surprised to see him.

'I just noticed your car was outside and I thought I'd pop around to give you my new mobile number. I realised I don't have yours so maybe you could just drop me a text so I have it if that's okay?'

'Course, yes, I'll do it now. I've just made some tea if you'd like one?' she asked on autopilot. Almost the very second the invitation left her lips, she could have kicked herself. Mel desperately craved her own company but would have felt rude not inviting him in. She consoled herself with the fact that a quick cuppa wouldn't be more than half an hour.

CHAPTER TEN

'Lovely. I don't often refuse tea. Milk and two sugars, please, Mel,' said Kev, his smile making happy little creases around his bright blue eyes.

Mel directed Kev into the lounge whilst she poured his drink. She had a fleeting moment of anxiety, worried that it might feel awkward with it being just the two of them. What if they struggled for something to say? It wasn't like they had stayed in touch much after Kev moved away. *Too late now*, she thought, and she took a deep breath and wandered through to the lounge.

'You're an angel,' said Kev as he took the mug from Mel. He went straight in for a sip and exhaled loudly. 'Now *that* is a good cuppa. A nine out of ten, that, Mel.'

'I've had years of practice!' said Mel as she sat back down on the sofa next to him. 'So how are you settling back to village life so far then, Kev?'

'Apart from it being bloody freezing, it's great. Not much has changed since we were kids, has it? I needed to be back for my dad. He's not admitted it, but I've sensed him starting to struggle. He's been telling me how much you've been helping him, so thank you for that.'

'Oh, I haven't done much, really, mainly because he's a stubborn old bugger, and he won't let me!' Mel said with a smile. 'Is there anything you're missing about Australia yet?'

'I really enjoyed my time there, Mel, but it was time to come home. Not just for my dad, I felt ready. So, no, there's nothing I miss and I'm looking forward to setting down some roots here now. I'll stay with my dad for a little while and then look for a place of my own nearby. Being back in my old bedroom is definitely not something I see as long-term,' said Kev with a chuckle. He glanced at the boxes that covered the coffee table as he sipped his tea. 'What's with the boxes? Don't tell me you're moving out!' His eyebrows raised in an exaggerated way for effect.

'No, nothing like that. I love living here, Kev. The boxes are the last of my nan's things. I've had them stored at my dad's since she passed away a few years ago. I've finally decided to go through them.'

'I remember your nan so well. I was really sorry to hear she passed. What a lovely lady she was. I was very fond of her,' said Kev softly, echoing the sadness she felt.

'She really was a treasure, but it seems there was more to her than met the eye. When I went through the first box, I found some photographs in a scrapbook, and it seems that my little nan was once a singer in an up-market London cabaret spot.'

'What? Are you serious? Your nan, a singer in London?' Kev's face was a picture of incredulity. 'You must have that wrong, surely, Mel.'

'I know. It's unbelievable, isn't it? I've had a few days to get my head around it now and yet I still can't quite do it. I showed the scrapbook to my dad and Liv, and they are both convinced it's her.'

'Can I see it?'

'Course,' said Mel as she went straight to the relevant box and fished it out for him to look at.

CHAPTER TEN

Kev slowly and silently thumbed through the pages; his eyes transfixed on the images.

'That's your nan, Mel. No doubt in my mind. And she kept this to herself all those years. I wonder why. If that was me, I'd be shouting it from the rooftops, not that anyone is ever likely to pay to hear me sing, mind you.'

'That's what me and my dad don't understand. Why the secrecy? So, I'm wondering what else I may find out in these boxes. I'm almost afraid to look!' said Mel with a grimace. 'I mentioned this to Tony and Jeff on Sunday and apparently, they've done some digging. Tony still has a lot of contacts in London, of course. He knew the place she performed in too and said it was where all the celebs used to go back then. I'm meeting up with them at Liv's tomorrow as they have news for me.'

'It's quite exciting, this! You'll have to keep me posted. Shit, I've just realised I'm holding you up. Anything I can do to help? I can go through some boxes with you if you like. Have you eaten yet? I could nip to pick something up if you want me to. My cooking would only stretch to beans on toast or scrambled eggs at a push. Or maybe it's best if I leave you in peace to crack on? Sorry, Mel,' rambled Kev.

'Seriously no need to apologise; don't forget it was me that invited you in! There's no need to leave unless you want to, and I wouldn't blame you. Sitting here going through boxes of old family photos isn't exactly the night dreams are made of, now, is it?' she said with a laugh.

A few minutes later, Mel was stirring a pan of beans on the stove as Kev buttered toast. Going through boxes of old photos may not have been the stuff of dreams exactly, but Kev decided that spending the evening with Mel sounded like a nice idea.

Over their meal, sat at the kitchen table, Kev asked about Liv, Tony, and Jeff. Kev mentioned that he hadn't seen any of them yet since coming home but was looking forward to catching up with them again soon. He hadn't been at all surprised the three had volunteered to help Mel research her nan's secret life in London. He knew how well they all got on and how fascinated they would be in a story like that. Secrets, intrigue, and drama would be right up their street.

After clearing up together, Mel and Kev went back to the lounge where they both took a seat on the sofa. They speculated about what Tony and Jeff may have uncovered. Some suggestions were logical, others ridiculous as they took things to the extreme. They fell about laughing when they each conjured up increasingly silly and outlandish reasons that Lizzie had left London.

What had Mel been worried about earlier, she wondered? Of course there wouldn't be awkward silences; they had known each other for years and sat here in her lounge it felt like no time had passed at all.

There were lots of family snaps in the box Kev had and the two amused themselves commenting on some of the more questionable fashion statements made by Mel and her family. There were large lapels and even larger flares aplenty on show. The photos in Mel's box were similar. Her grandad Bill regularly got his camera out and she was so glad he did. Looking through these

CHAPTER TEN

stirred up lots of memories of her younger years. Mel shared some of the stories behind these precious images that captured the happy essence of her childhood. The love Mel's grandparents had for her was clear. There were photographs of her doing the most ordinary of things, such as playing on her roller skates, sleeping on a deck chair in their garden, and riding her bike. They had also captured less mundane memories too, like her opening her Christmas presents, appearing in school plays, and dressing as a witch for Halloween. As Mel came to the last photo in the box, she suddenly thought how boring this must be for Kev, especially as they hadn't found anything useful. She closed the box and put it on the floor to the left of her.

'Well, that was a riveting half an hour or so for you, I'm sure,' Mel said with an eyeroll.

'Don't be daft. Seeing those photos of you looking so sweet and innocent when you were little, who would have predicted you'd turn into an indie punk type of teenager a few years later.'

'It's goth, actually!' she said, hitting him with a cushion in fake outrage. 'Not much trace of that left now apart from my Doc Martens and a couple of skull scarves. Saying that, a few months ago I went to see The Mission and Gene Loves Jezebel play live. Both were great gigs and Wayne Hussey and Jay Aston still sound fabulous. There's life in the old goths yet, me included,' she said with a playful smile.

'Nothing old about you, Mel, and you suit your Docs and skull scarves. Shall we do another box?'

'Why thank you, Kev, flattery will get you everywhere,' said Mel playfully. 'Are you sure? Haven't I put you through enough for one night?'

'Oh, come on. Let's do one more.'

Kev reached for the next box which was marked *Papers*. As they flicked through, they found lots of uninteresting things like receipts for household appliances and cars long since gone. Mel made a mental note that a lot of things from this box could be recycled. There weren't any profound or warm fuzzy memories attached to the receipt for the washing machine her grandparents bought in 1971!

After the initial disappointment, some more meaningful things surfaced further on in the box. There were some birthday and Christmas cards to and from both her grandparents that contained some heartwarming messages of love for each other. There were some of their wedding cards from friends and family wishing the couple a long and happy marriage. While it might not have been as long as they would have liked, it was, without a shadow of a doubt, happy.

Just as Mel thought this box held no clues to the hidden part of her nan's life, she found a fragile, old-looking envelope addressed to Miss A Miracle at her nan's old family home, Hen Bandy in Llanllyfni, Caernarfon. She carefully opened it and found a piece of paper inside with faded handwriting on it.

CHAPTER TEN

My Dearest Alice,

I hope this letter finds you. Firstly, I need to say that I am not looking for forgiveness, but I want you to know how deeply sorry I am. It's not an excuse but I didn't mean for any of this to happen in the way that it did. I don't expect you to understand or maybe even believe that, but it is the truth, nevertheless. All I can say is I would have never intentionally hurt or upset you. The fact that I have breaks my heart more than you could ever imagine. I would beg for a second chance if I thought you would take me back, but I know that's too much to ask.

I will never forget you, my darling Alice. Not a day shall pass that I won't think of you, miss you, or love you. With my whole heart, I love you. Since you left, nothing is right in my world. There is nothing and no one that makes me happier than you did.

I now know what I had and what I lost.

Always yours,

Maurice

Xxx

Both Mel and Kev were silent for a few moments, neither knowing what to think, never mind say.

'Your grandad was Bill, so... who's Maurice?' asked Kev, still gently holding the envelope in his hand.

Mel sat quietly, trying to take in what she had just read aloud to Kev. She re-read it as though she hadn't trusted that she had read it properly the first time, looking for mistakes.

'This probably sounds stupid, but I feel quite shaken. It's not that my nan had a boyfriend before my grandad, more the tone of this letter. This Maurice sounds so desperately sad. Almost broken. They must have had something special between them. What the hell did he do to mess things up so badly? For her to keep that letter for all those years, he must have been special to her,' said Mel as she felt the emotion well up inside her.

'Are you okay?' asked Kev.

'Yeah, I'm fine. Just a bit of a surprise, that's all. In all these years my nan never told me about him.'

'It must be a shock, especially as you two were so close. It seems there was so much that she kept to herself.' Kev paused to reflect for a few seconds. 'I can see why Liv, Tony and Jeff have been drawn into this. It's fascinating, Mel. If you want help with anything, I'd love to be a part of your little research team if you'll have me. I'm not half bad with tech stuff if that's of any use to you?'

'Course I'll have you,' Mel said without pause, putting her hand on his arm. 'I'm actually really glad you were here for that letter, so thank you. Not something I'd want to have read alone to be honest.' She moved forward to the edge of the sofa and checked her watch to find that it was nearly eleven. The following day was going to be busy, and she suddenly felt emotionally spent. The past few days had been intense, and she was wrung out. 'It's getting late, and I've kept you long enough already.' Mel hoped Kev would pick up on the fact that she needed to go to bed.

CHAPTER TEN

Sensing it was time to go, Kev stood up to leave. Mel thanked him again, and again he told her it had been his pleasure. After he had stepped out the front door, he turned and wrapped his arms around her and gave Mel a long cwtch before gently pulling away.

'I'll see you soon, Mel. Don't forget to drop me a text when you get time. How else am I going to be able to invite you out for that meal?' he said with a grin.

'Too right! I've cooked for you twice now; you owe me, mister!' joked Mel.

After closing the door behind Kev, Mel went back to the lounge and sat for a few moments in the fading orange glow coming from the log burner, trying to get her head around what had happened tonight. She mulled over whether she should invite Kev along to Liv's the following night and decided she probably would. She would check with Liv first to be sure it was okay before inviting him.

Reaching for the piece of paper Kev had written his number on, she picked up her mobile and added his details to her address book.

Goodnight Kev, and thanks again. Mel xx

Goodnight Mel. Sweet dreams. Kev xx

Not even a minute later the phone flashed again. Expecting a further message from Kev, Mel was surprised to see that it was from Liv.

Am I cooking for five tomorrow instead of four by any chance, darling? xxxx

How the hell does she know? thought Mel.

Yes, Liv. I think you are. M xxx

Chapter Eleven

Mel stepped outside the next morning and shivered almost violently as she closed the door behind her.

'Morning, Mel!' Andrea from number five and Suzanne from number six said cheerfully and in stereo.

Mel looked up and spotted them standing next to the post box, no doubt discussing this year's festive decoration that would adorn it.

'Morning, both! Is it that time already? What's it to be this year?'

'Ah, well, that would be telling, wouldn't it?' said Andrea, beaming.

'Yes, you'll just have to wait and see!' followed Suzanne.

'Whatever it is, I'm sure it will be fabulous, girls! Looking forward to your dazzling display.' Mel smiled and gave a wave as she jumped in her car to go to work. It really would be fabulous too, thought Mel. Andrea and Suzanne always did an amazing job, which seemed to just keep getting better each year.

FINDING A MIRACLE

Cat had just parked up outside the carers' centre when she spotted Mel heading for her usual parking spot. After getting out of her car, Cat went to the boot and retrieved the bags of prizes that she had wrapped the previous night at home. She had arranged a treasure hunt at ten am for the young people in their local park. *After all, what's a treasure hunt without treasure*, she thought. Cat smiled gratefully as she noticed barely a cloud in the blue sky. It was such a glorious winter's day. Everything felt a little brighter, she thought, not just the weather. Today *was* a better day, she decided. It might even be a good day, and she needed that.

'Hey, trouble, how's tricks?' called Mel.

'Morning, Mel. Canny, thanks, pet. I'm glad I've caught you. I'll be out all morning; we're doing a treasure hunt in Porth Park. I was hoping I'd see you so I could warn you not to buy any lunch today. I made a big lasagne last night and brought in the leftovers for us. As it turns out, I have more than I expected because Mike barely ate a thing last night, so I hope you've skipped breakfast as usual.'

'Is he ill or something? Not like him to be off his food.' Mel looked quizzically at her friend.

'He really wasn't himself, and to just pick at his tea I think he must be coming down with something. Usually, when I make lasagne from scratch, he devours it; it's his favourite. I made it to ease my guilty conscience for doubting him.' Cat's grimace was almost cartoon-like.

The pair walked towards the centre, continuing to chat as they went. A lunch date was set for one o'clock in

CHAPTER ELEVEN

the staff kitchen. Mel had indeed skipped breakfast and by lunchtime would be more than happy to help Cat deal with her homemade lasagne leftovers. Whilst Cat had a field trip that morning, Mel had admin in store and wasn't due to deliver a group session until two o'clock. Her plan for the morning was to use the time to start organising the Christmas party for her groups of carers. Seeing Andrea and Suzanne hovering around the post box earlier reminded her that Christmas wasn't *that* far away and so she needed to get a move on. Mel decided that her first task would be to compile a list of local businesses to ask for some gift donations so that each attendee would have at least one present to take away with them. To avoid any distractions, Mel locked herself away in her office as she knew from years of experience it would take a couple of hours to write all the emails and letters.

After checking the time a little while later, Mel was pleased to see that she had completed her first job with enough time to start planning other aspects of the Christmas party. Next on her to-do list was the venue. Needing to check her budget for the party, she went to speak to Janet. Funding events was often a headache, particularly for the adults. Raising money for children was always much easier. Christmas though often brought out the charitable side of people and they were blessed to receive more generous donations at this time of year than any other. She knocked gently on Janet's door and heard an invitation to enter from the other side.

'Hey, Janet. I've just popped in to ask when a good time might be to discuss the budget for the Christmas party for my groups,' said Mel tentatively. Janet was always so busy, and she hated bothering her, but needs must on this occasion.

'I've been expecting you. It's nearly that time of year again, isn't it?' Janet's voice dripped like honey. 'Actually, Mel, I have some good news for you. I've spoken to a few local businesses already, and we've had a few offers of help. The bakery is providing us with a free Christmas cake and one hundred mince pies. Anything else we want to order we will get at a special rate. The guys at the Red Lion have said we can have their function hall on the twentieth if we guarantee to be out by half past four. They kindly offered us a buffet with tea and coffee at a reduced rate. I need numbers from you so that I can get it costed.'

'Wow! *You* are a total legend, Janet! Thank you so much, my lovely. The Red Lion would be *perfect*. Their function room will already be decorated which saves us time and money and I'm sure they would put some music on for us as well. We don't have enough room to host it here at the centre anymore. I've already checked the numbers and we're looking at eighty people. I've contacted local businesses for a variety of donations as usual. Do you think we'll have enough in the funds?' Mel asked hopefully.

'It will be tight, but I *think* we can make it work. Let me do some sums and come back to you, darling.'

Mel went back to her office and sat at her desk, leaving Janet to work her magic on the numbers in peace. She felt hopeful that they could make it work as Janet had said. Her group members did so much for their loved ones all year round, so it felt important to Mel that their organisation did something nice for them. She checked

CHAPTER ELEVEN

her watch to find that it was close to lunchtime. She heard her phone buzz from the depths of her bag and went in search of it. There were two unread messages. One from her dad and another from Kev.

The text from her dad was just him checking in on her and asking if she had any more news about her nan's secret past. He also mentioned that he'd seen Kev that morning. Mel's reply was short and sweet. She told him that she was fine and explained that she should have more news for him in a few days regarding Lizzie. She added that she knew about Kev being back as she'd seen him a couple of times. Next, she opened Kev's text.

Hey Mel. Hope it's okay to text you at work. I wanted to ask if it would be alright to tag along with you tonight. If it's a yes, what should I bring? Kev xx

Hi Kev. No problem with you coming to Liv's later, I meant to send you a message to invite you along, but it's been a busy morning. Meet you at the front gate at 6.30. Liv is cooking, the boys are bringing wine, and I'm bringing dessert. Maybe bring chocolates or flowers for Liv? See you later, looking forward to it! M xx

Just as Mel pressed send, the door to her office opened and a frozen-looking Cat popped her head in. Her cheeks were a just-pinched pink, her nose was red, and her eyes looked watery. She announced that the lasagne was in the microwave and mentioned that Colin was joining them. Apparently, they needed extra help finishing off her wares as it was more than a two-woman job.

The kitchen was unusually quiet for that time of day. It was just Colin sitting at the table when they walked in.

The microwave pinged and Cat went to retrieve and serve up their food. Over a tasty lunch, the three chatted almost without pause. Mel mentioned the plans she had for the Christmas party. Cat told them about the fun morning her young people had had, hurtling around the park in search of clues and treasure. Colin admitted that if he spoke about his morning in the IT world his dining companions would glaze over before dying of boredom. Between bites, the three discussed their plans for that evening. Mel said that she was meeting up with her friends at Liv's, Colin was watching a film at home and having a beer, and Cat was expecting a quiet night at home with Mike with him seeming to be out of sorts. Cat's phone alerted her to an incoming text.

'Oh! Speak of the devil. It's Mike,' she said with a smile.

She opened the message and read it.

Hey Clare, hope you're having a good day. I'm feeling much better, so I think I will head to the gym tonight. I've got my gym bag in the car so I will head straight there from work. Don't worry about making anything for tea for me, just sort yourself out. See you later x

The colour instantly drained from Cat's face, leaving her ashen. She placed one hand on her chest as she read the message again, but aloud this time. Colin's expression was one of shock and confusion as he looked at Cat, then Mel, then Cat again. Mel sat up straight, her eyes alert and wide open. She instinctively leaned in towards Cat after what she'd just heard. And they had both heard it; there was no doubting what Cat had said. For a moment a pin

CHAPTER ELEVEN

drop could have been heard as they tried to make sense of it.

'Who's Clare?' asked Cat in a tiny, brittle voice, breaking the heavy silence.

Chapter Twelve

The text Cat had just received could not have come at a worse time. There was no mistaking the fact that it took all three by surprise and for once they all seemed a little lost for words. Getting a name muddled happened to everyone at times in conversation but was surely much rarer when sending a text message. Mel did her best in the time she had available to her to reassure Cat that it was probably nothing more than Mike's phone autocorrecting her unusual name. As the words left her lips, she wasn't sure she believed them. To protect her friend's feelings meant she had to find an excuse that in turn protected Mike and that part did *not* sit well with her. Not one bit. Mel apologised profusely for having to leave to go set up for her afternoon session, but she had no choice. She gave Cat a cwtch, mouthing *look after her* over Cat's shoulder to Colin before heading off to the group room.

Remaining unconvinced that Mike's faux pas was indeed some kind of typo, Mel's mind was racing. Trying to come up with a good explanation was more than difficult. By itself, a slip of the tongue, or finger, in this case, wasn't particularly concerning, but when combined with Mike's unusual recent behaviour, alarm bells rang loudly, and Mel couldn't quieten them for the whole of the afternoon.

CHAPTER TWELVE

For once she was glad when the session was finished and the last of her group members left, and she rarely felt like that. Mel's job was something she was extremely passionate about, but it had been hard to focus on the session and get the picture of Cat's crestfallen face out of her mind. Mel closed the door and exhaled loudly. She set about hastily clearing up, placing chairs on tables to help the cleaners who were due that evening. It bought her a little thinking time before having to face Cat. *What the hell do I say to her and who the hell is Clare?* Mel wondered. For half a second, she considered cancelling her plans for the night but then felt that wasn't particularly fair on Liv or the boys. Cat would need a friendly face tonight though, preferably someone she had confided in about what she suspected was going on with Mike.

Mel braced herself and went to Cat's office to look for her. Still not sure she had the right words, one thing she did know how to do though was listen and maybe that was all Cat needed from her. The door was ajar and from behind it, Mel heard hushed voices. She tapped on the door before walking in.

'Hey Col. Hi Cat, how are you doing? Any more from Mike?'

Col pulled out the chair next to him, inviting Mel to take a seat with them.

'Hiya Mel. I'm okay, I guess. I texted Mike back and said no problem, glad you feel better, have a good night. He replied saying thanks, you too, kiss, kiss. I think my gut instinct was right all along. I've thought about it and it's strange that after all these years his phone suddenly starts autocorrecting my name. It's not happened before so why now?'

'That's a good point.' Mel paused before continuing. 'And not something I have an answer for. I'm sorry, my love. Are you going to be okay on your own tonight?' Mel reached over the desk to give Cat's hand a squeeze. 'I've got a night arranged at Liv's tonight, there's a few of us going over. You'd be more than welcome to join us. I'm sorry that I can't cancel it, love.'

'Don't be silly, pet, I'll be alright. It's a kind offer but I'm not in the mood to be with a group of people tonight. Thank you, though.'

'You can always come to mine tonight, Cat. I'm having a quiet one at home. You'd be very welcome to join me in a takeaway and a film if you fancy it.'

Cat hesitated and was *almost* about to politely turn down Colin's offer until she clocked the stern look on Mel's face. She could read her like a book! That look meant business and without the need for words said *don't you dare say no*.

'Sounds good to me if you're sure, Col. Thanks,' Cat said with a hint of a smile.

Relieved that Cat had agreed to go to Colin's for a few hours, Mel got up to leave. She knew that Col would look after her and try to take her mind off things. Cat was definitely in good hands, and she didn't need to worry about her. Well, not tonight at least. Before leaving, Mel gave Cat a cwtch and wished them both a good night. She

CHAPTER TWELVE

explained that she had to dash to catch the bakery before they closed to pick up dessert to take to Liv's.

Luckily, there were still a few things for Mel to choose from at the bakery. She bought an apple and plum crumble and a chocolate and orange roulade. *Well, it is approaching Christmas,* she told herself as she considered the vast number of calories in the boxes she clung so tightly to. Mel's journey home took a few minutes longer than normal as she wanted to take no risks with her rather delicious-looking travelling companions carefully placed on the back seat. Nope, there would be no sharp turns or heavy braking tonight!

After pulling into the close and parking outside her house, Mel dashed up the few steps to her front door. She decided she had the time for a quick shower, to pop on some makeup, and to run the iron over a change of outfit. Forty-five minutes later, she checked her appearance once more in the mirror. A black shirt with black jeans and some pixie boots. *Not too bad for an old fart*, she thought with half a smile. She questioned the choice of eyeshadow, though. Was gunmetal eyeshadow a bit too much for a Thursday night gathering at Liv's? Possibly, but it was new, and she hadn't had a reason to wear it yet. Besides, it didn't half suit her and made her green eyes pop. A quick spritz of perfume and another layer of nude-coloured lip gloss later and she was nearly ready. She grabbed her black leather biker's jacket and a silver scarf to throw over the top. She'd taken advantage of the fact she didn't have far to walk, so she was able to wear a cute little jacket instead of a thick winter coat for a change.

FINDING A MIRACLE

Mel trotted down the steps, car keys in hand. She set about getting the goodies from the bakery from the back seat when she heard Dougie's front door open followed by, 'See you later, Dad.'

'Good timing, Kev. You can give me a hand with these cakes, please, love,' said Mel loudly.

'Happy to help, Miss Jones!'

Kev beamed at Mel as she turned to hand him two large boxes. He was already carrying a bag that he had set on the floor at his feet. After Mel locked the car, she instinctively picked up Kev's bag and they started walking towards Liv's house, chatting as they went. Liv's front door swung open before they had the chance to ring the bell. Mel walked straight into the open arms of her beloved friend. They cwtched tightly as was typical for them.

'Good to see you, girl, and damn I am *loving* that eyeshadow on you!'

Mel wandered through to the kitchen, noticing the boys were yet to arrive.

'Kev! How the devil are you?! Welcome home, darling! How long has it been? No, don't tell me, you'll only make me feel old and I am *not* having that.'

Kev walked in, carefully balancing the two boxed cakes and setting them down in the kitchen before giving Liv a kiss on the cheek. Mel had taken off her jacket and held out her hands, gesturing for Kev to do the same. She popped their jackets on the post at the bottom of the stairs. Seconds later came the arrival of Tony and Jeff. The sounds

CHAPTER TWELVE

of bottles clinking together and wicked giggles coming from the hallway made Mel smile. She loved nights with these people. *Her* people.

Kisses all around, glasses filled, lots of noisy chatter, and the scene was set for what was going to be a good night, thought Mel. Jeff, Tony, and Liv had lots of questions for Kev about his time in Australia and his decision to come home. Kev had said how pleased he was to be back and that he had no more plans to live overseas again. He told them he was going to look at his work options in the new year, and until then, he planned on spending time catching up with family and friends. Kev also had questions for Liv, Jeff, and Tony about what they had been up to during the time he'd been away. By the time Liv had taken the casserole pot out of the oven, put it on the table next to the rice, and warned everyone at least three times not to touch it because it was piping hot, they had pretty much caught up with the most significant happenings.

With plates all filled with Liv's delicious-looking beef stroganoff and rice, everyone eagerly tucked in. The conversation was light and bounced around the table during the meal and flowed happily between mouthfuls of food and wine. There was no mention of Mel's nan as they ate. It was as though there had been an unspoken prior agreement that there would be no talk of their research until after their meal was finished. It felt almost strange to Mel as she listened to Kev joining in with the chat and banter. He fitted in the little group so well, and she was pleased that the dynamic hadn't changed one bit. Sometimes, adding one extra person changes things, and often not for the better, but this certainly wasn't the case with Kev. Mel smiled as she looked at him across the table from her. He looked so happy and at home here, and she was glad.

Liv started to clear away the dishes and Mel automatically went to help. As Liv loaded the dishwasher, Mel took bowls, spoons, roulade, and cream to the table after reminding Liv to warm the crumble in the oven.

'Right then, boys, you've left us in suspense for long enough. Time to spill the beans on this research you've been doing.' Mel was keen to find out what they might have discovered. She was also looking forward to updating them on what she and Kev had found the previous evening.

Tony brought his fist to his mouth and cleared his throat for dramatic effect.

'Right, boys and girls, well, where to start? After you told us about your nan being at The Metropole, Mel, we decided to do some research on the old place. In days gone by, it was, as I mentioned, largely a cabaret and cocktail sort of place for the rich and famous. Their guest list was impressive back then. I checked out some of the acts that used to play there from some flyers I spotted online. Lo and behold, there were a few drag acts that performed there, would you believe, which of course meant I had a few ideas for potentially useful contacts.'

'Long story short?' Jeff interjected, aiming an elbow at Tony's ribs. He teased him that they would be here until this time tomorrow unless he gave the bare-bones version. Jeff had spent a good many hours checking things online and making calls the past few days and while it was all fascinating, not all of it would be relevant tonight.

CHAPTER TWELVE

'Good point, my beloved. I will keep it as short and sweet as possible. As I was saying, I thought about some of my older contacts back in London. The first that sprang to mind was Elsie Day. Elsie worked in *all* the best places when she was younger, usually as a hostess. She has some stories that would curl your hair, and what she doesn't know about the West End ain't worth knowing. So, I gave her a call and asked her if she had any information that could help us or whether she knows anyone that could put us in the right direction. Eighty-nine but bright as a button, she is. Turns out she worked at The Metropole; no surprise there. She was probably there a little after the time your nan was, though. Did you bring copies of the paperwork with you, Mel? I need to be able to give Elsie some names.'

'Firstly, thank you so much for digging around, darling. I can't believe you have tracked someone down who also worked at The Metropole at a similar time to my nan. That's amazing! I've not stopped the last few days, so I've not managed to make copies of the flyers yet; I'm so sorry. I'll take the stuff to work and do it for you all tomorrow. I think making a file for the originals to protect them would be a good idea, as some are so fragile.'

'Oh, that reminds me!' piped up Kev. 'I almost forgot.' He got up and went to get the bag that Mel had carried for him and left on the sofa. He reached inside and brought out a box of Lindt chocolates that he handed to Liv. 'For the lovely hostess, thanks for having me, Liv.'

'You're very welcome and if you bring chocolates next time too, you can come again!'

Next, he pulled out a ring binder and a pack of clear poly pockets and handed them to Mel. 'I thought these would come in handy to keep your things organised and protect them. Great minds, eh?' Kev said with a smile.

'Ahh, you're a star. Thanks, Kev, that's so sweet of you,' said Mel, genuinely touched by his thoughtfulness. 'I promise to get all the relevant paperwork copied tomorrow, scout's honour. Hopefully, your Elsie might be able to shed a bit more light on things.'

'Hmm. Why do I get the feeling you two are keeping something back?' asked Liv, her eyes narrowed and her attention focused on Tony and Jeff.

Jeff laughed and looked at Tony before telling him to put them all out of their misery.

'Okay, okay. Now, nothing is certain, so don't go getting your knickers in a twist, but when I told Elsie the story of your nan, Mel, she told me that she remembered hearing some gossip from The Metropole way back when. It was a proper scandal too by all accounts. Something to do with a love triangle. She seemed to recall a relationship between a new singing sensation and a band member.'

Kev's eyes were fixed on Mel, and she looked straight at him, too. Both wondered if the letter from Maurice to Mel's nan had anything to do with this love triangle that Elsie Day remembered. Mel proceeded to tell the group about the letter, doing her best to recount it as accurately as possible. The three listened intently, swapping knowing glances with each other. It was clear they believed that this letter *was* relevant and was very likely to be linked to Elsie Day's account.

CHAPTER TWELVE

'There's a bit more of Elsie's story that Tony hasn't mentioned yet,' said Jeff. 'Probably because he loves the drama and having the last word. But I'm going to steal his thunder now! What he hasn't told you is that Elsie mentioned that the singer involved in this love triangle of yesteryear disappeared suddenly and without a trace...'

'Not only that, but this singer also just happened to be Welsh!' interrupted an excitable Tony, determined to get the last word.

Chapter Thirteen

Before heading to work that morning, Mel collected the items of her nan's that she wanted to photocopy and put them carefully in the ring binder Kev had given her the night before. *What a thoughtful gesture that was,* she thought. Mel was dying for a cuppa. After just three glasses of red wine the night before, she wasn't hungover, but she did have a slight headache. *Probably just a bit dehydrated*, she assumed. Despite quickly falling asleep to her audiobook the previous night, the sound of her alarm that morning was no welcome visitor. She hit snooze three times, something she almost never did. Recalling her busy week at work and home, Mel felt it shouldn't be a surprise. *You're not twenty-one anymore, girlie, and you also need to drink more water!* She promised herself a hot candlelit bath later and a night alone. No ifs, no buts. Now drained of tea, her mug was rinsed and put in the sink to be washed properly later. Mel needed to get going so she could photocopy her nan's things before her morning group session. She thought gratefully what an inspired decision she had made not to run group sessions on a Friday afternoon. It usually meant she could finish early if she was owed any time, which was often the case.

CHAPTER THIRTEEN

An hour later, with her photocopying complete, the group session prepped, and the room set up, Mel decided she would pop in to see Cat.

'Morning, Cat. How are you, my love, and how was last night?'

'Hiya, Mel. It was canny, thanks. Col was a great host. He even let me choose the takeaway and the film, bless him.'

'He's such a star,' said Mel warmly. 'And how were things with Mike?'

'Mike got in just after me. He didn't ask what I'd done, so I didn't mention going to Col's. I didn't say anything to him about getting my name wrong in the text, and I don't think he's even noticed he did it. If he had, no doubt he'd try to cover his tracks or at least behaved a bit awkwardly, so I'm pretty sure it's like it never happened as far as he's concerned.'

'That's a good point. I think you're right,' said Mel, nodding in agreement.

'I've asked Col to go back to the gym again, and he's agreed. This whole "Clare" business has thrown me a bit, and I just want to be sure. So, I'm just waiting for Mike to say when he's going next.'

'Well, if it puts your mind at rest, it's worth it. If you need anything over the weekend, I'm a call away; you know that. I need to head off now, though, sorry Cat. I'll catch up with you later, my love.'

Cat was in limbo, and Mel knew how much all this was wearing her down. It wasn't right, and it wasn't fair. *She doesn't deserve this, not even close,* thought Mel with a heavy heart. *There's a lot to be said for being single.*

After her group left, Mel returned to her office and checked her emails. There were already a few responses to her requests for donations of Christmas presents, which was encouraging. Janet had emailed with the excellent news that they had enough funds for the Christmas party at the Red Lion, so she had provisionally booked it just in case another organisation beat them to it. A relieved and grateful Mel made a mental note to buy Janet a large bottle of Baileys for Christmas. After sending a few thank-you messages, Mel checked her mobile. There were a couple of texts, one from Liv and one from Kev.

Hey, darling. Let me know when you're leaving work and I'll make a snack for us. I was thinking of just a few sandwiches, and we could finish off the rest of last night's dessert if you fancy it. Lots of love L xxx

Mel thought that sounded good, as long as it was just a flying visit.

Hey Liv. That's great, thanks! I won't stay too long though, darling. I'm absolutely knackered, and I'm craving a soak in the bath and an early night. If you need me to pick anything up, let me know. See you around half past four. Love, love, love! xxx

She then opened Kev's text.

Hiya, Mel. I just wanted to say thanks for letting me join you last night at Liv's. I had a great time with you all.

CHAPTER THIRTEEN

I was wondering if you're free at the weekend. I thought it might be nice to take you out for that meal I promised if you're free and fancy it. K xx

That wasn't a bad offer either…

Hi Kev. Ah, you're so welcome; it was great to have you there. It was such a good night. By the way, I've already used the ring binder! I will drop off your copies of the papers this evening after work. A meal sounds lovely to me, Kev. I don't have plans for tomorrow night if that suits you? M xx

The afternoon passed reasonably quickly. Mel used the time to reply to emails and phone calls regarding the Christmas party and get on top of some general admin tasks. It was difficult keeping her mind on track, though, as her thoughts drifted off in several directions. It was like a competition was happening in her subconscious, with different things and people fighting for her attention. She wandered between thoughts of her nan's mysterious past and the situation with Cat and Mike. She couldn't help wondering who Mike's 'Clare' was. Struggling to focus, she went to the photocopier in the main office to print off the worksheets for Monday's sessions. *Do something practical if you can't concentrate,* she reasoned. Just as she had come to the end of her task, she saw Colin approach her. They had the room to themselves, which pleased Mel.

'Thanks again, Col, for last night. Cat said she had a nice time at yours.'

'Nothing to thank me for; it was nice having her round. She didn't say too much about the text or Mike. But she has asked me to go back to the gym. She just told me that our favourite fitness fanatic is going again tonight, which means I am, too. He's going after his dinner this time. I can't imagine being in Cat's shoes, sitting there sharing a meal with him, wondering where he's going after and who with. Surely he won't *really* be at the gym. I mean, who goes to the gym straight after eating their dinner?'

'Now *that* is a very good question, Col.' At that moment, Mel decided there would be no glass of wine at Liv's and none when she got home. Whilst she was still planning a quiet night in, if things went badly for Cat, she wanted to be able to jump in the car and collect her if needed.

'Will you keep me posted, please, love? I hope he's going where he says he's going and isn't up to anything. Even if he is at the gym, though, I still have a nagging feeling that something dodgy is going on. I just can't put my finger on what it is yet.'

'Course I will. And I agree. There was something odd when I saw him at the gym. He didn't seem to be doing enough work to be employed and not enough working out to be a customer. I have no idea what he's up to, but it feels a bit off.'

Mel nodded. There most definitely was something *off* about Mikey-boy. Mel thanked Colin again and squeezed his arm before heading to see Cat.

'Right, Cat, that's me done for the day, love. I'm calling in at Liv's on the way home but won't be there long. You know what to do if you need anything tonight, even just a chat.'

CHAPTER THIRTEEN

'I'm fine, honestly, no need to worry,' said Cat unconvincingly, unable to make eye contact with Mel as she spoke in a pointless attempt to put on a brave face. They both knew she had just told a lie.

A heavy blue-silver mist hung in the air and spun circles around Mel as she left the centre. It touched her face with ghostly fingers, sending a shiver down her spine. She pulled up the collar of her coat in defiance and sped up as she half walked, half trotted to the car park. As she settled in her car, she turned on the heater, plugged in her phone, and went to her playlist. She turned up the volume, and she instantly felt better. The long-familiar sound of The Mission put a smile on her face as Wayne Hussey serenaded and soothed her. Mel had loved them since she was a teenager, and they were still the band she had seen live more times than any other. They kept her company for her journey back home, and she stayed in the car after pulling up so that she could hear the end of 'Over the Hills and Far Away'. Mel grabbed her bags and walked across the front of Harlech Close towards Jeff and Tony's. As she got to about halfway, she noticed in the gloom that the post box had had a makeover. Of course, it was December first! Despite the cold, she wandered over to get a closer look at the handiwork of Suzanne and Andrea. A snowwoman. She looked fabulously glamorous! She wore a white glittery beret, had perfectly pouty red lips, and clutched a bejewelled handbag. Mel took out her phone and used the torch to see it better. *Earrings! Brilliant touch!* At that moment, Mel felt a little pang of festiveness. If this was one of those cheesy Christmas films, the snow would gently start to fall right about now, and a choir of angelic children would be singing about the night being silent or about a friendless reindeer with an exceptionally red nose, thought Mel.

Popping her phone in her pocket, Mel continued towards number seven. Seeing their car was gone and no lights were on, she assumed that Tony and Jeff were out. She rang the doorbell once, just in case. It was too cold to hang about, so she took their photocopies out of her bag and popped them through the letterbox.

Liv answered the door in what seemed like a nanosecond, and Mel dashed into the welcoming warmth of Liv's house. After dumping her bag and coat, she cwtched Liv and then wandered into the kitchen.

'Wine or gin, darling?' Liv stood in front of the cupboard where she kept her glasses.

'Tea, please, Liv. I'm bloody frozen.'

After sarcastically checking there wasn't something seriously wrong with her friend, Liv went to put the kettle on and started making some sandwiches. As she did so, they chatted about their day. Mel spoke a little about the arrangements for the Christmas party and Liv mentioned that she'd had four phone tarot readings and one via Zoom that day. Mel dug out the paperwork from the file Kev had bought her and put it on the kitchen table beside where Liv always sat.

Liv brought the pot of tea and sandwiches to the table and sat opposite Mel.

'So, last night was fun, and how lovely to see Kev. I bet you're glad he's home for good.' Liv's blue eyes sparkled as she smiled mischievously at Mel.

CHAPTER THIRTEEN

'Yeah, a good night as usual with you lot. Thanks for having us round. It *is* nice that Kev's back, but that's an odd thing to say. What are you suggesting exactly?' asked a suspicious and bemused Mel.

'Oh, I don't know; possibly that you two used to have a bit of a thing for each other in the past but never seemed to be unattached at the same time so could never do anything about it.' Liv faked innocence, but there was no hiding the wickedness of her smile. 'You're both young, free, and single now. Well, free and single, at least,' she said with a chuckle.

'You can cut that out when you like, Cupid. Kev and I are old friends, nothing more. I *like* being single. I have a good and happy life. Why the hell would I want to complicate things?' Mel's thoughts went straight to Cat and the drama she was currently going through.

'Hmm, maybe because the time is finally right for you and Kev. Come on, darling, you can't lie to me; I know you've had a thing for him since we were in school. And I don't need to use my psychic powers to know he had a thing for you, too.'

'Okay, I admit I did have a soft spot for him, but so did most of the girls and with good cause! He was gorgeous, and he's still a handsome guy now. You know how popular he was, and back then he didn't date anyone for longer than a month. It's one of the perks of being good-looking and a rugby player. He had his pick of girls and besides, I was never into the sporty types; I was more drawn to musicians, so it would never have lasted.'

'And that's exactly why he never asked you out, I'll bet. He didn't think you'd say yes! I don't know, Mel. Something in my bones tells me romance is on the cards for you and Kev.'

Mel laughed and rolled her eyes. She didn't have the energy to argue.

'Speaking of cards, why don't you put the kettle on for another pot of tea and grab the dessert leftovers while you're at it? I'll get my tarot cards. Let's see what they say about all this, shall we?'

'You're not going to let this go, are you, Liv?' asked Mel with a sigh and a smile.

After demolishing the remains of last night's roulade and crumble, they cleared and cleaned the space, ready for Liv to lay down her reading cloth. Liv then lit the candle that sat half burned on her table and asked Mel to meditate with her briefly before asking the question she had for the cards. They sat quietly, the only sound coming from the gentle hiss and breath of the candle and the rhythmic shuffling of Liv's precious 'Blushing Fool' Rider Waite Smith tarot deck. As Mel meditated, it wasn't a romance with Kev that was at the forefront of her mind. The images that sprang into her head all came from the boxes that sat on her lounge floor in the spot where her Christmas tree usually went. Photographs of her nan, the band at The Metropole Hotel, and the letter from her nan's lover played out before her, almost like a monochromatic film reel lost in time.

CHAPTER THIRTEEN

'Okay, I'm ready, Liv. I'm sorry to disappoint you, my love, but what I'd really like the cards to tell me is what happened to Alice Miracle.'

Chapter Fourteen

A love of tarot and oracle cards was a passion shared by both Mel and Liv. Having studied and practised tarot for a couple of decades, Mel was more than equipped to conduct a reading for herself. She adored the artwork of Pamela Colman-Smith, or Pixie, as the tarot community knew her, in particular. There was something special about being read for, though, and Liv was exceptionally good at blending mediumship with her intuition and her expert knowledge of the tarot cards' meanings. Mel knew she was in great hands.

Liv asked Mel to choose eight cards. Mel closed her eyes and ran her hand over the cards all spread out in a line on the table. She waited until she felt pulled to specific cards, and in no time, she had chosen the eight that Liv had asked for.

Liv took three long, deep breaths and cleared her mind a little more each time she exhaled. She began turning over the cards and laying them on her white reading cloth. As she turned over the last card, the spread reminded Mel of an arrow, with six cards in a row and a card placed above and below the fourth card from the left. Liv explained that the spread was set out like a storyboard that would offer

CHAPTER FOURTEEN

insight into her nan's relationship with Maurice from its start to its demise.

'Okay, so this is interesting. The first card, the Two of Cups, is such a romantic card, as you know, but it also encourages honest dialogue. Good communication is important for any relationship to succeed, and this one is no different. I feel that your nan and her young man had an instant connection and went on to discover they had a lot in common. I'm sensing their powerful physical and emotional attraction and that your nan's partner made the first move. He didn't charge in exactly, but he didn't waste any time either. He wasn't sure she would say yes and couldn't bear rejection. Hmmm, doesn't that sound a bit like our Kev, eh? Maurice was so captivated by her that he felt she was out of his league. I strongly sense that she took his breath away, and he was utterly charmed by her. The lion above and between them is telling me it took a lot of courage on his part to risk a possible rejection. Wow, go, Liz! Seems like she made a *huge* impression on him, love.'

'Well, she was the most amazing woman, but it's still weird to think of her in those terms, Liv.' Mel momentarily cringed at the thought of her nan being this desired woman. Lizzie being anything other than her nan was inconceivable, let alone the object of this mysterious man's affections. 'Keep going before I change my mind!' said Mel as she tried to shake off the thought of her nan being pursued by Maurice.

'Our second card takes us a stage further. So, they've met and got together, as we know. The next card, The Lovers, is particularly significant. The love they share seems so pure and innocent. If you look at the card, they are as naked as the day they were born, and above them we have an angel. It looks like they are being blessed not just by the angel and the heavens but by the sun that fills the sky. The connection between this and The Sun card is calling out to me. As you know, The Sun is one of the happiest and luckiest cards of the deck. I feel that they were completely lost in the warmth of their relationship. They were the only two people in the room when they were together. Maybe even the only two people on the planet. The future is looking bright at this point for your nan, and she feels adored and excited. But sadly, there is a but. The Lovers card also symbolises choice. So, it seems some decisions need to be made, and they aren't insignificant decisions either. This is a major arcana card, and we know that means we need to pay close attention. In the card's background, we see a rather large mountain springing up out of nowhere. This is suggesting to me that something happens that blindsides your nan. Storm clouds are gathering above The Lovers, but your nan's been so focused on the positives she hasn't noticed them. Something is about to come in and change everything, and she won't see it coming.'

Mel's heart missed a beat as she listened intently to her friend. She wrung her hands in her lap, fearful for what might be about to happen to her precious nan. She was no longer creeped out by the thought of them as a couple after hearing Liv describe their relationship as being so happy and loving, but she felt helpless and frustrated, nonetheless. Because this all happened long before she was born, there was nothing she could do to prevent the chaos heading toward her nan.

CHAPTER FOURTEEN

'And next we have The Moon. Another major arcana card, so we know this is really significant. This card deals with emotions, instincts, and things maybe not being as they appear on the surface. It can also be a card of deception or self-deception. There was something going on in the background that your nan didn't know about. Something was purposefully hidden away from her. Yet I feel she had an awareness building. Her instinct whispered to her that there was something in her life that wasn't quite right. She felt her intuition nagging at her like the moon draws the tides. At this point, she removed the rose-tinted spectacles and started to pay closer attention to life and the people around her.

'The next card is The Tower and another powerful card from the major arcana. It's a massive wake-up call to open your eyes and smell the coffee. Something happened so out of the blue that your nan could not have predicted it. It blindsided her and stopped her in her tracks. It literally shook her to her core. What was hidden in the shadows of moonlight in the previous card is now front and centre and in the spotlight. She has been forced to face something unavoidable. I feel that when this event happened, she turned inward and kept going over things in her mind. What had she missed? What had she not paid proper attention to? She had sleepless nights trapped in a cycle of overthinking and self-blame. What she doesn't realise yet is that what happened to her could have happened to anyone. She was not to blame. I feel she had been deceived, but she wasn't the only person that was a victim. Two people are falling from the tower depicted in this card. Not everything was exactly as it seemed with Maurice, but I'm getting a sense that he did not set out to intentionally hurt her. I think he got swept away on the tides of romance, but it backfired on him, big time. This may sound strange but the timing of this was a blessing. In the end, your nan felt relieved that her wake-up call happened when it did before things became even more serious. That doesn't mean she wasn't hurt and didn't feel very let down. But I feel that she took control of the situation and removed herself, head held high.'

'Oh, my poor nan! What the hell did he do? I want to throttle him and if I could I bloody would. How dare he mess my little nan about.' Mel wasn't upset, she was angry, but her anger had nowhere to land. Her tiny hands were balled into fists but just lay in her lap as her mind raced. It was clear to Mel that Tony's contact, Elsie Day, was probably on the right track about the rumours she had heard as a young woman. Rumours of a love triangle. A love triangle involving a singer from Wales. What didn't make sense to Mel was how Maurice could cheat on her nan when he was supposed to be so deeply in love with her.

'I know, Mel. It does seem like he's a proper shit to do this to Liz, but I also think there's more for us to uncover.

'So, the Three of Swords next. The image of a heart pierced by three swords tells us that your nan was heartbroken. She was let down badly, no doubt about it. Interestingly, though, I do have this strong sense that she wasn't the only one and that there were no winners. This was the moment of rock bottom for your nan *but* it was also a turning point. After feeling very disappointed, she decided what she needed to do was take the moral high

CHAPTER FOURTEEN

ground. Her resilience comes shining through, and she does the unimaginable. She forgives.'

Mel sat silently as Liv's words washed over her before sinking in. She knew how resilient her nan was – Liv was right about that – but to forgive? That must have taken every ounce of strength she had. The anger she felt turned to pride.

'Next up, we have the Eight of Swords. We see a woman blindfolded, bound, and standing at the sea's edge. This card, for me, is about accepting a challenge or choosing not to. Seven of the swords are behind this woman, which, in this reading, is suggesting to me that the worst is behind her. She has options. Does she free herself from what binds her, raise her sword, and turn back the tides that threaten to overwhelm her, or does she stay there and allow it to happen? Does she dig deep and move forward like a survivor or accept her lot and allow this moment to define her future? Well, we know what she chose to do, and she chose to grab that sword and move on like a proper little warrior.

'Another eight, this time it's Cups. In numerology, eight represents strength and power and is probably the most influential and lucky of them all. It also represents balance and flipped on its side, of course, it's the lemniscate or symbol of infinity. The figure on the card has turned his back on the eight upright cups on the ground behind him. His feet are firmly planted on the ground, and he carries a staff to help him on his journey. This suggests to me that while your nan's path going forward wouldn't be without obstacles, she had all she needed to progress and succeed. The decision was clear to her; she was guided by instinct. Look at where the figure in the card is headed towards. The mountains. Your nan went straight back to Wales with hardly a glance back at the glitz and glamour she left behind in London. Liz needed to heal and knew there was no better place to do it. I'm getting the image of Dorothy clicking those magical ruby slippers. There really is no place like home.

'And now onto our final card. This is the card that gives us the outcome of this spread. We have The Fool. The first card of the tarot and its number is zero. Your nan felt like she was starting from ground zero, much like The Fool. She wanted to have a complete change from what had gone before. Time for a clean slate. As we see on the card, this young man appears to be blindly walking himself off the edge of a cliff without any concern for his safety. It seems that he's not looking where he's going or aware of what might go wrong. He's enjoying the adventure and is optimistic about the next stage in his life. This suggests to me that your nan did her healing, took her time, and then was ready to take her next steps. She wisely decided to put the past behind her, remain open to new opportunities, and go looking for them! This is such a positive end to the reading, Mel. Look how carefree The Fool is! He has the sun on his back and is now standing on top of a mountain, not a care in the world. I feel like he's at the peak of the mountain from the previous card, the Eight of Cups. It tells us that she took on the challenge of the climb and thrived.'

'Wow, thank you for that, Liv. That was incredible. It all fits into place and I feel like we have our answers as to

CHAPTER FOURTEEN

what happened.' Mel paused momentarily in reflection. 'I feel much better about things now and am so proud of my nan. I can see why she decided to keep that all to herself. I think most of us have a chapter or two in our lives we don't want to revisit or read aloud. I have to say, though, I'm still intrigued and would love to find out more about Maurice and my nan's time in London.'

Mel took a deep breath and felt a world of tension and emotion leave her as she exhaled. A solitary tear fell from her eye, which she swept away with the back of her hand. Maybe it was the combination of things that had taken place over the past week, but she felt simultaneously emotional and drained.

'It may seem daft to want to know things ended well after London because I know she was more than okay. She and my grandfather couldn't have been a better fit or happier together. But I'm sure the time between London and meeting my grandfather was awful. I know there was a happy ending for her but it's still comforting to have that confirmed. Thank you, Liv.'

'My pleasure, darling girl. The cards never lie, do they, and neither do they let us down. It felt intense, didn't it? I was disappointed initially that you didn't ask the cards about you and Kev, but now I'm glad you didn't. This is all so fascinating about your nan. Not that *you* aren't fascinating too, of course!' said Liv with a cheeky smile.

They chatted for a few minutes longer before Mel admitted defeat and gave in to her tiredness. She thanked Liv for a lovely evening and told her it was time she went home. *Would it be rude to put the file of papers for Kev through the door and not knock and hand them to him?* Mel pondered the question as she prepared to leave and quickly decided it would be fine.

Just as she had buttoned up her coat and put on her scarf, she heard a text notification coming from her coat pocket. She instantly became more alert as her thoughts went straight to Cat. She checked her phone and saw that the message was from Colin.

Are you free, Mel? I've got some news about Mike, and I need to speak to you before I ring Cat. It's not good. Col x

Chapter Fifteen

'Hiya, Col. Sorry, I was at my friend's house. I'm almost too scared to ask, but what's happened?'

'No probs, Mel. Thanks for ringing. I need your take on this before I speak to Cat. Tonight was different from the last time. Mike was there as he told Cat he would be. I didn't expect him to be there, but I was wrong. Initially, I thought it was positive he hadn't lied about where he was going, but that didn't last. Mikey-boy set up camp on one of the stools at the end of the reception desk like a barfly. The same receptionist was on duty as the other night. She and Mike chatted non-stop; the only thing to interrupt them was the occasional customer wanting something. There seemed to be a mixture of talking and laughing, and they looked very comfortable together, I have to say. She showed him things on her mobile, and they appeared extremely relaxed in each other's company. Like people who know each other well. Very well. Like a couple.'

'Oh, hells bells, this doesn't sound good, Col.'

'There's worse to come, trust me. I decided I needed something more than just a vibe or a feeling. So, I went to the counter and asked the receptionist for a membership form and asked a few questions about some of the classes they do for women. I made up a story about one of the girls at work wanting me to get some information for her. I'd say the receptionist is in her thirties, probably about five foot six, with a short black bob. Mike didn't take his eyes off her the whole time she spoke to me, Mel. She had to walk to the back of the reception area to pick up the membership form, and on her way back to the counter, I noticed something. I couldn't fail to see that she's very obviously pregnant. Being behind the counter means you can only see her top half, or I'd have noticed last time I was there.'

'Oh, Col! This is worse than I thought. It would be bad enough if Mike was playing away, but this! I know this might be some weird mix-up and might mean nothing, but the worst-case scenario is about as bad as it gets.' Mel's heart sank as she thought about Cat and how this news would affect her.

'There's one last thing, Mel. I thanked the receptionist for her help and said I would pass the information on. I asked her what her name was so that my friend could give her a call if she had any questions. She told me her name is Clare Roberts. She's Clare, Mel.'

Chapter Sixteen

After the news had sunk in, Mel suggested that both she and Colin not say anything to Cat until they'd done more digging. There could be an innocent explanation for all of this and there seemed no point in worrying her unless they had actual proof. Col and Mel arranged to meet at the bakery in the village at eleven the following morning. In the meantime, Col would text Cat with the basic information that Mike was at the gym and there wasn't much to report so she didn't worry too much. He felt awful keeping things from her but agreed with Mel about gathering more evidence before potentially turning her world upside down.

Mel wearily locked the door and turned off the lights before she climbed the stairs. She lit some candles then poured in an indulgent measure of her Neal's Yard bubble bath before turning on the hot water tap. Minutes later she was immersed up to her chin and felt the day's stresses leave her for a heartbeat in time. The water was piping hot and already turning her pale skin pink. She struggled to hold on to that feeling of comfort for a little while longer but the issue with Cat and Mike pulled it away from her. Far away and out of reach.

FINDING A MIRACLE

As she lay in the water, Mel decided she needed some ideas on how to proceed with this. Her default was always to be a fixer and problem solver so making action plans was at the very core of her being. Mel's mind drifted back to the profile they had made for Lisa the fake Facebook lovely. She considered that Lisa could gather information they might not otherwise get. Lisa didn't necessarily need to be a flirty love interest; she could be just a friend Mike could talk to. A friend he would confide in, hopefully. Lisa could share a bit of her story about the recent break-up of her long-term relationship, and maybe Mike might start to open up about his situation. It may put him at ease chatting with someone who had recently gone through something similar. An idea came to Mel. She knew which bands Mike followed on Facebook because Cat had mentioned them when they discussed making the fake profile at Merola's. Lisa could approach him as a fellow fan. Colin could easily find photos of the bands or their album covers and use them in her profile images. Mel mulled this over in her mind, and the more she thought about it, the better the idea seemed. It didn't hurt that she was single, too. It left the door open just in case Mike was in the midst of a premature mid-life crisis and was playing the field with more than just Clare. Mel felt the beginning of a reasonably solid back story coming together, and it felt like a good place to start when she saw Colin the next day.

Mel forced herself to switch off from Mike and just try to enjoy her bubble bath. That felt easier to do now she had forged a plan. As she lay there, Mel's thoughts eventually drifted to the recent discoveries about her nan. She would arrange to catch up with her dad over the weekend as there

CHAPTER SIXTEEN

was a lot to update him on. Mel was certain he would be gobsmacked hearing what Tony and Jeff had uncovered and about the letter from Maurice. There seemed to be so much happening and Mel had barely any time to catch her breath lately. Despite being tired she was looking forward to her meal with Kev the following night. She smiled as she played with the bubbles and let the water run through her fingers. It was amazing just how invested Kev, Liv, Jeff, and Tony were in the mystery that surrounded Alice Miracle. She felt incredibly lucky as she thought back to her gratitude exercise with one of her groups a few days prior. She had fabulous people in her life and for that she would be eternally grateful.

It was only because the water was getting cold that Mel reluctantly dragged herself out of the bath. After drying herself with a big fluffy towel, she got into her soft jersey pyjamas and jumped into bed. She started to listen to a book on Audible but barely made it to the end of the chapter before entering the realm of dreams.

***

At just after eight the following morning, Mel woke feeling as bright as a button. She'd been so exhausted she had slept for at least eight hours. She heard her mother say, *'You must have needed it, love.'* That was precisely what she would say if she were here with her now. Thinking about her mother reminded her that she needed to arrange to see her dad. She felt guilty that she had barely spoken to him since he'd come over the weekend before for lunch. She decided to send him a text because if she called, they would be on the phone for an hour, as was often the case. There was also a high probability she would end up telling him all the news she had on the secret life of her nan, and she wanted to do that in person. Mel saw that she had a text from Kev thanking her for the photocopies and checking she was still okay to meet up that night. He suggested he pick her up at seven with a smiley face emoji. Mel guessed that meant he would walk from next door to knock on her door. She quickly texted back, confirming that she would be ready for seven and was looking forward to it before turning her attention to her dad.

Hey, Pops. Fancy coming over for lunch tomorrow? I still have some of Nan's boxes to go through in the morning, so shall we say two o'clock? I won't have time to make a roast tomorrow, so apologies in advance! xx

No roast?! Well, well. You've made it very clear that you no longer love me. I'm wounded, deeply wounded.

After the fake histrionics had passed, John announced he would tear himself away from binge-watching *Breaking Bad* for the second time to join her for lunch on Sunday, adding that he would just about cope with cottage pie instead of roast chicken. *One final little dig,* thought Mel with a laugh. He really was a wind-up merchant.

Mel put on a warm dressing gown, went downstairs, and made herself a quick cuppa. Once she had finished her tea, she opened the blinds in the kitchen to let in some daylight. She saw a flash of movement out of the corner of her eye. Dougie's cat, Mrs C, had landed on her windowsill, looking through the window in hopeful expectation.

CHAPTER SIXTEEN

'You can come in, but only for a little while. I've got a busy day, and I'm going out soon,' said Mel, fully realising that Dougie's little cat failed to understand what she had just said and neither did she care. She just wanted to get a fuss before some of the cat treats that Mel kept in the cupboard especially for her. She miaowed her approval as Mel opened the back door to let her in. Mel was well-trained by now and did what was expected before heading upstairs to get ready.

When Mel walked into the bakery an hour later, she saw that Colin was already sat waiting for her. There was an empty coffee cup in front of him, so he had clearly been there a little while. She gave him a wave before going to the counter to order a fresh latte for Colin and tea for herself. As she got to the table Colin stood to give Mel a cwtch.

'I'm glad to see you, Mel. I feel like shit keeping this pregnancy business from Cat. And when she finds out there really is a Clare, she'll be devastated,' he almost blurted out.

'I know, love, it doesn't look good. But, as I said last night, let's get some proof before landing her with all of this. What if we make Lisa a friendly, easy-to-talk-to person that Mike may choose to confide in instead of a honey trap? What do you think?'

Colin tossed the idea around in his mind for a few seconds as Mel thanked the waitress who brought over their drinks.

'Genius, Mel! That's a great idea! Befriending him seems way less sleazy than setting up a honey trap, especially if this is all some kind of mistake and he somehow finds out about what we're up to. It just doesn't feel as wrong. I know what we're doing isn't anywhere near as deceptive as he probably is, but if we can avoid stooping to his shitty level, then I'd rather we did. Although if push comes to shove, I think we're both ready, willing, and able to do what's necessary to get Cat some answers.'

'I must admit, I hadn't thought about it in those terms, but you're right. I was more focused on discovering what's happening rather than how it might appear to Mike if he caught us. So, let's crack on with this profile, shall we? I've brought the list I made with Cat a few nights ago for you to make a start on it. We can show her the profile on Monday and double-check that she still wants to go ahead before we get the ball rolling.'

'No problem. It won't take long to get it ready, especially as you and Cat have pretty much done most of it.' Colin took a sip of his latte, a crease forming between his brows. 'I think we need to make sure we arrange some fun things for Cat to do to cheer her up if it all goes to shit.'

'You're right, and I've been thinking the same. I read the other day that tickets are going on sale on Monday for an acoustic gig with Amy Wadge in Cardiff Bay. She and I both love her, and I considered getting her a ticket for Christmas. Fancy it?' asked Mel.

'Sounds good, count me in, thanks, Mel. I think I'll get a voucher for a manicure or something as well. She'll need things like that to take her mind off Mike.'

CHAPTER SIXTEEN

'Don't worry. We'll make sure she'll be okay if the worst happens. I'm just hoping we don't need to,' said Mel wistfully.

Chapter Seventeen

The rest of the day went by in a blur. Mel went grocery shopping and then caught up with laundry and house chores when she returned. After giving her home a good top-to-bottom clean, she arranged the bouquet of festive flowers she had treated herself to in a vase to put in the kitchen. The dark green and red added a lovely splash of colour and gave her a tingle of Christmas spirit. *Where has the year gone,* she wondered. How could it be December already? Planning for the next day when she knew she would be home, Mel went to the garden to gather logs from the shed. It would be good to have a fire while she went through the last of her nan's boxes. If there were any remaining clues to her nan's story, then the sooner she discovered them the better because it may save a whole lot of guesswork and investigation for her and her friends. Besides, she would need to clear the area under the bay window before too much longer so she could put up her Christmas tree as that time was fast approaching.

After lunch, Mel went to her wardrobe to pick out an outfit for her 'date' with Kev. He hadn't mentioned where they were going, but chances were it would be local and not somewhere she needed to get too dressed up for. She would wear flats or boots as they would most likely be

CHAPTER SEVENTEEN

walking. Heels felt like too much of an effort, and besides, the older she got, the less appealing they became due to the sheer discomfort. Mel selected a plain but well-cut knee-length scarlet dress to wear with thick black tights and some cute black ballet shoes. She would dress that up with bold silver earrings and her go-to Vivienne Westwood orb necklace. Her finishing touches were a black clutch and her black winter 'going out' coat that she kept for best. Not having had time to get her nails done at the salon, she fished out her trusty Caught Red Handed nail polish, ready to apply later. Mel contemplated whether she would wear a statement lip or a smoky eye, finally deciding on a red lip and a subtle eye look with just mascara and black eyeliner for definition. She was looking forward to their night together and hearing about what Kev had been up to in more detail.

As she'd had so little time to herself over the past week, Mel took the opportunity to relax with a good book that afternoon. She took her time getting ready as she had done nothing but rush around for days. By a quarter to seven, she felt refreshed from having relaxed a little and was ready. At seven o'clock sharp, there was a knock on the door.

'Good evening, Mel. Your chariot awaits.'

'Evening, Kev. Chariot?' replied Mel quizzically.

'Yes, I will be whisking you away in my courtesy car to a top-secret location if that doesn't sound too sinister! said Kev playfully. 'I'm waiting for the paperwork to go through on the car I've bought, so for now I've got this one.'

'Top-secret location it is, then. How exciting! Lead the way.'

Kev opened the car door for Mel and closed it once she was safely inside. *I could get used to that,* thought Mel, as it had been a while since a man had done that for her.

'So where are we going?' asked Mel, trying her luck and hoping to get an answer this time.

'Nice try, but you'll just have to wait and see, won't you.' Kev tapped the side of his nose and gave a knowing nod.

Mel sighed and shrugged her shoulders in exaggerated disappointment at her failure.

'Thought it was worth a go. I hoped you'd have dropped your guard or cracked under the intense pressure of my questioning, but no such luck.'

Kev gave her a side eye before letting out a dramatic mock sigh of exasperation aimed very much at her. She laughed and noticed he could not hide the smile that crept on his face, although he had tried his best to look serious.

The two made small talk as they drove through the village, which was now bright and sparkly thanks to an array of Christmas lights and decorations in the shop windows. They spoke about Christmas and how it seemed to start earlier each year and general chit-chat about how little the village had changed over the years. Kev mentioned how pleased he was to see the graffiti at the side of the butcher's shop hadn't been removed or become lost in time to the weather. It had long been a talking point in the

CHAPTER SEVENTEEN

village since it first appeared. Someone had scratched the message *Johnny, you are late* on the wall in the early 1980s. Remarkably, it had stood the test of time and was still going strong. Whoever had scraped the message on the wall at the side of the shop had done an excellent job of it. Everyone back then had wondered who this Johnny was. It had been and still was a mystery and the stuff of urban legend in their part of the world. Had Johnny been late today, there would only have been a shirty text message with an angry-faced emoji to emphasise the author's level of annoyance, and no one else would have ever known a thing about it.

Soon, they were headed into the countryside, and fairy lights gave way to a black velvet sky littered with stars. The roads were becoming narrower as they drove up into the mountains. About twenty minutes later, the car tyres scrunched onto a gravel car park outside a gorgeous old country inn called The Brynglas. Mel had been there numerous times, but it had recently closed for a complete renovation. The Welsh word *Brynglas* means blue hill, a nod to the wild bluebells that grew in the woodland to the right of the pub's car park. The smell of smoke from the open fire came tumbling out of the big chimney, making the perfect winter scene. Both Mel and Kev took a moment in silence to drink in the view.

'Shall we?' prompted Kev. His arm stretched towards her with his hand moving to the small of her back. Mel nodded happily, and they walked inside. In less than a couple of minutes, they were escorted to their table close to the fireplace. The place already had a lively atmosphere, with almost every table filled. Mel was pleased that the refurb hadn't changed the energy or character of the pub as she didn't particularly enjoy the sort of eatery where you felt the need to whisper. The Brynglas had a happy little buzz about it without being *too* noisy. *Ten out of ten for venue choice, Kev,* thought Mel. Kev quickly shrugged off his coat and placed it at the back of his chair before helping Mel with hers.

'You look gorgeous, Mel. That dress is beautiful, and you don't half suit red. It's your colour, that.'

'Thank you. You don't scrub up too badly yourself, mister.' A hint of pink blushed Mel's cheek for the briefest of moments.

The waiter came over and collected drink orders and brought them a couple of menus.

'Great idea this, Kev. I've always loved this place. I hadn't realised it had reopened. What made you think of coming here?'

'Glad you like it,' said Kev with a broad smile. 'I went to see an old rugby friend who has a car dealership in Trehafod a few days ago, and we came past here when I was test-driving the car I've bought. He happened to mention that it had just been done up and that they had a new chef. He had heard lots of good things about it, so I thought it might be an idea to give it a go.'

They perused the menu, both finding it difficult to pick something as there were a lot of great-sounding options to choose from. Mel mentioned how she often succumbed to food envy when someone else's food looked

CHAPTER SEVENTEEN

better than hers. Amused by this, Kev admitted to suffering from the same condition and suggested they make a pact to swap starters if that happened to them that night.

Having made their decisions, they were free to sit back, relax, and enjoy their drinks and each other's company. Mel had opted for a lime and soda as Kev wasn't drinking alcohol due to being the designated driver. Drinking alone was never much fun, she'd always thought, plus it didn't seem fair to be knocking back the wine when Kev was only having a lemonade.

'So, how's work going, Mel? I'm assuming you're still at the carers' centre.'

'I am and still loving it as much as ever. I work with a great team that are more friends than colleagues. My boss is amazing and so supportive and encouraging when I suggest new workshops or activities I want to run. She lets me get on with it, which is such a blessing. I would hate to be micromanaged!'

'That's good to hear. It's so important to be happy in your job.'

'What's your plan now you're back?'

'I've decided to have the next few weeks off to settle down and catch my breath. Christmas is never the best time to look for a job, so I'll spend the time wisely catching up with people I've not seen in forever. I'll contact some recruiters in the new year. I need to start looking for a place of my own, too. It'll be a busy time in January, so I fully intend to make the most of my time off until then.'

The starters arrived, and both were pleased with their choices. Mel happily began tucking into her baked camembert, and Kev did the same with his pâté.

'It must be quite exciting. A fresh start somewhere familiar. Where are you thinking of getting a place?' Mel asked.

'Ideally, I'd like to find something between here and Cardiff because I'll be looking for work there. I want to be close to my dad as well. I need to see how he's managing on his own and what he may need help with because, as you know, he won't ask for it!'

Mel smiled inwardly as she remembered Dougie saying exactly that to her dad. *No flies on you, Dougie*, thought Mel as she nodded and agreed that it was a very good idea.

'Living with the old man has its perks, though. It's not as sad and tragic as it sounds: a fifty-something, single bloke living with his dad. He's got a great neighbour. Not only is she an amazing cook, but she's a lot of fun and rather easy on the eye, too,' said Kev with a cheeky laugh.

'Bloody hell, Kev, did those cheesy compliments get you very far in Australia? Please tell me the women there had more sense! I see what you're up to. Don't think for one second, you've got me fooled. I know what you're after is a regular invite to a roast dinner on Sundays. You're just like your dad; you'll say anything to get fed!' Mel said with a chuckle.

'I'm hurt, Mel. Shocked and hurt!' said Kev, laughing and shaking his head in staged disbelief.

CHAPTER SEVENTEEN

'Oh really?' asked Mel with one eyebrow raised.

'I meant what I said, although I can't deny that I knew I raised my chances of being invited around again when I said it.' Kev's face had a playful expression, and Mel couldn't deny how handsome he looked. A little older, naturally, than his schoolboy days, but still the same twinkly eyes and cheeky grin. 'The Australian women were wise to me too. I was in a relationship for a while, but that ended a good while ago. So, it looks like you have a fair point. I need better chat-up lines, clearly!'

'You'd better get a move on then, you're not getting any younger!' joked Mel, well aware they were the same age.

The two chatted without pause throughout the evening. Kev asking Mel about people they knew from their younger years and catching up on local news and gossip. Having finished their main meals – steak for Kev and chicken in a mushroom sauce for Mel – Kev settled the bill, not even allowing Mel to leave a tip. He helped Mel with her coat before putting on his own as they weaved through the tables and outside into the night.

As they pulled up into the close and Kev parked the car, Mel thanked him for a lovely evening. Again, she waxed lyrical about what an excellent choice he had made and how lovely the meal was.

'The night is still young yet, Mel. Fancy a nightcap at the Red Lion?'

Mel paused. She didn't want the night to end but wasn't sure about going to the pub.

'Or we could just have a drink at mine,' suggested Mel.

'Sold! Lead the way.'

Chapter Eighteen

The sound of hailstones battering her bedroom window woke Mel sharply. She checked the time; it was just after nine. She had hoped for an earlier start, but it had taken her longer than usual to fall asleep the previous night. *Time to get up,* sighed Mel. It would have been lovely if she could lie there a little longer, but she had a busy day ahead. She mentally arranged her to-do list in order of priority. First breakfast, make the cottage pie ready to warm in the oven later, light the fire, and go through the last of the boxes before taking them upstairs. Her dad would be coming to hers at around two, so she had more than enough time to finish everything if she made a start now. *Perfect,* thought Mel as she grabbed a jumper to pop over her pyjamas, tied her hair up, and put on a pair of the slipper socks that Suzanne from number six had knitted for her. Now nice and toasty, she peered out of her bedroom window that overlooked the Green. It was beautifully carpeted in white with a mixture of frost and the heavy burst of hailstones that had woken her so abruptly from her slumber. Mel shivered and wrapped her arms around herself as she looked out on the wintery scene below before turning away and heading towards the stairs.

After perusing the contents of the fridge and then assessing what she could be bothered making, Mel decided on a mushroom omelette for breakfast with a glass of orange juice and, of course, her usual pot of tea. She hummed contentedly as she set about chopping mushrooms and beating eggs. The sounds and smells in the kitchen started to sharpen her senses: the kettle boiled noisily, and the mushrooms hissed and crackled in the pan, filling the air with a mouth-watering aroma that said, 'Eat me.'

Mel picked up her mobile to check for messages while eating breakfast. Nothing. She was relieved that there wasn't a message from Cat. *No news is good news*, she hoped. A few seconds later, her phone beeped and flashed with a text alert. *Spoke too soon,* she thought despondently.

Morning, Mel. I just wanted to say thanks for a lovely evening last night. We must do it again soon. Let me know if you find anything interesting in your search this morning. Have a great day, lots of love, K xxx

Good morning, Kev. It's me who should be thanking you! I had such a lovely time. I have a couple of chores to do before starting on the boxes, but I will keep you (and L, T & J) posted if I discover anything juicy. Speak soon. Love M xxx

Mel took a moment and reflected on the previous night. She and Kev had managed to polish off a nice bottle of red before he went home around midnight. She'd had a good time and was pleased he seemed to feel the same as he suggested doing it again. *Was* there something to what Liv had said about her and Kev? *Don't be stupid*, she thought. She quickly dismissed the notion with an involuntary shake of the head as she needed to get cracking.

CHAPTER EIGHTEEN

After breakfast, Mel set about the tasks on her mental to-do list. She fired up the log burner and opened the curtains in her lounge to let the pale morning light trickle in. With the fire beginning to spring into life, Mel returned to the kitchen to make a start on the cottage pie.

With her chores almost complete, she could finally make a start on the three remaining boxes belonging to her nan. The first box held nothing significant about her nan's life as Alice Miracle. There was a mixture of letters, postcards, birthday cards, and cinema tickets. Mel smiled as she looked at the strips of black-and-white photographs that had been so popular years ago, long before the invention of mobile phones and selfies. These strips captured her nan living her best life with various friends throughout the years, and all exuded love and happiness. Not a pouty duck face nor filter in sight. They looked vibrant, beautiful, and carefree and glowed with contentment. This was most definitely the memory box of her nan's friendships. It warmed Mel's heart to see all the mementos she had kept, and it confirmed to her just how much love she'd had for them. Family may have been Liz's priority, but she still always found time for her friends. Mel's mother, Anne, had also valued her friendships greatly and made time to see friends, particularly her best friend, Elaine. *When people matter to you, you make time, not excuses.* Anne's voice spoke gently to Mel. Without a doubt, the pattern continued with her, too. Mel smiled as she thought about her two wise owl role models and felt grateful for them as she placed the lid on the box.

As Mel lifted the second box, she wondered what treasure she might discover within. Tentatively, she opened it and was filled with hope and apprehension. There was a mixture of receipts and letters on the top that were of no sentimental value and would, in time, find their way to the recycling bag. Further down, there were old passports, programmes from shows Liz and Bill had gone to see, and souvenirs from holidays and day trips they had taken over the years. *So far nothing of great significance*, thought Mel, unsure whether she was disappointed, relieved, or a bit of both. The next item was a small coin purse in a silvery-gold colour. Something was in it, but it didn't feel like a coin. When she opened it, Mel saw a lock of golden hair tied in a white ribbon. Attached was a piece of paper in her mother's handwriting. *Melissa's first haircut.* Her nan had kept it all those years. A lump in Mel's throat quickly became a tear in her eye. She truly had been raised by the most loving women, and the hole they left was unfillable.

The last item in the box looked like a scrap of white material folded into a bundle. Mel felt something inside it as she lifted it out of the box. Carefully, she unwrapped it and saw it contained a pendant on a chain with a small piece of paper beneath it. The chain was a bronze colour with an emerald green charm attached to it. The stone was large and beautifully faceted to reflect light. As she held it up towards the window, it exploded into life. *To look this good after all this time, it must have been expensive*, Mel thought. The charm had a wide bale, and Mel thought how striking it would look if worn as a choker. She was mesmerised as she watched the light show it made on the wall of her lounge with every move of her hand. It looked like it had been crafted over a hundred years ago and had to be a vintage piece. Mel went to wrap it back up in the white cloth for safekeeping when she saw the initials *MN*

CHAPTER EIGHTEEN

embroidered on one corner. It wasn't a cloth; it was a silk handkerchief. *Maurice's* silk handkerchief? Mel felt her heart rate speed up as she took the folded note from the box.

My dear Alice,

I saw how lovingly you looked at this, so I had to return to the antique shop and buy it for you. If it means half as much to you as you do to me, I'll be a happy man.

With all my love,

Maurice

xxx

Maurice wasn't all bad perhaps, thought Mel as she picked up the third and final box. At first glance, it looked like it contained chiefly letters. On top, there was a bundle tied neatly in a red ribbon. Mel recognised the elegant handwriting in an instant. It was her grandad's. How a man built like a barn door with shovels for hands could have such beautiful penmanship always puzzled Mel. He had always had a flair for art and being creative in general. Mel felt a little twinge of sadness as she remembered her grandfather. When she was a child, he had built a miniature garden chair for her; when she was a little older, he had made her a sledge for the snow. *A man's man but a heart of gold*, Mel thought as she traced his handwriting with the tip of her finger. She set this bundle of letters aside for the time being. For some reason, reading letters from her grandfather felt like a much greater invasion of her nan's privacy, and the irony did not escape her.

There was a collection of recipes written in faded handwriting that Mel assumed may have been her great-grandmother's. Mel knew Liz's handwriting, and whilst this wasn't it, there was a resemblance. It would make sense that she'd kept them if Liz's mother had written them. Carefully turning the fragile pages, Mel had the strongest feeling that these recipes had been given to Liz by her mother when she got married to her grandfather, Bill. Many of his favourites were there: leek and potato soup, apple tart, and Welsh cakes.

Next, there was a bundle of miscellaneous paperwork covering anything from health care appointments to solicitor's letters relating to the purchase of Liz and Bill's home. Mildly interesting but nothing too noteworthy, Mel thought. She put them to the side to shred later.

Strangely, the following items were at odds with the rest. There was a scarf and a pair of gloves wrapped in tissue paper. *Why were they hidden away with old letters?* Mel wondered. Although they looked very old, they appeared unworn and made from good-quality material. The scarf was still bold and made up of a striking autumnal colour palette. Autumn was Liz's favourite time of year, so whoever bought that for her had been paying attention, Mel assumed. As she lifted them from the box, she noticed a tag still attached that bore a small crown logo that read *Frasers of London*. London! Mel's mind and heart raced in competition. Maybe Liz bought these for herself while living there, pondered Mel, but then she discarded the theory like yesterday's newspaper. If she had bought them for herself, it made no sense that they would be stashed unworn in a box. Money was tight back then, and if you

CHAPTER EIGHTEEN

made a purchase, it was usually driven by necessity and not some fleeting fancy. So, had *she* bought them, she would have worn them without question. They *must* have been a gift. A gift she couldn't bring herself to part with. A gift from someone very special to her. A gift from Maurice, no doubt.

Underneath the gloves and scarf was what looked like lining paper. It was clear to Mel there was something concealed below it, something oblong-shaped. Mel lifted the paper and saw two letters. Both bore London postmarks, but the handwriting did *not* belong to the same person. More than one letter bearing the same writing made perfect sense to Mel, given her nan's relationship with Maurice, but a letter from a different person puzzled her. She gently opened the first envelope and took out the letter.

Dear Miss Miracle,

My name is Rose Newman and, as I am sure you are aware, I am the wife of Maurice. It is my understanding that you have been spending a great deal of time with my husband outside of your work commitments with him. Therefore, I must inform you that I demand that any social activities must cease at once. Any contact or interaction is to be purely professional from now on. This is because it has come to my attention that you have romantic feelings for my husband that are completely unreciprocated and unacceptable as he is a happily married man. My preference is that you stay away from him and that you do not come back to The Metropole at all. This situation has caused me a great deal of upset and stress, which, given my condition, is intolerable.

I am asking you, politely, to please stay away from my husband. You have made things exceedingly difficult for him, and your behaviour could tarnish his impeccable reputation should you persist. He is a kind and polite man and was embarrassed by your unwanted and unrequited attention. I am expecting our first child in just over a month, and I want nothing more than for you to leave us alone as a family. I trust you will do that.

Yours,

Mrs R Newman

Mel sighed and put the letter down. *Oh Maurice, what the hell did you get my nan tangled up in?* Knowing her nan as she did, there would be no way she would have tried to steal someone's husband. Mel picked up the second letter.

My Dearest Alice,

I do hope this letter finds you well. I realise I owe you an explanation and an apology, so I will try to do that as best I can.

I was wrong for not telling you I was married; I am sorry for that. The truth is that, for my part, the marriage was one of convenience and, I am ashamed to say, to further my career as a musician. My wife's uncle, Reginald, is a highly influential and well-respected figure in all things theatrical, and he made it clear that he could help me if I so chose. It became apparent that his niece, Rose, was attracted to me, and Reginald mentioned that it would benefit me if I decided to pursue a relationship with her. He talked about the fantastic opportunities that could come my way and the important

CHAPTER EIGHTEEN

people he could introduce me to. I know how awful this sounds and how weak this makes me seem, but I didn't know how to say no to this man. I was aware that he could make or break my career. The truth is, I do not come from a wealthy background, and so having the Newman family's backing was an opportunity I could not refuse. I am embarrassed to say that I took 'Newman' as my stage name to please him and attach myself to such a successful family in show business. Admitting all this to you makes me feel utterly ashamed.

When I met you, I fell for you in an instant. You were everything I didn't realise I needed and wanted. My marriage was a duty, and as time passed, I spent more time at work as it was preferable to being at home. This was the case before you ever breezed beautifully into my life. I felt free and happy when we were together, as if anything was possible. I knew almost at once that I loved everything about you, and I still do. Not seeing you every day, not hearing your angelic voice, crushes me to the core of my being. I am living in a world beyond sadness. If it were just the case of my career being ruined, I would take that and not look back to be with you. In a heartbeat, I would. Unfortunately, the decision is out of my hands because Rose is pregnant. If it were just Rose I was leaving, I would do so, but to leave my child is different. I have a responsibility to this little soul that I cannot abandon.

I must apologise that my wife wrote such a cruel letter to you. She told me what she had written, and I am so sorry. I explained that she was mistaken in assuming you were the only one with any feelings, but she would not accept it. I'm afraid it is easier for her to blame you than face the reality of a loveless marriage. I have tried speaking to her several times, but she will not listen and makes excuses for me. She wants to believe you tricked me and weaved a wicked plot to steal my heart. The truth is that nothing about you is wicked. You really are enchanting, Alice, and I gave my heart to you freely and without doubt or question.

I do not expect to hear from you as it's more than I could hope for. I'm sure my days will be darker without you in them, and that is what I deserve. If only things were different, and I hadn't made such a mess of everything. Oh, how I wish I had met you sooner.

I hope you have a bright and happy future, my dearest Alice. I will love you every day of my life, and more than anything, I hope you know that you will remain forever in my heart.

Yours always,

Maurice

After carefully folding the letter, Mel placed it on the coffee table next to the letter from Rose. She wasn't sure how to feel after reading them. Confused by her emotions, she rubbed at her temple as though that might summon answers like a genie from a lamp. The end of this relationship sounded hard for Maurice, but Mel was in no doubt it would have been harder still for her nan. Trying her best to be logical about the situation, she consoled herself remembering just how well things turned out for her. She had gone on to marry a fantastic man whom she undoubtedly loved with her whole heart and who had loved her with the same, if not greater, depth of feeling. When looking at things this way, Mel felt comforted. She tucked her feet underneath her on the chair and relaxed

CHAPTER EIGHTEEN

back into it. There were still questions chasing around in her mind. What happened to Maurice and Rose? Did they stay together? If not, did Maurice ever try to win Lizzie back? Could it be possible that Maurice was still alive? That last question was pushing it, Mel conceded. While it may seem like it was case closed, there was a curiosity building that Mel knew would not fade until she found out what had become of Maurice Newman.

Chapter Nineteen

Mel returned to the kitchen and began mashing potatoes on autopilot. She had to taste them to check whether she had added salt or not, having no memory of having done so. It was a good job she had checked as she had already added a generous amount in her fugue state. Mel then went upstairs to take a shower in the hope it would clear her head. She stayed there longer than normal as she processed what she had read in the two letters. She had felt quite shaken after reading them and needed time to compose herself. Mel loved being in or around water of any description, so the shower helped to soothe her and calm her senses, but only just. There was now a clear sense of what her lovely little nan had been through, and Mel felt it emotionally and physically.

She quickly dressed and dried her hair, wanting to read the letters for a third time. By the time she reached the lounge, the room was already beginning to feel warmer and brighter, and she welcomed the comfort it brought her. She settled down and picked up the letters to read them again. Mel couldn't wait to update her dad when he arrived and wondered if she should message Kev, Liv, Jeff, and Tony. They would want to know about this latest development. Was this perhaps the end of their little

CHAPTER NINETEEN

group investigation, though? While *she* was interested in discovering what happened next, she wouldn't blame her four friends for not feeling the same. Mel set about sending a group message to them.

Hey there, my lovely Miss Marples in the making. I've looked through the last of my nan's boxes and uncovered some interesting letters. I can't go into detail now because my dad is due soon. It's significant, though; I can tell you that. When might be a good time to meet up? The sooner the better, if that's okay. Love, M xxx

Twenty seconds later, Mel's phone erupted in a barrage of texts.

Are you kidding me? I repeat, ARE YOU KIDDING ME?! You can't leave us dangling like that, you little minx! X (one kiss and no love whatsoever!)

Mel felt the cartoon-like explosion of frustration coming from Liv, and it made her laugh out loud. She needed that.

Well, we are definitely meeting tonight then, aren't we? You can't leave us in suspenders like that. The last time we wore suspenders was the Rocky Horror Picture Show in Cardiff, and I don't mind telling you there was more than a bit of uncomfortable chafing! Love J & T xxx P.S. Liv is right, you are a little minx!

Looks like you're on the naughty step, Mel, you little tease! Good job these guys have no influence over Santa's lists, or it might be slim pickings for you in a few weeks. A question for you – your place or the Red Lion? Kev xxx

Wow, get off the fence and tell me how you really feel about me, you lot! So how about I drop you a text after my dad leaves, and you come here this evening then? Love, love, love (even though you don't deserve it!) M xxx P.S. The big guy in red just phoned and told me I'm nowhere close to being on the naughty list, thank you very much, Kevin!

Their reaction both pleased and amused Mel in equal measure, particularly Liv's. *Safe to say they wanted the update then*, she mused with a smile. Her friends had managed to lift her mood with just a few messages, and she felt blessed.

In what felt like no time at all, her dad arrived, full of chat from the second he walked through the door. Mel took his coat, and John wandered straight through to the kitchen. After checking what he wanted to drink, she poured them both a glass of lemonade before retrieving the bubbling cottage pie from the oven and setting it down on the dining table.

'That looks delicious, Mel, but hotter than hell itself. Tell me about your week while it cools a bit.'

Mel dished up a steaming plateful of food for them both and sat down opposite her dad.

'Well, buckle up, Pops, I have a lot to tell you.'

John sat in silence as he took in the sheer volume of information that Mel and the four other Miss Marples had gathered in the last week. Digesting what Mel had told him would take a little longer than his dinner, he thought. They decided to sit in the lounge to relax a little after

CHAPTER NINETEEN

eating. John settled down on the sofa next to his daughter. As was his routine, he'd grabbed one of Mel's blankets from the basket she kept them in and put it over his legs.

'I'm stunned. I can't believe just how much you lot have uncovered in a week, Mellie. A huge well done to you and your little gang. It seems to me that you've found out exactly what happened, so the mystery is solved. I wonder if the reason she kept the whole "singing in a fancy London hotspot" quiet was that it was also linked to such an unhappy time in her life. It looks like this Maurice character turned her world upside down, swept her off her tiny little feet, and then broke her heart. Poor Lizzie.' John paused in thought for a moment before continuing. 'Then again, she landed an absolute diamond in Bill, so it all worked out well for her, and that's the main thing. I'd still like to give that bloody Maurice a piece of my mind if I could, though. He didn't half make a mess of things. Sounds like he paid a hefty price for it, mind you. Imagine a life sentence of being trapped in a loveless marriage for the sake of his career. From his letter it sounds like his biggest regret was losing his relationship with your nan, and who can blame him?'

'Telling you all this has made me realise just how much we have uncovered between us. I suppose we have solved the mystery, or at least most of it anyway.'

'Why do I get the feeling you're about to tell me you aren't ready to stop digging just yet, little Miss Adelie?' asked John, with a wry smile lighting up his face.

'Well, the thing is, Dad, we don't know what happened next for Maurice and Rose, do we? I'd love to find out how things panned out for them. I've not yet had the chance to update the others on the things I found today, but they'll be calling in later, so I'll do it then. I have a feeling that they will be keen to find out what happened to Maurice, too. It's even possible that Tony's contact from London, Elsie Day, might know something about him. I'd love to know why Nan used the name Alice Miracle, too. It sounds more like the name of a circus act or a magician. It's an unusual choice, don't you think?'

'It *is* an unusual name for a singer from back then. Anything goes now, but it was a bit flamboyant for those days. I'd love to know what became of Maurice Newman. I wouldn't mind betting this Elsie Day may be able to shed more light on it, or if not, one of Tony's other old contacts from London. It's better than any soap opera on the telly, all this,' said a pensive John.

It was obvious from what Mel had said to him that she would be determined to uncover whatever could be found. *A dog with a bone, just like her mother and her nan for that matter*, he thought fondly. Father and daughter chatted on for an hour longer as they often did, putting the world to rights, before John decided it was time to make a move. He was planning to stop in at the Legion for 'just the one pint' before going home to watch a bit of telly before bed. They both knew he would be 'persuaded' to have at least one more and that he wouldn't put up too much of a fight.

As Mel walked her dad to the front door, she had a question for him.

CHAPTER NINETEEN

'So, you know Christmas is coming…well, I just wondered if you fancied donning a Santa outfit to hand out presents at the centre's Christmas party again this year? You went down a storm last year. It's at the Red Lion.'

'Is that your way of telling me I need to drop a few pounds, Mel? That's a cruel blow, especially as you just fed me!'

'No, don't be daft. There's more fat on a butcher's pencil than there is on you! I've never worked out how someone with an appetite like yours never manages to put on weight. It's not bloody fair, I know that much. I just thought you might fancy it. I'm sure it'll be a good day, just like last year. Of course, we would need to get you a costume and pad your belly out. No pressure, have a think about it. I'm sure I could get someone else if you don't fancy it.'

'I'll have to check in with my agent for availability, Mel; after all, I'm a man in demand! Text me the date when you get time, and I'll see if I can squeeze you in. Thanks again for a lovely dinner, love.' John kissed his daughter on the cheek before trotting down to his car and telling her to go inside because it was 'bloody freezing outside'. Seconds later, John was on his way. Mel hadn't gone in, of course; she waved him off as she always did, and he flashed his hazard lights as a last goodbye, just as he always did.

Chapter Twenty

After checking her watch, Mel decided an hour would be more than enough time to tidy up in the kitchen and get herself ready. She texted her friends and invited them over for seven.

With fifteen minutes to go, Mel was ready, so she set about lighting candles, dimming the lights, and throwing extra logs on the fire. As she had just put the remaining cottage pie in the fridge, it prompted her to text Cat and Col. They had also set up a WhatsApp group, which made contacting each other much more convenient.

Evening, you gorgeous pair. How are you both doing? I hope you're having a nice weekend. Unless I hear to the contrary, I will bring in lunch for us tomorrow. I made a huge cottage pie earlier that you're welcome to join in with. Do we have a date, darlings? Love, love, love. M x

Within five minutes, Mel heard back from both Cat and Colin, happily accepting her offer of lunch. This would be an excellent excuse to check how Cat was doing and for them to discuss going live with Lisa's Facebook profile. A lot was resting on Lisa. How the hell were they going to catch Mike if he didn't take the bait? It was one thing uncovering a scandal from the last century, but

CHAPTER TWENTY

catching Mike out may prove more difficult, even with today's technology. So far, he'd been covering his tracks well, with only the odd slip-up. Mel was determined that they would be ready to pounce on any future faux pas he made.

Her train of thought was abruptly disturbed by her first arrival of the night. She assumed it would be Liv and was surprised to see that it was Kev instead. He was almost instantly joined by Jeff and Tony. They didn't walk into Mel's; they wafted. They smelled expensive, like how she imagined the perfume hall at Harrods would smell. Without need for invitation, they trooped into the lounge after discarding coats and giving cwtches and kisses to Mel and a 'man cwtch' to Kev.

'What does everyone want to drink?'

Jeff and Tony decided they would join Mel in a G&T whilst Kev opted for a beer. Just as Mel took the cap off the gin bottle, the doorbell rang to announce Liv's arrival. A comment was made by Jeff, who declared, 'That woman can smell a bottle of gin being opened from more than three miles away, I swear it.' He placed his right hand on his heart with his left held up to heaven.

'I've made Welsh cakes, but I haven't decided whether or not you can have one yet.' Liv gave Mel the sternest of looks as she handed her a plate covered in kitchen foil.

'Come in, darling, you're just in time for a gin and tonic.' Mel smiled and kissed her friend. She was clearly still not completely forgiven for keeping them dangling.

'Good job I love you a little bit, isn't it?' said Liv with a laugh. 'Come on then, you, get pouring these drinks so we can get started.'

The group settled in the lounge, drinks in hand, and decided to dispense with any small talk. There was no polite conversation tonight, no asking each other if they'd had a good weekend or discussing how cold it was. Mel smiled as she saw the eager, almost impatient looks on their faces.

'Thank you so much for coming over at such short notice and generally for helping me with this search. Finding a Miracle, you might say! It's been quite the emotional rollercoaster, and I could not have picked four more fabulous companions to share the ride with me...'

'Oh, someone please stop me from going over there and shaking her, will you?' Liv looked around the room for the support of the others before diverting her attention back to Mel. 'I know what you're doing, you naughty little sod. This is like watching the painful reveal of who's being sent home on *X Factor* or *Britain's Got Talent*! Spit it out, woman, and stop your games!'

All four erupted in belly laughs. Soon enough, four became five as Liv joined in, unable to resist their contagious mirth. Labelling Mel 'a proper bloody wind-up merchant', Liv threw a cushion at her, almost taking out her drink.

Feeling suitably told off for taking too long and being, in her mind, unfairly accused of being a tease, Mel told her friends about the letters she'd found. Without

CHAPTER TWENTY

delay, she read out the letter from Rose first before passing it around for them all to have a look. Mel had decided to put the poly pockets that Kev had bought her to good use to protect the ageing and fragile pages as much as possible. Just as well with flying cushions being aimed in her direction, she thought.

Mel gave them a moment to reflect on the first letter and let it sink in. All were suitably horrified that Maurice had hidden the fact he was married from Mel's nan.

'Absolute shithead doing that to Lizzie,' said Liv, her face like thunder. 'She must have been so hurt and upset. Everyone in The Metropole would have known he was married. Not just married but expecting a baby! Why the hell didn't someone tell her? She must have been devastated.'

Kev, Jeff, and Tony nodded in solemn solidarity.

'Things might make a bit more sense when you hear this next letter.' Mel proceeded to read out the letter Maurice had written to Liz. All four listened intently, and for once they were silent, their eyes as wide as the moon.

'Wow, Mel, those two letters are quite the bombshell,' said Kev. 'I'm not sure Maurice came out of this much better than your nan. It sounds like he was so unhappy in his marriage, not that it's any excuse for what he did. It's just so very sad. All three of them were unhappy at the end by the looks of it. Rose was totally blinkered and wanted to keep Maurice at all costs, which is tragic.'

'There's just one more thing. God, I sound like Columbo now! All this detective work is clearly having a terrible effect on me!' said Mel and then handed Kev the pendant and asked him to pass it around before handing him the note that had been stored with it. After the four had seen both, Jeff passed them back to Mel.

'Well, my darling, that wraps things up, doesn't it? I am so pleased that your nan went on to have a great life. I don't think Maurice was *all* bad; he was conflicted, and yes, he made a few bad decisions. I'm sure, though, he didn't set out to deliberately hurt your nan or his wife for that matter. To me, it sounds like he was heartbroken he had to end it with Liz because she was the love of his life,' said Tony.

'Oh, come on, Tone! You can't go sprinkling glitter on this and hope it shines. He knew what he was doing. A perfect case of wanting your cake and eating it too, if you ask me. I agree that his intention wasn't to hurt anyone, but that's exactly what happened because he put his selfish wants and needs before those of the two women in his life.' Jeff folded his arms impatiently. He was clearly feeling far less forgiving than his soulmate, Tony. 'But I do agree this is all very sad, and I can't bear a sad ending,' he added quietly.

'At least things got better for Liz, though. She met Bill, and I'm so pleased she did because had that not happened, then we wouldn't have our Mel,' said Kev, trying to lift the mood in the room. 'And at least we know now exactly what happened, so we can put it to bed.'

CHAPTER TWENTY

'Hmm, not quite, Kev,' said Mel. 'We might know how things turned out for my nan, but we haven't a clue what happened to Maurice and Rose. Aren't you guys the least bit curious? I know I am.'

There was a slight pause while the group considered what Mel had said about there still being some unanswered questions. There were nods of agreement all around that told Mel that they, too, were interested in finding out what had become of Maurice Newman.

'Good point, Mel, and yes, it would be good to complete the picture, so to speak. I've got to say, I'm wondering where your nan got the name Alice Miracle from, too. I know it might not be a top priority, but I'd *love* to know. It's a *fabulous* stage name,' said Tony.

'Aren't we overlooking something here? Forgetting something *extremely* important?' asked Liv, who for once had been uncharacteristically quiet as she sat there taking it all in. 'Rose was pregnant. That means there might well be a living relative of Maurice out there just waiting to be discovered.'

Chapter Twenty-One

Half an hour before her alarm announced it was Monday morning, Mel woke. She had slept deeply and felt rested. Deciding there was no point in just lying there, she got up and got herself ready for work before heading downstairs to the kitchen. Thoughts of the previous night's conversations about her nan, Maurice, and his family disappeared as she put three portions of cottage pie in a container ready to take in for lunch as well as the remaining Welsh cakes Liv had brought the previous evening. Mel's focus had switched to Cat and the situation with Mike. She popped the remaining cottage pie back in the fridge and took out the milk to make herself a cuppa before heading off to the centre. She had a session that morning focusing on the creation of vision boards. Her groups always seemed to enjoy that activity, and because of that, so did Mel. Her involvement would not be quite as intense as most other sessions she ran, as the group members did most of the work in this one. They would, Mel was sure, chat away happily as they chose images aligned with their future goals, cut them out and glue them to their vision board. Today Mel was pleased it was a gentle start to the week as there was every chance, she may feel a little distracted. Besides, just like Bob Geldof, she'd never been a fan of Mondays.

CHAPTER TWENTY-ONE

A little while later, safely ensconced in her office, Mel fired up her PC before heading off to the kitchen. After putting their lunch in the fridge, she set about looking to see if Colin was in. She had spotted neither his nor Cat's car in the car park, but as Colin sometimes cycled to work, that didn't necessarily mean he wasn't in. Mel knocked on his office door to double-check, but the darkness of the room had already given away the fact he hadn't arrived yet. Back in the kitchen, Mel filled the kettle and put it on to boil. The next stop was Janet's office, and Mel didn't doubt she would already be at her desk.

'Good morning, Janet. I come bearing gifts!' said Mel, putting a couple of foil-wrapped Welsh cakes on her desk.

'Ooh, you bad girl, Mel. You're a wicked little temptress! I've treated myself to a new dress for the Christmas party that only *just* fits, so I am forced to keep whatever you brought me for lunch and not have a second breakfast. I'm sure it will be far more exciting than the tin of soup I had planned! Thank you, mwah!' Janet blew a kiss to Mel from behind her desk.

'You're welcome, my lovely. I hope you enjoy them. They're way more appealing than a tin of soup, I can vouch for that.'

'How's everything going with the gifts for the Christmas party?' Janet purred.

'Everything is going well, thanks. We've had most of the gift donations already. I'll spend one evening here soon to get them all wrapped and labelled, and then we're all set.'

'That sounds like too much for one person. Let me know when you plan on doing it and I will stay behind to help. I'm sure we can get some extra pairs of hands involved too. Keep me posted.'

Mel thanked Janet and left her to her spreadsheets. After making her tea she went back to her office and checked her emails before heading into her group room to set up the activity for that morning. Just as she'd finished getting the room ready, Colin walked straight in and, seeing the room was empty, closed the door behind him.

'Morning, Mel. I'm glad I've managed to catch you before your group. I'm all set for the lunchtime reveal of Lisa's profile. I'm pleased with how it's turned out. The back story of Lisa wanting a fresh start has really helped because I've been able to keep parts quite vague. Right, well, I won't keep you. I'll see you at lunchtime and thanks for bringing in food for us.'

'That's all sounding good, thanks, Col. I'm about to go and book tickets for the Amy Wadge gig. I should be done with this session by half past twelve, so I'll see you in the kitchen around one.'

With tickets bought, Mel went to the group room ready to welcome her carers for the morning's activity. She didn't have to wait long for them to start arriving. Soon, the room was turned up a few notches with the noise of people chatting and laughing. After the last stragglers turned up, Mel set the group the task of the day. She explained how useful it could be to have a constant visual reminder of the goals they wanted to achieve in life. Having it displayed somewhere they would see it every

CHAPTER TWENTY-ONE

day would help keep the vision of their future firmly in their mind. It didn't take them long to start discussing the kinds of things they wanted to achieve or do. They went through the array of magazines that Mel had provided and chose images and words to cut out that reflected their plans. The lively session went by in the blink of an eye, and afterwards Mel thanked the last group member who had stayed to help her tidy the room.

Col and Cat were already sat in the kitchen when Mel walked in. She went straight over to Cat and gave her shoulder a squeeze. After putting their dinner in the microwave to warm, Mel sat down and asked Cat how she was.

'I must be honest, pet, it wasn't the best weekend. I just can't get Clare, whoever the hell she is, out of my mind. I spent more time dejunking my stuff, did a few drop-offs at the charity shop, and gave the place a good clean. I did some research on prices for van hire and packing boxes too, just in case. Col has filled me in a bit about the profile. It's all set now. I think it's best that I take the role of Lisa. I know Mike better than anyone, so it makes sense for me to do it.'

Mel caught a nervous glance from Colin. He looked more than a little uncomfortable. Mel stood, excused herself, and went to the microwave to check on their food. It hadn't pinged, but she needed a few precious seconds of thinking time. Maybe it was for the best that Cat took control of the profile. If there was bad news, perhaps hearing it for herself would be helpful.

'Mike's going to the gym after work and Col has agreed to go again to see if there's anything else to find out. I was thinking of sending the first message from Lisa tonight, Mel. I wondered if you could be with me when I do. I think I might be a bit nervous, to be honest. Only if you're not too busy, though, pet.'

'Of course, I'm not too busy. Tell Mike you're having tea at mine; let him sort himself out,' said Mel, feeling less than charitable towards Mike.

The plan was made that Col would call around to Mel's after the gym to update them.

***

Once in Mel's kitchen that evening, Cat sat and made herself comfortable at the table. Mel offered to cook or order a pizza, but neither had much of an appetite, so they settled for a hot chocolate. Mel suggested it would be wiser to not crack open a bottle of wine as they needed clear heads just in case Mike responded to the message from Lisa.

Cat had set the scene with Mike just after lunch, texting him to say she wouldn't be home until much later. He had replied saying he would sort out a quick tea for himself and for her to have a nice evening with Mel. It seemed so cordial between them now, like passing ships in the night. Cat felt in her core that their ships were more sinking than just passing and wondered whether Mike felt the same. Maybe he was as relieved as she was when they were apart. They didn't have to pretend things were normal.

CHAPTER TWENTY-ONE

'Right, Mel. If I don't do this now, I may bottle it,' said Cat, reaching for her mobile. She logged in as Lisa and began to type.

Hi there, Mike. How are you doing tonight? I hope you don't mind me messaging you, but I saw your profile on the fan page of The Bolshoi, so I thought I'd say hello. I absolutely love them, and it's always good to meet fellow admirers!

Cat read the message aloud to Mel and looked at her for approval. Mel nodded, and Cat pressed send.

Chapter Twenty-Two

Mel discreetly checked her watch. It was just after half past eight. It had been well over an hour since Cat sent Mike the message from Lisa and there was still no reply. Mel had done her best to distract Cat to take her mind off things but hadn't managed to stop her from checking her phone every few minutes. When the doorbell rang, Mel almost leapt to her feet to answer it. Colin had a grave look as he came in through the front door that told Mel instantly he didn't come bearing good news. She directed him towards the kitchen.

'Hi, Col. Thanks for coming over. What happened? Was he there? Tell me everything and don't keep anything back, okay? I don't want you trying to spare my feelings. If there's anything I need to know, please don't filter it.' There was no hiding the sheer desperation in Cat's voice. Her words had spilled out of her mouth without pause. She, too, had clocked how serious Colin looked when he walked in and expected the worst.

'Hi, Cat,' said Col as he took off his coat and went to sit at the table opposite her. He swallowed hard. 'Okay. I will keep it brief and tell you as much as I know. Just the facts. So, in the few times I've been to the gym, I've noticed that while Mike does use the machines, he also seems to

CHAPTER TWENTY-TWO

spend a fair amount of time standing at the reception desk chatting to the woman who works behind the counter. He did the same tonight up until the time I left, pretty much. Now, there's not been any hand-holding, touching, cuddling, or anything at all that suggests they're a couple, but they seem pretty chatty and comfortable with each other.'

'Okay. That's not too awful so far,' said Cat with a trace of hope in her voice.

'There's a bit more to it, Cat,' said Col gently.

'Why do I get the feeling this isn't going to be good news?' asked Cat, her tone apprehensive. Mel reached out and put a comforting hand on hers.

'The last time I went, I noticed that the woman was very obviously pregnant. I hadn't spotted that fact before because the counter is quite high, so I only saw her from the chest level up. It wasn't just Mike with her tonight; she had her daughter with her, a girl who looked about eight years old. I get the impression she's a single parent, because she introduced her as "*my* daughter, Samantha" and mentioned having no childcare for her tonight. The final thing I need to tell you, Cat, is that I found out the woman's name. She's called Clare Roberts. Her being called Clare could be some kind of strange coincidence, of course, so bear that in mind, okay?' said Colin, desperately trying to offer some reassurance.

Cat's defeated expression showed he had failed miserably.

'No wonder Mike hasn't replied to Lisa's message yet; he's too wrapped up with bloody Clare.'

'Now look, Cat, we haven't got any proof of that at the moment,' Mel said firmly. 'We need to stick to what we do know, okay? All the guesswork under the sun isn't going to help us. There are still a thousand scenarios that could be playing out, so there's no point trying to fill in the gaps.'

Cat's stony reaction took both Mel and Colin by surprise. There were no tears; there was no angry outburst. They waited, but nothing happened. It was like she was in shock.

Calmly, she asked, 'And you're sure there's nothing else, Col?'

'Scout's honour, Cat. I'm keeping nothing back, I promise you. As I was leaving, I noticed that Mike was paying close attention to his phone. Has he replied to Lisa's message?'

'Nothing. Well, not the last time I checked anyway, which wasn't long before you arrived. So, not just a Clare, but a *pregnant* Clare. This really does draw a line between Mike and me. I know what you two are about to say, and while I appreciate it, I don't want to hear any excuses or reasons why I'm jumping the gun. His locked phone, getting my name wrong, never being home, and most importantly my gut instinct is telling me something is most definitely going on between Mike and his pregnant Clare.'

CHAPTER TWENTY-TWO

'I hear you, love, I do, but there's no proof of that. As Col said, this could be a misunderstanding,' said Mel, filled with concern. Both she and Colin felt a little uneasy about Cat's demeanour as she was *way* calmer than either would have predicted.

'Look, why don't you stay the night, Cat? You could always tell Mike you decided to have a couple of drinks. It's not like it's the first time you've done that, so it wouldn't raise any eyebrows.'

Cat sat and contemplated. She realised that there would be no hiding how angry she felt tonight. Mike would know there was something wrong, and with the mood she was in now, there was every chance she would blurt everything out in a tirade. No, that wouldn't be the right way to handle this. She wanted to be calm and clear when it came to confronting him, and she also wanted actual proof. Mel was right; they had none. As it stood, all she knew for sure was that he knew a pregnant woman called Clare. Not exactly a slam dunk case. Even though it was a bitter pill to swallow, she had to have hard evidence before accusing Mike of cheating on her. Mike, the man she thought she'd marry, maybe have kids with. Mike, the man she thought she'd grow old and wrinkly with.

'That's probably sensible. I think if I'm to get *any* sleep tonight, then wine will be required. Thanks, Mel.'

Mel rose to her feet, went to the cupboard to get glasses, and grabbed a bottle of red from the wine rack. Realising they hadn't eaten in hours, she felt it wise to grab a selection of crisps and nuts from the cupboard, too. Col refused wine as he was driving, so Mel poured him a lemonade despite him saying he needed to head off soon. She settled back on her chair and then poured her and Cat a large glass of wine each. She noticed Cat pick up her mobile. She sent a quick text to Mike to let him know she would be staying the night at Mel's. He soon replied, wishing her a lovely night.

'Thanks for the wine, Mel. I think I needed this,' she said before taking an almost medicinal sip from her glass. 'Right, let's see if Mike has replied to Lisa, shall we? I'd like to think he can at least stay faithful to one of the women in his life.'

Cat logged on and went to Lisa's profile page. Her stomach lurched and flipped like an Olympic gymnast.

'Lisa's got a message,' she said, and with the click of another button, she saw who it was from. 'And surprise, surprise, it's from Mike. Seems like he couldn't resist a pretty face.'

'What's he said?' both Mel and Col asked in stereo.

Cat pushed her phone towards them and took a large sip of wine.

Hi Lisa. Thanks for your message. It's always good to hear from another fan of 'the best band most people haven't heard of!' Have you liked The Bolshoi for long? I discovered their music in my teens, and they are still a firm favourite. I'm wondering if we have anything else in common, musically. I'm looking forward to hearing more about you. Lovely profile picture by the way.

Speak soon,

Mike x

CHAPTER TWENTY-TWO

'Well, it's a start. Nothing I could nail his balls to a tree for, but it's a start. He's taken the bait. I have a feeling it won't take long for this to escalate. He has the house to himself, assuming he's not with Clare, so I'm guessing he thinks he's free to play message ping-pong all night with the lovely Lisa. Well, Mike, your wish is my command,' said Cat with icy determination, sounding stronger and braver than she felt. She picked up her phone again, her hands trembling, and pressed reply.

CHAPTER TWENTY-THREE

Both Mel and Colin urged Cat to take a moment before she replied to Mike. They were concerned by the steely look etched on her face. Mel reminded her firmly that Lisa was to appear friendly and encouraged Cat to take a few deep breaths before replying. Cat took her friend's sage advice onboard. Mel was right; she needed to pitch this perfectly and try to park whatever feelings she may have for now. Cat gave Mel an appreciative smile and then began to type.

Hi there (again), Mike. Great to hear back from you. I think you are probably right about us potentially having more shared interests. I like all sorts of music, really. Some mainstream and some less well-known. Here are a few examples for you... Throwing Muses, The Pixies, Belly, Bob Mould... I could go on! Any crossovers? I've not been a Bolshoi fan for as long as you. I'd say I first heard them maybe five years ago. My ex-boyfriend introduced me to them. One of the few things I can thank him for! Thanks for the comment about my profile pic. Yours too is a lovely photo. Lisa x

Mike had added a kiss at the end of his message, so Cat felt it acceptable to respond in kind. She read out the reply to her co-conspirators, who sat in impatient silence. Mel asked that she read it through a second time for good

CHAPTER TWENTY-THREE

measure. She and Col exchanged glances, and both gave nods of approval. Not wishing to waste any time, Cat hit send.

'How are you feeling, love?' asked Mel tentatively. Her friend had gone from borderline hysteria to ice queen in two shakes of a lamb's tail. Not typical behaviour for her, but then this wasn't exactly a typical situation.

'Numb. I feel exhausted and numb. I just want this all over and done with now. It's draining the life out of me.' Cat finished off the wine in her glass and put her hand across it when Mel instinctively went to top her up. 'I don't think I want any more, pet, but thanks. I may have a cuppa in a bit.'

Mel's reply was interrupted by the buzz from Cat's phone. All three jumped as the sound was loud and jarring, even though it was expected. Col looked at Mel, his eyes narrowed in disapproval. She felt she could read his thoughts as they reflected her own. *Someone's bloody keen.*

Hi again yourself, Lisa. Well, I guessed right! I have albums by all those bands! I can't take too much credit, though. It wouldn't be hard to predict you have great taste in music, knowing you like The Bolshoi. Sounds like your boyfriend had mixed taste to me, though, musically sound but a daft bugger for letting you go! Do you get to go to many gigs, Lisa? I don't think you can beat live music. I have seen hundreds of bands over the years but don't get to see as many as I used to. Whereabouts do you live? I'm near Cardiff. Mike x

FINDING A MIRACLE

'What do you guys think so far?'

'Nothing too incriminating, but I'm interested to see if he mentions the ex-boyfriend again. When it's written down, it's harder to know if he's being polite or flirty,' said Mel.

'From a bloke's point of view, Col? And please be honest, pet,' asked Cat.

'I'm on the fence, like Mel. I could see myself saying the same thing without any hidden agenda or, with the intention of testing the waters, I suppose. We need a bit more from him, but so far, he hasn't said anything conclusive.'

Cat looked at Col, her expression serious and thoughtful. She turned her attention to her phone.

Hey, hey. Yeah, my ex-boyfriend wasn't the best. I had to make a new Facebook profile because he became a nuisance. It's hard to make a fresh start when someone's holding you back in the past. I live in Chester now. I moved here last year, and I'm settling in well. My main friend that lives near me is pregnant, so my social life is basically cinema, shopping, or a meal out now! My musical tastes aren't shared with many, lol, so not been to a gig in ages. What about you? Is there a Mrs Mike? Lisa x

'I just want to know, and I don't want to wait forever. His next message will be telling, I think. I've been direct there. If he denies he has a girlfriend, then I think we will know for sure that he is attempting to flirt with Lisa. There would be no other explanation for him pretending I don't exist.'

CHAPTER TWENTY-THREE

'I don't blame you, Cat. I'd want to tear off the plaster, too. No playing cat and mouse, just get on with it, that's what I'd do. No pun intended, by the way, and I'm not calling Mike a mouse,' said Col clumsily. 'I call my three-year-old nephew Teddy "Mouse" and he's great.' Col grimaced and raised his eyes to heaven, annoyed with himself for prattling on.

Cat was about to pick up her phone when it buzzed again.

Oh, that's a shame that your wings have been clipped due to your friend's pregnancy. Someone I know is currently pregnant and she's all about watching box sets these days. Sorry to hear things went so badly with your ex. I hope you're okay and things get easier going forward. I'm sure your Mr Right is out there waiting to sweep you off your feet. I don't have a Mrs Mike, as in I'm not married, but I've got a girlfriend, and we live together. It's all a bit complicated at the moment, though. Mike x

After Cat finished reading Mike's message aloud, she sat there in silence, her mind spinning as she tried to process his words.

'Complicated? What the hell does he mean by "complicated"?' she asked her friends.

'I don't know, love, but if you can face it, this is the perfect time to ask him,' said Mel as she topped up Cat's wine glass with the remainder of the bottle. This time Cat didn't stop her.

Ha! Your friend sounds a bit like mine! Her vodka money is now going towards books and baby things. I didn't see that happening at all; she loves vodka! I hope you're right about my Mr Right, Mike. I'm fine for now but hope to find someone to grow old with one day. Hmm, not sure what to say about the situation with your girlfriend. I don't want to pry, but is everything okay? Lisa x

Cat felt like she was holding her breath until Mike's reply landed. The same was true for Mel and Col. Both thought she was extremely brave, and both reached out to her.

Heaven forbid, trading in vodka for nappies! Lol. I'm sure it will all be worth it for her, though. Don't worry about finding someone. I wouldn't mind betting your knight in shining armour is out there looking for you as we type. His satnav is having problems finding its way around Chester, that's all! Things were okay…better than okay, they were great. A few months ago, though, I ran into someone from my past, and it kinda turned my world upside down. Mike x

Cat's fingers barely kept up with her thoughts.

Turned your world upside down in a good way or a bad way? Lisa xx

The answer to this question could make or break their relationship.

I think both to be honest. Seeing her again has changed absolutely everything…there's no doubt about that. If I'm honest, my head's been in a mess since she first came back. I might not need to swap vodka for nappies like your friend, but preparing to become a dad was the last thing I expected. Mike xx

CHAPTER TWENTY-THREE

The phone dropped from Cat's hand with a thud, and her hand went to her mouth as she took in a shocked breath.

'A dad! He's preparing to become a *dad*! It must be with that Clare; it must be. I can't believe he would do this to me. To go behind my back like that and get someone pregnant. I've finally got my proof now. There's no coming back from this. We are well and truly *done*,' said Cat flatly.

'Darling, I am *so* sorry. What an absolute *bastard*. I knew things seemed off, but I had hoped that you'd got it wrong. That we all had. I didn't see him doing this; he just never seemed the type.' Mel put her hand on Cat's arm and gave it a squeeze.

'He's an idiot, and he doesn't deserve you, Cat. It's as simple as that,' said Col, angry at Mike and devastated for his friend.

Without any tears, Cat picked up the phone and started typing.

Oh wow, well, that must be exciting for you! Congratulations! Is this your first child? L xx

Thanks, Lisa. Yes, I'm very much in at the deep end without a clue. I think I'm more terrified than excited. It's probably going to change a lot of things, including things I wish would stay the same. God, look at me going on at a total stranger. Sorry for offloading all that. You must think I'm a proper oddball! I'm not usually, honestly. You're very easy to talk to…or type to, rather. M xx

Cat swallowed hard as emotions began to build. She sent replies quickly, no longer stopping to check for Mel and Col's approval.

Well, I think you will be a natural, Mike. You don't come across as odd in any way. You're very easy to talk/type to as well. I'm glad I reached out to you. L xx

That's so kind of you. I've bottled up so much lately, so I appreciate having someone to talk to, so thank you. M xx

If I hadn't had a friend to talk to when I was going through all that shit with my ex, I don't think I'd have coped, to be honest. We all need a listening ear sometimes, Mike. L xx

I think that makes us new friends then. I've bent your ear enough for tonight, and in the hope that I do get to chat with you again, I think I should bid you a good night and not scare you away completely! Sweet dreams, Lisa. M xx

Speak soon, Mike. Sweet dreams to you too. L xx

Cat put the phone down and let out a long, slow breath.

'I don't know how you managed to keep your cool, my lovely. Well done, seriously,' said Mel, who felt absolutely spent. It felt like all the energy had been sucked right out of the room, leaving a vacuum in its wake. No wonder she was so cautious about getting into a new relationship. This kind of thing was why she felt being single was for the best. *When the person meant to love you the most hurts you like this, what's the point?* she thought.

CHAPTER TWENTY-THREE

'Who wants a cuppa?' Mel asked before getting up from the table to put the kettle on. Usually, something as serious as this would require something far stronger, but right now, for once, she couldn't stomach it and didn't think her two friends could either. Cat nodded at her suggestion of tea.

'I'm going to head off now and leave you girls to it. But thanks for the offer, Mel,' Col said before turning his attention to Cat. 'Mel's right; you were remarkable then. I think I'd have phoned him and had a go at him. But this way you have your answers and you've bought yourself time. When you confront him, it will be on your terms, in your own time, and you'll hold all the cards.'

'Thanks, Col. I'm so glad you told me about Clare being pregnant. That couldn't have been easy for you, but it would have totally floored me to find out in a text meant for Lisa. I have time to get my head around things and then work out what to do next. I don't suppose the offer of your spare room lasts for more than one night, does it, Mel?' asked Cat tentatively.

'Course it bloody does. I can't believe you'd even ask me that. You can stay with me for as long as you want, darling. I'll look after you. We both will, won't we, Col?' said Mel, covertly gesturing to Colin to encourage agreement. She walked over to Cat, wrapped her up in her arms, and kissed her on the top of her head in an act of almost motherly love. 'You will be absolutely fine. I promise you. Granted, it might be a bit pants for a little while, but we are with you every step of the way and will help in any way we can. Right, Col?'

'Course we will, Cat. You're going to be great; we will make sure of it,' Col replied eagerly, nodding firmly as he spoke. In equal measure, he wanted to reassure Cat, of course, but he also did not want to feel Mel's wrath for not agreeing quickly enough or with enough conviction for her liking! 'I'm going to make a move now, but if you need anything, I'm a call away. You stay there, Mel, I'll see myself out.'

As Mel poured them both a mug of tea, she asked Cat what she wanted to do in the next day or so. Cat felt that taking the next day off would be necessary because she knew she wouldn't be able to function. It would also give her time to go and collect a few of her clothes and other essential belongings to tide her over for a few days. Proof of Mike's infidelity might not have been a shock exactly, but that didn't make it any less sad. Mel was in no doubt that her friend would be dealing with a whole mixture of feelings right now and that, in the coming days, it would probably turn largely into grief. Grief for the loss of her relationship and for what, until today, had been a certain future.

Mel suggested they would be more comfortable sitting in the lounge. She took a detour before joining Cat and nipped upstairs to put a pair of pyjamas on the radiator in her spare room. She grabbed a fluffy blanket from the airing cupboard and laid that over the bottom of the bed for extra warmth. Cat felt the cold quite badly, which Mel found unusual for a woman who came from the northeast of England. She wanted her to be at least warm and cosy tonight. The final touch was a box of tissues that she placed on the nightstand next to the bed.

CHAPTER TWENTY-THREE

Mel joined Cat on the sofa and shared the blanket that Cat had already covered her legs with.

'I think I'm going to get a few bits from the house tomorrow, then spend the day here if that's okay. I'm sure work will cope without me for a day or two. I'll say it's a stomach bug for now. I can't face talking to management about it at the moment. I need to speak to Mike first anyway. I'll be there when he gets home from work tomorrow and will tell him I know what's been going on and then come back here.'

'That seems like a decent plan, love. No good would come from delaying things. You have the truth from the horse's mouth now. In your shoes, I'd want it over and done with as soon as possible. I'm so bitterly disappointed in him.'

'You and me both, Mel. Maybe we had become a bit too comfortable. Neither of us put the effort in that we used to, but I always trusted him. I never stopped loving him. This feels ridiculously out of character.'

The two chatted for a little longer and shared a comfortable silence before Cat announced she was ready for bed. Mel was drained, and she too was looking forward to getting into bed. Before they went upstairs, Mel ran through everything Cat needed to know about the house, how she should help herself to anything she wanted and generally make herself at home. Mel gave Cat a final cwtch and told her to try to get some sleep before wishing her goodnight. As Cat went into what was to become her room for the foreseeable future, she felt touched seeing the additional blanket that Mel had draped over the bed.

FINDING A MIRACLE

It was the sight of pyjamas warming on the radiator for her that loosened the first silent tear from her eye, though, and it was very quickly joined by many more as the floodgates opened.

Chapter Twenty-Four

It had been hours since Mel last looked at her phone. Just after getting into bed, she checked to see if she had any messages. She quickly scrolled through the copious number of adverts that had descended on her email inbox and decided she wasn't tempted by any of their *Amazing Offers Inside*. There were a few messages on WhatsApp. All were from her little group of sassy sleuths.

Hey there Miss Marples. I wondered when you might be free for a catch-up. I've done some investigating and want to update you. I can't be certain, but I think I may have found living relatives of Maurice Newman! Kev xx

Liv, Tony, and Jeff were all suitably surprised, impressed, and hungry for details, as was Mel. She was also touched to think Kev had decided to do some unprompted research. Mel had come under fire in their messages for being the only person who had not replied yet. Reading those messages lifted her mood. The group had taken it upon themselves to arrange a catch-up on Wednesday evening in the Red Lion. After weighing things up, Mel decided that she would be able to pop along, even if only briefly. There was no doubt that she wanted to be there, but she also wanted to be available for Cat as it would almost certainly be a difficult night for her.

SORRY! Just seen your messages. Kev, I can't believe you've found living relatives! Thank you, you're a legend. I will see you all at the Red Lion. Love, love, love M xxx

Before charging her phone, Mel decided to fire a quick text to Kev.

Hey Kev. Hope you're doing okay. I just wanted to say thanks for investigating for me. You're an absolute star! Under normal circumstances, I would be rushing around and knocking on your door demanding information, but I have a few things on at the moment. One of my friends is staying with me for a few days and I will need to be around for her for a little while. No need to reply, my eyes are already closing. Goodnight, M xx

***

The next morning, unfamiliar sounds of someone moving around in the house woke Mel from what had been a surprisingly deep sleep. She hadn't heard her alarm, so it was a good job that Cat was up and about, or she may have slept even longer. There was a gentle knock at Mel's bedroom door before it opened slowly.

'Morning, Mel. I wondered if you wanted me to bring you a cuppa. I'm about to make one and go back to bed for half an hour.'

'Thanks for the offer, but I'm running a bit late. Did you get any sleep?' asked Mel, though she already knew the answer judging by how washed out she looked.

'Not much, but I think I cried myself to sleep eventually.'

CHAPTER TWENTY-FOUR

'I'm sorry I can't take the day off to spend with you, love, but if you need anything, just text.'

'Don't be daft, I'll be fine. Thank you, though. I'm going to leave you to get ready.'

Just under an hour later, Mel was through the door and on her way to work. Soon after Mel left, Cat went downstairs to get her shoes and coat on, ready to go back to her flat to collect a few of her things. She went to the kitchen to pick up her bag and noticed that Mel had left her a spare key on the table. Cat didn't have a clue what she would have done had Mel not offered her a room. She didn't want to think how vulnerable that made her feel; instead, she chose to focus on how blessed she was to have Mel. *Everybody needs a Mel*, she thought.

The flat was silent as she let herself in. It took three attempts to get her key in the door because her hand was trembling. Once inside, she felt a chill creep down her spine. This felt wrong. Cat felt like she was trespassing and had no right to be there. She went to her wardrobe and retrieved her suitcase from the top of it and placed it on what used to be *their* bed. She quickly filled it with clothes, jewellery, makeup, and essential items like her passport and birth certificate. Once filled, she took the case straight to her car. Feeling overwhelmed, she couldn't wait to get back to the homely hive that was Mel's house.

The day had dragged on for Mel. It felt endless. She had checked in with Cat at lunchtime, who was already back at the house with a case of her belongings. Cat told her that she had arranged to see Mike at the house after he finished work that evening and that she planned to get there before him.

Mel texted Cat again just before she left the carers' centre for the day.

Are you okay, Cat? xx

I'm fine, thanks, Mel. I just arrived, and Mike's due any minute. I'll text you later. xx

As Cat heard the key turn and Mike walk in, she stood up. She wanted to meet this challenge head-on and there was no way she would be sat down for this. He called out his familiar greeting of 'I'm home' and it momentarily rocked her resolve, knowing it would be the last time she would hear that. Ever. The finality of this moment came crashing down like waves on a stormy night. She swallowed the lump in her throat and dug her nails into her palm for strength. *Do not bloody cry, don't you bloody dare,* she warned herself.

'Ah, there you are. Good day?' asked Mike as he dropped his bag on the floor and put his jacket on the chair. Her lack of response made him look up at her as he started taking his shoes off. Cat's stony expression caught him off guard. Why was she standing in the lounge with her coat on and almost looking straight through him?

'When were you going to tell me, Mike?' Her tone was accusatory.

'Tell you what? What's going on?' said Mike, feeling confused and ambushed.

CHAPTER TWENTY-FOUR

'Well, it doesn't matter now because I already know. I've saved you the trouble.'

'Know what? What the hell are you talking about?' Mike felt panic rise inside him, his heart rate through the roof in an instant. It couldn't be *that*; it must be something else, surely. Nobody knew, so how could *she* know? His mind raced and scrambled for answers like a cornered rat looking for an escape route. He saw the determined look on Cat's face and knew this was serious and there would be no escape.

'Ha!' Cat's laugh dripped with animosity; her cold eyes held him in a vice-like grip. 'You really want me to spell it out for you, Mike? I know about you and Clare. I also know about the *baby*.'

Mike reached out to steady himself, his mouth suddenly as dry as a desert wind.

'Nothing? Really? Not even an "I'm sorry, Cat, it's not how it looks"?' She almost spat the words at him in a mocking tone. Cat was angrier than he had ever seen her and by quite some margin. Her face barely concealed her rage.

'What baby, and what about Clare?' His voice was small and broken.

'Progress. At least you've not denied there is a Clare.' She clapped her hands slowly, her voice loaded with irony. 'Let's give Mike a gold star, shall we?'

'I...I...I do know Clare, yes. She's an ex-girlfriend from years ago.' Mike's whole body trembled, and he was pretty sure Cat could see his fear with her eyes closed.

'There's a little bit more to it than that though isn't there, Mike? You've been spending a *lot* of time with her lately, haven't you, eh? Probably because you're having an affair with her and she's carrying your child.'

'What?! No! An *affair*? God, no! She most definitely is *not* having my baby! Absolutely not! Look, Cat, I do have something to tell you. Would you give me five minutes to explain, please?' Mike sat down in the armchair next to him, unsure his legs had the strength to keep him upright.

'I'm all ears,' said Cat icily, folding her arms in defiance.

'Okay, so there is something I've been meaning to tell you for a while now, but I've found it difficult. Impossible really.'

'Clearly!' interrupted Cat angrily.

'A few months ago, I ran into Clare by chance at the garage. We dated for six months about nine years ago and broke up when she moved to Manchester. We lost touch, and I hadn't seen or heard from her in ages. Her brothers are joint owners at Pulse Gym and one of them told me that she had gotten married and moved again to Abergavenny. This was a good few years ago. So, when I met her, it was a surprise to know she had moved back here about three months before. We swapped numbers and said we would meet up. That was more out of awkward politeness than anything. If I'm honest, I never expected to follow through with it and arrange to see her.'

CHAPTER TWENTY-FOUR

'Because you always arrange to meet your ex-girlfriends and choose to not mention it to your current girlfriend, I suppose?' said Cat.

'It wasn't like that, honestly. Anyway, a few days later she rang me and asked if we could meet and that it was important. I met her after work that day, and that's when she dropped the bombshell. She told me there was a chance that her eight-year-old daughter could also be *my* daughter. I was gobsmacked and didn't know what to think. Long story short, I did a paternity test, and a week or so later, the results came back. I *was* the father of Clare's daughter. I *am* the father of Clare's daughter. Cat, I was shellshocked. I had absolutely *no* idea. I needed time to process it, to get it straight in my head before telling you.'

'An eight-year-old…and she tells you *now*?' said an incredulous Cat.

'I know, I know. It was a massive shock. Clare hasn't told her daughter yet. Well, *our* daughter, I guess. She wanted to give me time to get used to the idea first. I've met her a couple of times but haven't been introduced as her dad. Just talking about this is bizarre and hard to believe. She's eight years old. How the hell am I supposed to become a father to an eight-year-old girl? I don't know the first thing about parenthood, and I really am turning up late to the party.'

'Well, don't look to me for answers,' said Cat coldly.

'I'm so, so, sorry about this, Cat. I've been confused, and I've been a coward for not telling you sooner, but I have *never* cheated on you. I could never cheat on you.

Clare is pregnant with her ex's baby. She moved back here for a fresh start after they split up. I know I've been absent from us for a few months, Cat, but finding out about Samantha is the *only* reason for that. Keeping this secret from you has been hell, and I've tried to tell you so many times but then bottled it. I was scared it would change how you feel about me and us. The *last* thing I would want is to lose you.' Mike wiped away his tears on the back of his sleeve. He seemed to have aged twenty years in the past twenty seconds, thought Cat. His eyes were trained on her face, searching for a clue as to her reaction to this news. She stared down at him, making him feel even smaller than he already did. He'd screwed up, big time, and he knew it.

'Okay,' said Cat quietly. She was exhausted from trying to keep a lid on the wide range of emotions she felt.

'Okay? Is that it?' he asked cautiously, his voice thin and desperate.

'I'm not sure what to say or how I feel, Mike. This was a shock to you, and so obviously it's a shock to me too. Keeping all this from me makes me question *everything* about us. I thought we were better than this. I'm going to need to come to terms with the disappointment of how you handled things, and I can't be around you while I work out what I want to do. I'm going to stay at Mel's, and I'm not sure when I'll be back. Honestly, I'm not even sure that I will be coming back. I don't know what to think or how I feel about us. I need space, so please don't try to contact me. Goodbye, Mike.'

Chapter Twenty-Five

As Cat had said she wanted to go alone to Mike's, Mel decided the best thing for her to do was to keep busy. She made a Mexican chicken casserole with her signature dish, her infamous mashed potatoes with cheese and leeks. Mel knew this would be a safe bet. She had lit the fire when she got home from work, and the lounge was warming up a treat. Mel wanted Cat to feel as welcomed and nurtured as possible when she got back to hers. She paced around the house, looking for things to do to help burn off a fraction of the nervous energy that had built steadily over the course of the day. After what seemed like an eternity, Cat arrived.

Mel ushered her in, offered her a drink, and asked her how it went all within one sentence and without pausing for breath. Within mere moments, Cat was sat on the sofa and recounting all that had been said between her and Mike. Mel sat in total silence, absolutely transfixed. The news that Mike was not about to be a dad to a newborn but an eight-year-old girl took her back at a rate of knots.

'Wow, well I didn't see that coming, Cat. That's a bit of a shocker, isn't it? How do *you* feel about it?' said a stunned Mel, struggling to come to terms with what she'd been told.

'I'm not sure I feel much of anything. To be honest, I'm a bit numb. I've never been hugely maternal; I spend enough time with kids at work as it is. But we'd said that one day we would have kids. I just haven't reached that point yet, and I've always assumed I'd know when the time is right. I also assumed that when I had a baby, it would be with Mike, and it would be *our* first child. A first for us *both*. This might sound crazy, but I feel like I've had something taken away from me. Having a baby with me could never be as special to him now.'

Mel reflected and focused on the more positive aspects of the situation. He hadn't cheated and had no intention of cheating. The fact he had kept it a secret for as long as he did was because he was scared that this news would change things between them. That showed how much he loved Cat and cared about their relationship. Mel reminded Cat how visibly upset she said Mike had been. Another sign he was utterly genuine.

'I think this is a *far* better scenario than Mike cheating, all in all, Cat. I know it's not ideal and not what you'd choose, but it could be a lot worse. Before you go throwing in the towel on what has been, until recently, a great relationship, give it some thought. I can't imagine how hard this will have been for Mike. I feel for him, Cat, I'm sorry, but I really do. I never imagined for a second, I'd be saying that to you tonight. Take your time and think about things before you do something you might regret.'

'In your shoes, Mel, I would probably be saying the same. I just feel that staying with him would be a *huge* compromise. I'm sure he will want contact with

CHAPTER TWENTY-FIVE

his daughter, and so inevitably she will be coming to the flat, maybe even staying over. Worse still, his ex will now be a part of our lives. Part of *my* life but uninvited and unwelcome. We will be expected to go to school plays, parents' evenings, carol concerts, and all sorts. I didn't sign up for this, Mel, and I'm not sure I can do it. Having this little eight-year-old reminder of his past relationship shoved in my face makes me feel uneasy and resentful. We were fine as we were, just the two of us. Life will never be the same again, and it will never be as good. Mike's a decent bloke deep down, so I know he will want to do his best as a father. It's obvious that I will never be his priority again. He would always choose her first if push came to shove, and I didn't get with him to be his number two. If we both had kids, it would be different, but we don't. This changes *everything*.'

'I hear you; I really do.' Mel sighed. 'I think what you've said is extremely honest and brave of you. This is all fresh and new, and it's good that you've got how you feel off your chest but give it time to settle. You may feel differently in a few days, and it might be that you decide this *isn't* worth losing Mike over. You need time to think, and you will need to explain exactly how you feel about it to Mike. He might reassure you and put your mind at rest, and he deserves that chance, my lovely. For now, just let it all sink in and try to relax a little. I'm going to dish up some casserole and mash for you now because you need to eat something today, and I'm not taking no for an answer. While I'm doing that, are you up to letting Col know what's happened? I know he will be on pins, just as I was.'

Cat agreed and texted Colin, giving him a brief

update as she did not have the energy to phone him and go through everything in full a second time. Mel summoned Cat to the table, and she gingerly picked at her meal without her usual enthusiasm for anything Mel cooked. It was the first thing she had eaten all day, she realised, and that just wasn't her.

'I wonder how Mike is,' said Mel tenderly.

'I'm not able to think of him and how he's coping,' said Cat despondently. 'I feel like he's gained a daughter, and I'm now forced to share him with her. If I'd known about her before we got together, that would be different. I'd have been able to decide for myself whether or not I wanted to be with a man who had a kid. The thought of all the change is horrible. It's been pushed on me, and I feel like my voice won't be heard from now on. There would be whole weekends now when the kid would be with us. No more Sunday morning lie-ins. It'll be taking her swimming or dancing or whatever the hell eight-year-olds do at weekends. Having a child is the biggest decision anyone makes. And I haven't been part of the decision-making process.'

'And neither was Mike,' said Mel firmly. 'This child wasn't planned, and yet he's now landed with this huge and unexpected responsibility. *You* have a choice; you can walk away from Mike and not look back. He doesn't have the luxury of that option with his daughter. I'm guessing that poor bloke is distraught, sitting alone in his flat right now. No doubt hoping and praying that he will have your love and support as he tries to come to terms with this massive change in his circumstances. He's probably

CHAPTER TWENTY-FIVE

terrified. Terrified of having to become a dad overnight and terrified of losing the woman he loves. I know you didn't ask for this, Cat, but neither did he, so try not to lose sight of that.'

Cat took in all that Mel had said. Her words stung a little, and there was no avoiding seeing things from Mike's perspective now. Mel laid it all bare and she was right; Cat knew that, but it didn't make this situation any less awful for her. Thinking of Mike sitting alone in their flat, surrounded by their belongings and their memories, hurt her heart. *She* at least was surrounded by love tonight while he was left to deal with the fallout by himself. Needing to have a little time to process things, Cat excused herself, saying she was tired and needed an early night.

Mel made herself another cuppa and went and sat in the lounge to try to relax a little before going to bed herself. She thought about the complications that now existed in Cat and Mike's relationship, and it made her think of her nan and Maurice. She couldn't help but compare. Had Rose not been pregnant, then her nan's life may have been very, very different.

CHAPTER TWENTY-SIX

As Mel finally decided on a suitably amusing Christmas card for her dad, she then went to the friends section. She didn't send many cards these days but still sent them to the handful of people she knew would be disappointed to not get one. It didn't take long to find what she was looking for, and she then went on to pick out some silver bows, tags, and ribbons in preparation for wrapping presents. Mel always put effort into decorating her gifts. After the heaviness of the previous day, she was pleased to be doing something more uplifting, or as she would describe it, 'fluffy'. Wandering around and looking at all the festive items put a smile on her face, and the thought of seeing her friends later put an even bigger smile on her face.

Mel decided to go and grab a sandwich from the bakery before heading back to the centre. As Cat had been sleeping soundly before Mel left for work, she didn't even make a cup of tea, never mind breakfast, for fear of waking her. Mel doubted that she had slept particularly well and did not want to disturb her. As she walked into the bakery, Col was on his way out clutching the mother of all corned beef pasties.

'Hey, Mel. I'll wait for you to walk back to work.'

CHAPTER TWENTY-SIX

'Great. I won't be long.'

Mel picked out a cheese and tomato baguette as it was already made, and she did not want to keep Col waiting. She also picked up some cookies to take home for Cat. If she was still picking at her food, Mel felt sure she would at least manage those.

'How is Cat doing?'

'She's in shock, I think, Col. She's going to need a bit of time to come to terms with things. If Mike's smart, he will give her all the time she needs. She'd gone back to sleep when I left for work, and I've not texted her this morning in case I disturb her. I'm hoping that she will be feeling a bit better about things when I get back tonight. Now it's a question for her to decide whether she can cope with the idea of Mike having a little girl, really.'

'I hope they manage to patch things up. I feel sorry for Mike. This must have totally blindsided him.'

'I agree, Col, and said as much to Cat last night.'

When they got back to the centre, Mel went to her office to have her lunch. She decided to check in with Cat.

Hey Cat, how are you doing today, darling? Do you need me to pick anything up for you on my way home, love? xx

Hi Mel. Thanks for being there for me last night. I don't know what I'd have done without you. I feel a bit more settled today, pet. At least I know what's going on now. The not knowing was worse than how this feels. Mike has sent me a few texts. I read them but haven't replied yet. He's taken the day off sick, too, apparently. He asked if we could meet to talk later. I'm considering it. Perhaps best to get it over with, I'm not sure. I will keep you posted, though xx

Okay, well, I'm glad you feel a bit better. Sleeping on things always helps. I'll briefly be home a bit later tonight. Sorry it's rubbish timing, but I'd already made plans. Although having the place to yourself might be nice if you decide not to meet Mike. I'll be dropping my car off and walking back to the Red Lion. It won't be a late one though. You take care, and let me know how you're getting on xx

Just as Mel had pressed send on the text to Cat, she received a text from Liv.

Hey, you. Have you got plans for this weekend? If that's a yes, then cancel them NOW! Xxx

Mel half laughed and half groaned. What the hell was she up to now?

Why? Xxx

Can't say. Just trust me. Xxx

That sounds a bit cloak and dagger. And trust you? Hmm, why would I ever do something that stupid? Trusting you hasn't always been the wisest move I've ever made now, has it??? I haven't forgotten the time you wheeled me round the village in a shopping trolley or the time we fell over when you wore me like a backpack! xx

You make some good points but shush and do as you're told. See you tonight. Love you xxx

Love you too (a little bit) xxx

CHAPTER TWENTY-SIX

Mel was intrigued by the cryptic message from Liv. Whatever she had up her sleeve was bound to be fun, and she was sure she'd get it out of her later. She couldn't keep a secret from her for long.

The afternoon was a busy one for Mel as she had a group session. Today, they looked at stress management, and Mel led the group in a guided meditation. It helped relax her too and take her mind off things. She was glad of the distraction as apart from worrying about Cat, she had become eager to hear more about what Kev had discovered about the Maurice Newman clan. After the session, as she started packing up for the day, she got a text from Cat letting her know that she was about to leave to meet Mike and she would see Mel later. She was pleased that Cat had decided to meet him. Whatever the outcome, Mel felt it was positive that she was prepared to at least talk to him.

After parking her car, Mel nipped into the house to quickly freshen up. A top-up of perfume, a dusting of powder, and some lipstick later, she was back downstairs. She left the cookies on the kitchen table with a note that said *Enjoy! X* before trotting down the hallway and heading back out into the dark December evening.

When Mel walked into the Red Lion it was already lively. The pre-Christmas buzz had started and the pub was busier than it would be midweek at any other point in the year. She glanced around and saw her lot at the large table at the back. Kev spotted her and went to meet her at the bar.

'Great to see you, Mel,' he said after bending down to kiss her cheek. 'I didn't get you a drink because I wasn't sure if you would be driving later, so what are you having?'

'I am most definitely not driving and will be having a gin and tonic, thanks, Kev. Good to see you. I can't wait to hear your news on Maurice's relatives.'

'Not long to wait now. Why don't you go and sit down with the others, and I'll bring your drink over.'

There were lots of comments like, 'Good of you to join us' and 'What time do you call this, then?' despite her friends only having arrived shortly before her. They never wasted the slightest opportunity for gentle ribbing. Mel took her place next to Kev's empty seat. The four said their hellos and checked all was well. Kev appeared with Mel's gin and tonic in one hand and a few bags of crisps for them all to share in the other. Barely giving him a minute to sit down, Liv immediately badgered him to 'get on with it and give up the goods'. Not wanting to disappoint, Kev began telling the group what he had discovered.

'It's a bit of a long story, so I'll keep it to the bare minimum to avoid boring you to death. Okay, so I Googled how to find birth records in the UK and discovered a website that gives information about marriages and deaths as well as births. So, firstly, I searched for a child born to Maurice and Rose Newman, and it came up blank. Initially, I thought that was the end until I remembered in Maurice's letter that he said he adopted the name Newman. So, I searched again, this time for a marriage between a Maurice and a Rose Newman. There were four. Fortunately, though, it was clear fairly quickly it was

CHAPTER TWENTY-SIX

unlikely to be the marriages in Devon and in Edinburgh, not only because of the location but also because the dates were way out. The remaining two were in Greater London. One was in Lambeth in 1984, and the final one was a Maurice Bird marrying Rose Newman in Greenwich in 1946. Bingo!'

'Fantastic work, Kev. A *huge* well done for remembering that Maurice had a different surname!' interrupted Mel, unable to quell her enthusiasm.

'Thanks, Mel. There's a bit more to come, though,' said Kev with a smile before continuing. 'Next, I searched for a child born to a Maurice and Rose Bird. As far as I can tell from the records, they only had one child. That sort of fits with what we know about their marriage not being the best. They had a son in 1948 they named Alton Bird. I carried on with the search to see if Alton got married. The good news for us is he did. In 1972, Alton married Julie Danvers.'

Kev paused to take a drink, and it tickled him to see the concentration on the faces of his four friends. They were transfixed and uncharacteristically quiet.

'I think you know where I'm going next with this,' he said with a chuckle. 'I searched for any children born to Alton and Julie Bird and again struck lucky. They had two children. Morgan Newman Bird in 1973 and David Newman Bird in 1978; both born in Greenwich. Unfortunately, the records end in 1992, so I wasn't able to find out if Morgan and David got married or had kids, sorry.'

'Sorry? You've got nothing to be sorry for, Kev; you've done amazingly well! I thought you were an accountant, not a private investigator,' gushed Mel.

'That's seriously impressive, Kev. Well done, mate. That's incredible,' said Jeff, nodding as he complimented him.

'Thanks, but honestly, I'd not have managed to find much if we were looking for a Smith or Jones. Not only are they uncommon surnames, but their first and middle names are pretty unusual, too. I mean, how many Altons do you know? If we had not been blessed with such unique names, our search would have been impossible at worst and a struggle at best.'

'Well, I still think you've done brilliantly, regardless. It's a shame for it to end here, mind,' said Tony thoughtfully.

'Nope, not happening. We're not giving up; we just get our heads together and find a way, that's all,' said Jeff.

'Social media!' said Liv in an excited, shrill pitch. 'We might struggle a bit with David, but how many Morgan Birds can there be? How about we finish our drinks and head to mine? I've got a laptop, I've got wine, and it'll be quieter than here.' Liv nodded towards the bar area, which had become infinitely busier in the short time since Mel arrived.

The group seemed happy and so a plan was formed. Tony nipped across the road to order some pizzas from Merola's so they could spend as long as they needed to at Liv's and not have to dash off to make their tea. When he

CHAPTER TWENTY-SIX

got back, he told them he demanded their attention and announced they had a little surprise for Mel.

'So, darling girl. We have arranged a little trip for this weekend. You need to be packed and ready to leave at lunchtime on Friday. We know that you can take time off on a Friday afternoon, so no arguments, please.'

'It's all arranged so you only need to think about what you want to wear,' added Liv.

'So can I ask where it is we're all going?' asked Mel.

The four looked at each other, big smiles planted on their faces.

'London,' said Liv.

She was joined half a second later by her three co-conspirators.

'We're going to The Metropole!'

Chapter Twenty-Seven

It didn't take long for them to have a quick bite to eat before starting on their mission for the evening. Or as Liv referred to it, *Project Bird-finder*. They chatted excitedly about their upcoming trip to London between bites but soon calmed themselves as it was time to get down to the business of finding Maurice's living relatives.

'I think Kev should take the lead on this as he's got the ball rolling on it. What do you all think?' asked Jeff. All three agreed that was a good plan. Liv slid her laptop in Kev's direction and volunteered to take notes for him. Mel stifled a laugh, seeing the serious look on Liv's face. *She's really loving this detective lark*, thought an amused Mel.

'Well, it's a group effort, but thanks for the vote of confidence! Okay, so I think that, as Liv said, Morgan will be the easier of the two to track down, with David being a much more commonly used name.'

All four nodded in agreement and so Kev signed into his Facebook account. He typed 'Morgan Bird' in the search bar and was surprised to see a lot more people with that name than he expected.

'Hmm. Morgan Bird is a way more popular name

CHAPTER TWENTY-SEVEN

than I would have guessed,' said Mel, her voice giving away the disappointment she felt.

'It is more popular, Mel, but this is doable. Don't forget we can check to see if he has a "David Bird" in his list of friends and relatives, and we can also check for any Newmans. We also know they have links to Greenwich, so we have a few aces up our sleeve yet,' said Kev in an attempt to reassure Mel. He gave a slow, knowing nod with the intention of portraying a demeanour of calm confidence. The truth was, he was far from confident and not convinced they would actually find their man. He didn't want to let Mel down, though and would keep trying until there was no stone left unturned.

'You see, *this* is why you were a good choice for lead detective!' said Jeff. He puffed out his chest, looking rather pleased with himself for nominating Kev. 'I'd just like to point out that one of my many, many talents is being able to spot talent in others. I'm basically the Welsh Simon Cowell,' he said, smiling proudly.

'Shame you didn't have his Hollywood mansion and bank balance, my love. You're more of a pound-shop version of Cowell at best,' teased Tony.

'I'm hurt by that Tone, but luckily, I am also very, very brave. Please continue, Kev, while I regain my composure after that rather vicious and uncalled for verbal attack from my other half,' said Jeff, trying, but failing dismally, to keep a straight face.

'Right, you naughty lot, let's get stuck in, shall we?' said Kev, doing his best to restore some semblance of order to the room.

Kev filtered his search to remove all females named 'Morgan Bird', which, the group was relieved to see, reduced the numbers significantly. Next, he narrowed the search options to those living in the UK. Again, the numbers reduced. One by one, he went through the list, explaining why each Morgan did not fit. There were a variety of things that made them incompatible, age being the most common by far. Kev willed success with every stroke of the key. Over two dozen failed attempts later, there were signs of promise.

'So, this is looking better. This Morgan appears to be about the right age, judging from his photograph, and it says he lives in Greenwich! So far, so good. Now, let's see if he has any Newman relatives.'

Kev went to the friends and family section of his profile and typed in 'Newman'. There was a collective intake of breath as he pressed search, followed by some noisy cheering as it became clear that he did, in fact, have a few Newman relatives. The reaction was that of a lottery-winning syndicate that just discovered they'd hit the jackpot. After the celebrations calmed, Kev continued. His face was back to being serious and businesslike. Liv once again picked up her pen, poised and ready for action despite not having yet written a single word.

'Okay, this is promising, but now we need to find out if Morgan has a David in his friends and family list.'

Once again, Kev typed, and the group held their breath, eyes trained on Kev, waiting for a reaction.

CHAPTER TWENTY-SEVEN

'Got him!' said Kev, raising two arms in the air. 'We don't just have a David Bird on Morgan's friends list; we have a *brother* called David Bird. They *must* be our boys, surely?'

All five Miss Marple wannabes looked from one to the other excitedly, their expressions asking, *could it be?* Hardly believing their luck, they sat back in happy disbelief.

'There's only one way to find out for sure whether he's our man or not. We contact him and ask,' said Mel, grinning from ear to ear.

'Let's do it!' said Liv, slamming her unused pen onto the table.

Not wasting any time, Kev began to type.

Hi Morgan,

I'm sorry to bother you, but I'm helping my friend research her family tree, and we have discovered a connection with a man called Maurice Bird. He was a musician who used the name Maurice Newman. His wife was Rose Newman. I wondered if Maurice was related to you. I believe he and Rose had a son named Alton.

Many thanks,

Kevin

'How does that sound?' asked Kev.

They all gave their approval, and so he pressed send. For the next twenty minutes, Kev pressed refresh on Liv's laptop at least once per minute. Tony joked that he hadn't been this nervous since he crossed the Severn Bridge to move in with Jeff many moons ago.

The conversation returned to their trip to London. Tony mentioned that he had managed to get five tickets to a show at The Metropole on Saturday night and reminded everyone they needed to wear something 'fabulous'. It hadn't escaped Mel's attention that, other than this piece of information, they were rather scant on details. Despite her asking a few questions, none of them were particularly forthcoming. They were being sneaky, and Mel knew it. *You little sods,* she thought, wondering what the hell they had planned.

Thinking it was about time to call it a night as they could be waiting a lifetime to hear back from Morgan, the group all got up to leave. Kev was made to promise that he would update the group the second he received a response. As they all went in search of coats and scarves, Mel decided to quickly check her phone for messages. There was one from Cat that she had sent a few minutes before telling Mel that she was fine and to not wait up because she would be spending the night at the flat. Mel replied, saying that she hoped Cat was okay and that she would be in touch the next day.

As the four left Liv's house, Jeff and Tony went to the right and Mel and Kev to the left. Liv mentioned ringing Mel the next day to discuss their outfit choices for Saturday night before waving them off and closing the door on the heavy mist hovering over the Green.

Chapter Twenty-Eight

It had been quite a surprise for Mel to see Cat's car parked in her usual place the following morning as she hadn't expected her back at work. Mel rushed into the centre to escape the cold. Cat had noticed Mel's car pull into the car park from her office window and so went to make her a cuppa.

'Swap?' Mel asked with a smile as she handed Cat a paper bag containing the cookies she hadn't returned to the previous night, holding out her hand for her steaming mug of tea. 'Got a few minutes?' Mel was pleased to see that Cat looked *so* much better than the last time she'd seen her. She was still a little pale, but the dark circles under her eyes had all but gone.

Once out of earshot of the rest of the team and safely behind the closed door of Mel's office, she was able to ask Cat how she was doing and what had prompted her decision to stay at the flat the previous night. While her staying there might have seemed positive for their relationship, Mel couldn't shift the niggling doubt that it wasn't a sign necessarily that things were completely back on track for the couple just yet. She hoped she was wrong about that.

FINDING A MIRACLE

'Oh Mel, it was a tough one yesterday. Mike was a total mess when I got to the flat. It absolutely broke my heart to see him like that. We had a good long chat. I was completely honest with him about my feelings. He said if it was possible for positions to be reversed, then he might well feel similarly. He admitted that after the initial feeling of utter shock, he's now pleased he has a daughter, but that's tinged with guilt when he thinks about me. Basically, he's saying he doesn't want to lose me but realises this situation is unfair to me. He does seem to understand how I feel; I'm convinced of that from his comments yesterday. I stayed last night because I think we both needed the comfort of being near each other. I know he loves me, and I still love him.' Cat sighed. 'Having said that, I'd like to stay at yours tonight, though, if that's okay, Mel. I need more time to think things through. The changes in his life impact me hugely, and I need to work out if I can handle that. I have a massive decision to make, and being around Mike would only make it more difficult for me.'

'You can stay as long as you want, love. If you want a weekend with total peace and quiet, you'll have the place to yourself. I'm going on a trip to London with Liv and some other friends. They sprang it on me last night. I'm so pleased you've had that chat with Mike; it sounds like it was what you both needed. I guess it boils down to whether you love Mike enough to accept his daughter or not.'

'Thanks, pet. A few days on my own sounds perfect. You're absolutely right; it's as complicated yet as straightforward as that.'

CHAPTER TWENTY-EIGHT

'Whatever you decide, you will be more than okay, darling. Now, go and get yourself sorted for your session. What's in store for the kids today?'

'We're making calendars for next year with the older ones, and the younger ones are writing letters to Santa. What's your session today?'

'We're doing a review of their achievements this year to help them see just how much they've accomplished as well as setting goals for the next twelve months. I'm really looking forward to it. Getting them thinking and talking about what they've done this year really sets them up for planning the things they want to do next year. We never seem to focus on what we've done, only on what we've failed to do, so this is a nice little reminder and confidence builder. I always feel inspired after this session. I've got some Christmas music lined up too!'

'Sounds canny. I wouldn't mind sitting in on that myself! I'd better go, though. Thanks again for the cookies, Mel.'

After her session and with everything tidied away in the group room, Mel went back to her office to get ready to leave. She checked her phone and saw that she'd had a missed call from Kev. She sat at her desk and then dialled his number. It rang three times before he answered.

'Hiya, Kev, how are you doing? I've just noticed a missed call from you.'

'Hi, Mel. Thanks for ringing me back. I've got an update for you and wanted to tell you as soon as possible.'

'Ooh, that sounds interesting. I'm all ears!'

'I've heard back from Morgan Bird, and he confirmed he is the one we're looking for. We found him, Mel!'

'That's fantastic, Kev! Well done, you. Really, well done. Now, tell me everything,' said Mel enthusiastically.

'Okay, well he replied this morning and confirmed that he is Alton's son, as we suspected, and that Maurice and Rose were his grandparents. He asked how you and his dad were connected, so I explained that your nan was a friend of his grandfather, Maurice. I told him that they worked together at The Metropole and mentioned that we were going there on Saturday. I explained that you wanted to see where your nan worked all those years ago and that you were curious as to how life turned out for Maurice after your nan left London. It didn't take him long to reply. He told me that his dad has photos of Maurice and stills from a film he appeared in.'

'A *film?*' said Mel, taken aback. 'I wasn't expecting *that.*'

'I was shocked at that, too. Morgan suggested we swap numbers and have a chat over the phone, so that's what we did. He said he'd ring Alton to tell him about you as he thought he would love to speak to you. It seems that Alton was really close with his dad, so hopefully he'll be able to tell you a lot, Mel. Apparently, Rose wasn't a particularly well woman, so Alton spent more time with Maurice than her. Anyway, about fifteen minutes after I texted him my number, he rang. He said that he'd phoned Alton in the meantime, who is really pleased that you're interested to

CHAPTER TWENTY-EIGHT

hear more about his dad. He said he'd be more than happy to have a chat with you, and when Morgan mentioned you were going to The Metropole, he wondered if you wanted to meet during the day as you're sort of in the area. They asked if there was a chance that you could nip south of the river to meet up with them both. That's if you want to, of course. I said I'd need to check and get back to him.'

'Wow!' said Mel in mild shock. It took a few seconds for her to process this. 'Of course I want to meet him. Kev, you've done amazingly well. Things have moved so quickly I'm a bit lost for words to be honest.'

'I know. It's a lot to take in, isn't it? If you're sure you want to meet Alton and you're happy for me to make arrangements, I can give Morgan a ring now.'

'Yes, please, if you wouldn't mind. For some reason I feel nervous about it, but this chance might not come along again so I need to be brave. I'll have you guys with me for moral support so I'm sure I'll be fine. I can't thank you enough, Kev.'

'No need for thanks, Mel. I'm happy to help. Now, get yourself packed for London, and I'll update the others. Have a good night, Mel.'

As she hung up, the reality of the situation dawned on her. Not only was she going to visit The Metropole, but in less than forty-eight hours, she was going to meet Alton, the son of Maurice. The son of her *nan's* Maurice.

Chapter Twenty-Nine

On Friday afternoon, at two o'clock on the dot, the doorbell erupted. Mel grabbed her case and went to the door. Outside was a minibus waiting with its engine running.

'Come on, Mel, we have a train to catch!' said Kev with a huge smile. He helped her with her case, not able to resist teasing her on the weight of it and checking that she realised they were only away for two nights.

Within fifteen minutes, the group were at Cardiff Central station. Once safely settled in their seats in first class, which had been pre-booked by Kev, Mel thanked her friends for arranging the trip and for joining her on the final part of this adventure. There were similar responses from all her Miss Marple wannabees. They were all happy to be there, wouldn't miss it for the world, and looking forward to it very much. Mel sat next to Liv, with Kev opposite and Jeff and Tony occupying two seats at the next table to the side, so they were able to have a proper group conversation.

Mel was just about to comment on how nervous she felt about meeting Alton the next day when her train of thought was interrupted by a loud 'woohoo' coming

CHAPTER TWENTY-NINE

from Tony and Jeff's table. Tony had the foresight to pack chilled cans of gin and tonic in a cool bag and started to hand them out. *Oh, dear,* thought Mel, *we are starting early!*

Conversation flowed for the duration of their journey, rather like the gin and tonic, and before they knew it, the guard announced that the next and final stop would be London Paddington. Once outside, Tony, back on his home turf, hailed a black cab and asked the driver to take them to an address in Covent Garden. Having a Londoner to help with picking the most practical area to stay in was certainly an advantage. He did not make a bad tour guide either, as he pointed out some attractions and theatres along the way. It was a short walk to the hotel, and again Tony took the lead in getting them all checked in.

'Right, Mel, you've got about forty minutes to get yourself ready, love. The good news for you is you need less than half that to look ravishing,' said Tony, handing her a key.

'Err, thank you, and great, but where are we going? I need to know what to wear. Are we talking casual or fancy?' asked Mel.

In unison, the reply from her four friends came loud and clear. 'Fancy!'

Less than an hour later, all five were dressed to the nines and being shown to their table. Tony had recommended a tapas place in the West End, which Kev had duly booked. The bubbles from the Cava were certainly doing their job, and the group gave rave reviews about their delicious meal.

It didn't take too long for them to start talking about the meet-up with Alton the following day.

'What time are we meeting, Kev, and where are we going?' asked Liv.

'We're meeting Alton and Morgan at one o clock in a pub called The Market Porter, near Borough Market.'

'Excellent. We'll get back with plenty of time to get ready for our night at The Metropole. And Morgan's sure it's okay for us all to tag along?'

'Yeah. In fact, Morgan said Alton would love it. The more the merrier,' replied Kev.

'I need you lot with me, so that's just as well!' said a relieved Mel.

She sat quietly, listening to her friends, taking in every detail of the evening. She was having a wonderful time and didn't want the night to end.

'Shall I order us another bottle, or would you prefer something else?' asked Mel.

'Normally I'd say yes, of course, but sorry, darling, we'll be leaving soon. Very soon, actually,' said Liv, checking her watch for the time.

'Oh, already? It feels like we were just getting started,' said Mel, not feeling remotely ready for bed.

'Afraid so, my love. We have a busy day tomorrow, so we need to get going.'

CHAPTER TWENTY-NINE

Kev wandered over to the bar, to order more drinks Mel presumed. This lot would never be going to bed *this* early surely. *They're up to something,* she thought. This was confirmed when Kev returned and asked if they were nearly ready, as he had just settled the bill. Not ones to be wasteful, all four finished their drinks before putting on their coats.

When they stepped outside, Covent Garden looked magical. Twinkly Christmas lights in every window reflected a kaleidoscope of colour on the pavements below. Near the Piazza, there was a group dressed in Victorian outfits holding candlelit lanterns and singing carols. The moment took Mel's breath away. She hadn't felt this festive in a *very* long time.

'Confession time, Mel. We aren't exactly going to bed just yet,' said Kev, smiling down at her with a mischievous grin.

'Well, I did wonder who had swapped you lot for a better-behaved version of yourselves.'

'Rude, but true,' Liv conceded. 'You know how you've been calling us your Miss Marples? We thought it might be fun to try and solve a murder West End theatre style, so we, my darling, are off to see *The Mousetrap*!'

Mel put her hand to her mouth in total surprise. Seeing *The Mousetrap* had been on her bucket list for the longest time. She felt totally blindsided; she had not seen that coming. If anything, she'd expected them to hole up in the nearest good pub for a few hours. She couldn't believe they had arranged all this in a few days, and she was even more astounded that Liv had managed to not let the cat out of the bag in her excitement of being in on such a fun secret.

'Really?' she asked, hardly believing her luck.

'Really,' said Tony. 'Now let's get a wriggle on; we don't want to miss curtain up.'

Chapter Thirty

When Mel woke, her thoughts took her back immediately to what an amazing time she'd had the previous night. *The Mousetrap* was everything she had hoped it would be, and their seats were excellent. Mel had absorbed every second and knew the memories she'd made in St. Martin's Theatre would last her a lifetime. A knock on the door brought her sharply back into the present moment. She hopped out of bed to answer it as the person on the other side of the door knocked again, but more insistently this time. It *had* to be Liv.

'Liv! What a surprise!'

'Hey darling, got any paracetamol? My head's banging, and my mouth's as dry as chalk. Oh, and you need to get ready. We are doing "outside stuff" this morning, apparently. Damn, those bubbles in that Cava. They went straight to my head last night, and I feel like the buggers stayed there.'

Mel smiled fondly at her friend as she realised not only was Liv more hungover than she had seen her in a while, but she might even still be a little tipsy.

'Yes, love. I've got some in my bag. Help yourself, and there's some water on the table. "Outside stuff" sounds like I'd better get myself ready then.'

Liv couldn't answer as she was busy guzzling the bottle of water Mel had offered. She gave a thumbs up of agreement. Liv had already had her shower in the vague hope it might wake her. It wasn't exactly a case of mission accomplished, but it had helped. For the job to be done properly, she needed coffee. Strong coffee, and lots of it.

After a short deliberation, Mel decided on a black knee-length dress paired with black opaque tights, ankle boots, and her favourite Vivienne Westwood scarf in grey. She grabbed her thick black coat and her cross-body bag and headed down to the reception area. She was the last one to arrive and was greeted with cheers. Mel correctly assumed this was more about their need for caffeine and breakfast than their unbridled delight at seeing her.

'Good morning, my lovelies. What do you fancy doing this morning then, abseiling down the Shard or bungee jumping from Tower Bridge?' asked Mel with a big grin. There were groans from Liv and Kev, who looked a lot more fragile than they had the night before. As usual, Jeff and Tony were as fresh as daisies. Years in the pub trade equipped them with a spectacular resilience to late nights, early starts, entwined with too much alcohol. It really was sickening how well they looked, and their friends reminded them of this regularly.

'Well, as bungee jumping and abseiling aren't sounding popular, I propose something a little less adventurous. Breakfast and a wander around Covent Garden or a

CHAPTER THIRTY

wander around Covent Garden then breakfast. What's it to be?' asked Jeff.

'If I don't get coffee in the next five minutes at the very least, I'll turn feral, and people will get hurt,' Liv said quietly but with total conviction.

'I'm with Liv. All I can think about is a sausage sandwich and a vat of builder's tea served with a side of aspirin. I never drink Cava, and this morning I realised why,' muttered Kev, hoping for some sympathy.

'Come on then, you gorgeous lot, let's get some breakfast,' said Tony.

As they stepped outside the hotel, the brightness of the day was almost startling. It was deceptively cold, though, and the crisp weather was the perfect pick-me-up. Mel, Kev, and Liv followed Jeff and Tony as they led the way. The three chatted about the previous night and what a good time it had been as they strolled past the Piazza, the entrance to Jubilee Market and the London Transport Museum. Just as they took a left turn, they saw Jeff and Tony disappear into a building that had large red canopies over each window. All three found an extra gear and sped up at the promise of caffeine and carbs.

The five were shown to a large table towards the middle of the restaurant. Mel was struck by the opulence of the place with its expensive-looking furniture. There was a tasteful mix of wood panelling adorning the walls, the gold light fixtures were highly polished, and the seating was sumptuous red leather. Tuttons certainly had the wow factor in the most refined and elegant way.

'I'm expecting good things from this place, Tony,' said Kev, looking around him. He was as impressed by Tony's choice of breakfast spot as Mel was. 'Nothing beats the smell of freshly brewed coffee in the morning, and the coffee here smells particularly good.' The group piped up with a few additional suggestions for great morning smells, such as freshly baked bread and sizzling bacon, and struggled to pick just one. The one thing they did manage to agree on, however, was what a blessing it was that Tony knew such great places.

The food easily lived up to their expectations. The table was laden with hot dishes, and the group happily tucked in to sausage sandwiches, bacon sandwiches, scrambled eggs, and pancakes with maple syrup. Feeling way more human and ready to face the day, they decided to go for a meander around Covent Garden before heading over to meet Alton and Morgan.

The shops looked fabulously festive, and the whole area had a lovely vibrant energy despite it still being quite early. Mel felt like she was on a film set; it had that kind of feel to her. Too idyllic to be real. They took their time exploring, window shopping and going in to leisurely browse in the shops that particularly took their fancy. Tony pointed out what had once been one of his favourite haunts to see live music. Sadly, it had closed many moons ago and was now a shop selling high-end mobile phones and laptops.

'This place is where The Rock Garden used to be. I saw more gigs here in my misspent youth than I care to remember. A lot of great indie bands chose this as their first

CHAPTER THIRTY

London venue back in the day. I saw Adam and the Ants here, Patti Smith, The Police, Orange Free State, Suede.' There was a nostalgic, almost wistful look in Tony's eyes as memories of his colourful past played out like a movie in his mind's eye.

'Anyone for a sit-down and a cuppa before we head off to meet Mel's lads?' asked Jeff, linking arms with his love, Tony. All agreed that was a good idea, and so Tony suggested they walk up to The Nags Head. He figured the coffee shops would be swamped by now, and it might be easier to get a seat in a pub at this time, just before the lunchtime rush started. As usual, his instincts on such matters were on point.

'How are you feeling about meeting up with Alton and Morgan, Mel?' asked Kev, once they were all sat down, before taking a sip of his latte.

'Honestly, I haven't had that much time to think about it. It's been so busy since we got here that I've been happily distracted. Now that I *am* thinking about it, I am a little apprehensive. Who knows what, if anything, Alton knows about his dad's links to my nan. I hope he has something interesting for us,' said Mel quietly.

'I think it's bloody exciting. I can't *wait* to hear what stories he may have. I know you'll handle the situation perfectly, darling, so no need to be apprehensive.' Liv smiled warmly at her friend, who blew a kiss in her direction.

'I'll go and ask the bar staff to book us a cab. We won't risk getting a black cab at this time of day. Are you happy if we set off at about midday? It allows for traffic and means we can grab a table if we do end up getting there before them.' The group agreed that seemed like a sensible idea and thanked Tony for once again being chief travel planner and tour guide.

'He's such a legend, Jeff. You landed an absolute diamond there. Mind you, he's done alright for himself, too,' said Mel as she watched Tony walk over to sweet-talk the barmaid into booking them a ride.

'Oh, I don't know what I'd do without him, love, I really don't. It sounds cheesy, perhaps, but I feel like he really is my other half. The better half, if I'm honest. He's my North Star. Wherever he is, I'm home,' said Jeff, smiling.

Jeff's words touched Mel's heart. While she was happy being single, she would trade it in a heartbeat for the kind of relationship Jeff had with Tony. She could not deny there was something magical about being in love.

'You two have the sort of relationship the rest of us dream of having, Jeff, and you bloody deserve it. I propose a toast.' Liv cleared her throat for dramatic effect and raised her nearly empty coffee cup. 'Here's to Jeff and Tony, and here's to us three finding our own North Star.'

'To Jeff and Tony and us finding our own North Star,' said Mel and Kev in unison as they clinked their mugs together.

By a quarter to one, the group were all settled around a table in The Market Porter. Kev had gone to get some

CHAPTER THIRTY

extra chairs for Alton and Morgan for when they arrived and had texted Morgan to let him know they were already there. His phone buzzed.

'Okay, everyone. I've just heard from Morgan. They're in the car park and on their way in, so I'll nip outside to meet them.'

Mel felt her stomach make all the moves of a young Olga Korbut. She grabbed her bag, retrieved her mirror, and refreshed her lipstick before putting her bag back under the table. She let out a long, slow breath, attempting to calm herself.

'This is more nerve-wracking than a blind date,' she said stiffly as her heart threatened to burst through her chest. In stereo, she heard a chorus of 'You'll be fine' from her friends. Liv reached for her hand and gave it a reassuring squeeze as she saw Kev walk through the door, followed closely by Morgan and Alton.

The pub was getting busier, and Kev manoeuvred his way to their table, glancing back periodically to check Alton was okay. Mel stood up first, quickly followed by the others. Mel walked towards Alton, unable to take her eyes off him.

'Hello, Alton, I'm Mel. Thank you so much for coming to see me.'

'Oh, the pleasure is entirely mine, my dear.' He reached out both of his hands in front of him, an invitation for Mel to put her hands in his. His skin felt paper thin, and Mel felt the bones beneath, but his eyes were bright and youthful. She couldn't believe just how like his dad Alton was. It was just like seeing an older version of Maurice.

Chapter Thirty-One

After handshakes and introductions, Alton positioned himself between Mel and Liv, declaring himself to be a thorn between two roses. Within seconds of meeting him, Mel felt so much better. He had a wonderfully warm energy, and she felt much more at ease.

Kev went to the bar to get a lemonade for Morgan and a large brandy for Alton. As Kev brought the drinks back, he was pleased to see the whole table engaged in conversation. He handed Morgan and Alton their glasses and took a seat between Liv and Morgan.

'Your good health, everyone, and thank you so much for giving me an excuse to put my glad rags on,' said Alton, tugging at his crisp white shirt. 'Cheers to you all.'

The group responded in kind with exuberance. It was obvious that they had all taken a shine to Alton already.

'Now then, Mel. I believe your real interest isn't in me but in my dad. So, I will tell you a bit about him, and if there's anything I've left out, then you've only to ask.'

Mel couldn't take her eyes off his face. He was a carbon copy of the photos of his dad she'd seen, apart from the lines and wrinkles that graced his face and his shock of snow-white hair. He was handsome and charismatic, and Mel could only imagine that he followed his dad in more than just looks.

'That sounds perfect, Alton,' Mel said with a warm smile.

'Okay then, I'll start at the beginning. When he was a boy, my dad, Maurice, loved music. He loved all aspects of music, but his true passion was the piano. His parents were poor working-class folk and didn't have the money to send him to lessons. There was certainly no piano in the house either for him to practise on. My grandmother, though, was a smart lady. She managed to land herself a cleaning job for an elderly man who *did* have a piano. Apparently, he was a lovely old fella who was happy for my grandmother to take my dad along when she cleaned. He allowed him to play the piano while she did her work. He even gave him some lessons and passed on his knowledge. My dad was a very quick learner; some might have called him a child prodigy had he not come from such humble beginnings. Fast forward to him being around twelve years old. He managed to get a regular spot playing piano in one of the local pubs, The Salutation Inn near Greenwich Park. That was the foot in the door he needed. From there, he worked in many pubs in the area, including this one.'

'That seems so young to be working in a bar. Was that normal for back then, Alton?' asked Mel.

'Oh yes, Mel. Money was tight, so employers took on minors because they got away with paying them less. My dad was shrewd, though. Each time he took a new job, he made sure he was getting closer and closer to the

CHAPTER THIRTY-ONE

West End. A few years later, through some contacts he had made, he landed himself an audition with Reginald Newman. Now, this was a big deal for my dad, a very big deal indeed. Reginald was a top theatrical agent back then. He attracted some of the biggest names in show business, and even getting an audition with him felt like a blessing from heaven. So, my dad went to The Metropole one Sunday morning to audition. It was the place to be and be seen in those days, and the only time it wasn't packed to the rafters was a Sunday morning. My dad was given a few pieces of music to play for Reginald, who was sat with a few other people. After he had finished, they discussed his performance quietly amongst themselves. All at once, Reginald stood and strode over to my dad, who was absolutely terrified at this point. Reginald was, by all accounts, a large, stern man. The type of man you just wouldn't want to get on the wrong side of; he was powerful in all senses of the word. As he approached my dad, he held out his bear paw of a hand and said, "Welcome aboard, son. Now speak to my niece Rose who will give you all the details. You're starting tomorrow night at seven, and you'd better be on time.'"

Alton recounted this memory as if he had heard it and repeated it hundreds of times before. The whole table was in the palm of his hand; they hung off his every well-spoken word. Every inch the performer himself, it would be easy to believe he had spent years treading the boards of the West End, rubbing shoulders with all the greats. This was more like being in an actor's masterclass than listening to some old man chatting down the pub, and the group was mesmerised. Alton paused to take a sip of his drink that was slipping down nicely and warming his chest. He didn't usually drink brandy before five, but this felt like a special occasion.

'My dad did as he was told, of course, and went over to speak to Rose. She took him to the back of the hall with paperwork for him to fill out. She took his details, name, address, date of birth, next of kin, and so on. Rose told him he would start on three days a week with a view to that increasing if he proved popular. He performed Monday to Wednesday every week for three weeks before being given an extra day, Thursday. Rose attended every performance. My dad didn't think anything of it because she was part of Reginald's staff, or so he assumed. The truth was that Rose was a legal secretary and wasn't employed by Reginald at all. She had just happened to be at The Metropole that Sunday with her parents, who were sitting with Reg at the time of my dad's audition. The reason she went every night to watch him perform was because she was absolutely smitten with him! Reginald decided to get involved and play Cupid, to give things a nudge in the right direction. He hinted in the strongest possible way that his niece Rose had designs on my father, who had been blissfully unaware. Soon after, my dad was given the weekend slot at The Metropole and headlined with his very own band.'

'Your dad really was shrewd, as you said. It seems like his plan to get to the West End went well for him,' said Mel as she noticed the look of pride on Alton's face.

'You're right, Mel. Things had been going very well for him. Sometime later, my mother broke the news to my father that she was pregnant. He did the right and proper

CHAPTER THIRTY-ONE

thing and married her, of course. It was the done thing back then. A short while after the wedding, it came to pass that my mother, Rose, had in fact been...let's say *mistaken* about the pregnancy. But, within a year, she did become pregnant, and nine months after that, I came along.'

The regular sips of brandy had resulted in an empty glass. It was Jeff this time who went to the bar. He didn't ask what anyone wanted because he did not want to interrupt Alton, who was in full flow. Besides, he could take an educated guess as to what might be acceptable. Jeff did not want to miss a word of Alton's story but decided the others would fill him in on what he had missed later.

'My mother and I didn't have the closest of relationships, if I'm to be completely honest. She had a few issues that caused a lot of problems in the house, and my parents' marriage was strained for the entirety of it. There was the rumour that my mother had made up the first pregnancy to push my father into marrying her, which, I believe, he felt bitter about. My father spent most of his time at work, and my mother spent most of her time just waiting for him to come home. He and I were inseparable, and my mother was more than a little jealous of that, unfortunately.'

Alton paused momentarily and felt a tinge of sadness for the poor relationship he'd had with his mother when he was growing up. Deciding not to dwell on that aspect of things, he changed the topic.

'When I was around seven, my father appeared in a film called *The Swindler*. It was a farce about a con artist and his accomplice that hardly broke box office records, but he was excellent in his role as the policeman. He took me to the set as often as he could, and I absolutely loved watching him and the other actors perform. I felt so lucky to be there, and I was so immensely proud of him.

'Later in his career, my father became the manager of the Melville Theatre in Rotherhithe. He attracted many incredible acts during his time there. It was his first stint as a theatre manager, and he made a huge success of it thanks to the connections he had made at The Metropole and my great uncle Reg. He still performed and played piano occasionally. He loved his role as manager, but I don't think anything could beat the excitement of being on stage for him. And the Melville Theatre is where the story ends for my dear dad. He passed away there suddenly at midnight after a show. He had gone to the office after the place had cleared, and that was where he had a heart attack and died. He was not found until the following morning when my mother went to the theatre to look for him. She was a shell of a woman after finding him like that, and she passed away too within eighteen months.'

Stopping to take a fortifying drink from his glass, he then asked Mel if she had any questions.

'Thank you so much, Alton. Your dad sounded like the most amazing man. I really can see why you had such a close bond with him. I wondered if you knew much about the band he had at The Metropole.'

'I do know that playing with that band was the happiest he ever was career-wise. I've brought some photographs of him with his band, actually. Morgan, have you got them, son?'

CHAPTER THIRTY-ONE

'Yes, Dad, here they are.'

Alton took the envelope of photographs and leafed through them until he found what he was looking for. He passed one to Mel of Maurice with his fellow musicians on stage at The Metropole. Then he passed another with the same people on it but in a different pose. The next was a photograph of them performing live with a male singer. Mel passed them along the table for her friends to look at. Alton looked through the next few and handed them to Mel. They were the publicity photographs of her nan with Maurice and the band. She had seen most of them before, but she almost forgot to breathe as she thumbed through them. It felt altogether different looking at them with Maurice's son.

'These photos here, Alton. This lady...the singer... this is, this was, my grandmother.'

'Oh well now, isn't that interesting. What a beauty. You really take after her, Mel.' The look on Alton's face changed, suddenly becoming softer. 'What happened to your nan, if you don't mind me asking?'

'Not at all. She was originally from Llanllyfni, a small village in Caernarfon, North Wales, before going to London. I'm not sure how she ended up singing there. I only recently found out about her time in London after going through her belongings, as she never mentioned it. I don't even know how long she stayed in London before going back to Wales and settling outside Cardiff. She met my grandfather, they got married and had my mother. Sadly, she and my mother have both passed away now. My nan was an incredibly special person, and I believe she was very fond of your dad.'

Alton took one of the photographs back from Mel and studied it more closely.

'The Enchanting Alice Miracle. Well, they chose the perfect name for her, didn't they? Any idea where it came from?'

'Absolutely none. It's a complete mystery. My nan's name was Lizzie Jones, nothing so glamourous as Alice Miracle.'

'She really is quite beautiful, Mel. Hmm…the way my dad is looking at her in this photo, I'd say he's noticed that, too. I'd say he was rather fond of her in return.'

Alton smiled as he passed the photograph back to Mel. She passed it around the table for them all to see.

'I wonder why your nan left London, Mel?' Alton spoke softly and tentatively, as though he was almost afraid of the question.

'I wish I knew. She never told me anything about this,' said Mel, pausing cautiously before she continued. 'Is there a reason you asked?' Her tone mirrored Alton's, and she was aware of the shift in energy between them.

'I hope I'm not speaking out of turn here, so please, if I am, forgive me. Many years ago, before I was born, my mother discovered my dad had met another woman. Not just met her but fell in love with her. My understanding was that my mother forced my father to end the relationship

CHAPTER THIRTY-ONE

and practically ran the woman out of town. Is it…is it at all possible that the woman I am referring to was your grandmother, Alice Miracle?'

Mel gulped, and she felt her face drain of colour. She didn't know what to say but had to think of an answer quickly.

'I think it might be possible, yes.' Mel wanted to undo the words the moment they left her lips. 'I'm sorry, Alton.' Tears pricked at her eyes.

'My dear girl, you have *nothing* to be sorry for. Most of the time, my mother liked to pretend she and my dad were the happiest couple in history, but there was the odd time I recall her using my dad's affair to punish and control him. As I said earlier, she had her issues. I could understand anyone being hurt and angry that their partner had betrayed them, but her tricking my dad into marrying her was the worst kind of betrayal. She never stopped to question why he hadn't noticed her staring lovingly at him every night. The reason for that was that he had barely noticed her. Great Uncle Reg was not a man anyone wanted to disappoint, and my dad hinted at the fact that this was the reason he and my mother got together in the first place. Whomever the lady was that my dad fell in love with, I have nothing but gratitude towards her. She probably made him happier than he had ever been with my mother, and I am so glad he had that. I hope that Alice *was* this lost love of his, Mel, I really do.'

'I'm glad you feel that way, Alton. If that's true then I'm happy for them and the love and joy they may have shared too, however brief,' said Mel, her voice loaded with emotion. She felt like the weight of the world had been taken off her.

'Very well put, my dear,' said Alton as he placed a reassuring hand on Mel's and smiled at her affectionately.

The group chatted for another hour or so. Kev explained to Alton and Morgan how he had managed to find them, and both were suitably impressed. Morgan mentioned how his brother David would have enjoyed meeting everyone but that he was working in Germany right up until Christmas so was not able to join them. Alton shared a few more childhood memories about his dad, and Mel told him a bit more about her family, too. She toyed with the idea of telling him everything contained in the letters, feeling guilty for keeping it from him, but ultimately decided that it might be better to wait and perhaps speak to Morgan about it first. She did not want to overwhelm Alton, and despite her instinct telling her that sending him copies of the letters would be the right thing to do, the tone and content of Rose's letter to her nan gave her some concerns. Mel did not want to further tarnish Alton's memory of his mother.

'Today has been a total delight, but I think I'd better head off now, Mel. If I stayed any longer, I'd only drink more brandy, and then I'd end up going to The Metropole with you lovely people tonight!' The twinkle had returned to Alton's eyes, and his smile lit up his face. 'Would it be okay for us to keep in touch, do you think, my dear?'

'I would absolutely *love* that, Alton,' said Mel, who promptly gave her address and phone number to Morgan and took Alton's in return. 'I can't thank you enough for

CHAPTER THIRTY-ONE

coming to meet us; it's been an absolute pleasure.' She kissed Alton on the cheek.

'Well, if I knew I'd be getting a kiss, I'd have turned up an hour earlier!'

'Stop your flirting, Dad, I can't take you anywhere, honestly!' said Morgan despairingly.

'Too old to change now, my boy, and there's life in the old dog yet.' Alton winked cheekily at Mel.

Morgan helped his dad to his feet, and they both said their goodbyes to the group. Alton brought Mel in close and embraced her. As he did, he said quietly, just for her to hear, 'Thank you, Mel, and raise a glass tonight to Maurice and Alice for me, would you?'

Mel felt a lump in her throat.

'Of course I will, and I'll make it champagne.'

Chapter Thirty-Two

'Well, guys, I don't know about you, but I feel like Elvis just left the building. What an *amazing* man. Such a character! I felt I could listen to him all day. He could read the phone book and make it sound interesting.' Mel's tone dropped and became less exuberant. 'How do *you* think that went, and be honest. I nearly bloody died when he first started asking questions about my nan, and I'm sure he will have picked up on it,' she said with a grimace.

'I think it went *very* well. He's a lovely bloke, and he was clearly taken with you, darling,' said Tony with a laugh.

'As predicted, you handled it *perfectly*. You chose your words well and cleverly, darling. When you told him that your nan had never mentioned her reasons for leaving London, I had to stop myself from applauding,' said Liv with an expression on her face that backed up how impressed she was by her friend.

'You did superbly, Mel. I honestly don't think that could have gone better. I know you were worried about potentially upsetting Alton by revealing his dad's affair with your nan, but it sounds like he's known about it a lot longer than you have. He walked away with a smile on his

CHAPTER THIRTY-TWO

face, probably because he got your number!' said Kev. His words and his broad smile removed any remaining traces of doubt Mel felt.

'I don't half wish he *was* coming to The Metropole with us tonight,' said Jeff. 'I think we'd be fighting about who gets to sit next to him. I absolutely loved him! And the guys are right, Mel, it couldn't have gone better, and you were pitch perfect, love. You should be very proud of yourself.'

'Is anyone else starving or am I the only bottomless pit?' asked Liv. Mel was pleased she had asked the question not only because she was ready for something to eat but because she needed to talk about something else while she processed their time with Alton.

They sat chatting whilst waiting for cod, chips, and peas for five. Mel and Liv were deep in conversation about what they would wear that evening, discussing the options they had brought with them. Kev, Jeff, and Tony were discussing the logistics of getting back in time to go to the club. Tony pulled a few strings and managed to secure the VIP booth next to the stage for them. They were to arrive at eight, and the show started at nine.

Over their meal, Mel was at the sharp end of some serious leg pulling about her and Alton. The group operated like a tag team, and they were relentless in their teasing. Mel had to admit they were rather funny.

'Right, now stop it, you lot. He's old enough to be my father! Tony, save me will you, and get us a taxi? Actually, get two. One for me and one for you bunch of piss-takers.'

FINDING A MIRACLE

The journey back to Covent Garden was idyllic. The icy blue sky had descended into pitch black, and the Christmas lights everywhere shone like jewels. The group was quiet, contented, and taking time to recharge their batteries a little. All too soon, they reached their destination and stepped out into the frosty air.

'I think we will need to meet in reception by seven thirty. Are you happy with that, Tony?' asked Kev.

'Yes, but no later. You've got just over an hour, so use your time wisely, people. The dress code for tonight is fabulous, so do yourselves proud!'

The group separated and scattered to their rooms. Mel and Liv had rooms across the corridor from each other, which was helpful for second opinions or tricky zips.

Mel decided she had time for a quick shower before putting on her makeup. As this was a special occasion and Tony had used the word 'fabulous', she had brought along a set of false eyelashes. It was a good excuse to make a special effort. She curled her hair and set it with a whoosh of hairspray. Pleased with her results, she began to apply her makeup. With her foundation looking flawless, she added a little highlighter to accentuate her cheekbones, followed by a light dusting of powder to brighten. Turning her attention to her eyes, Mel decided to add colour and definition to her brows and applied primer to her lids. To finish the look, she added black eyeliner and applied the false eyelashes. Normally, she found them fiddly but, as luck would have it, tonight they caused her no such problems. Next, she applied a generous amount of her favourite perfume and let that settle while she looked at

CHAPTER THIRTY-TWO

the three dresses she had brought for tonight. Mel tried on each one in turn despite having worn them all several times before. After careful consideration, she chose the fitted black dress with the Bardot neckline. As everything was relatively plain to this point, Mel knew she could get away with a large pair of statement crystal earrings and a complementary bracelet. With minutes to spare, she carefully applied a bold scarlet lipliner and completed her look with matching lipstick. Mel took one last look in the mirror, then grabbed her clutch bag and went for a spectacular pair of heels that she knew would destroy her feet within half an hour. Finally, she put on her coat and exited her room, ready for the night ahead.

Mel knocked on Liv's door, who answered it with her arm in one half of her coat. Liv looked beautiful in a midnight-blue velvet dress.

'You look absolutely stunning, Liv.'

'Thank you, darling. You're looking rather ravishing yourself! Well, the boys *did* say we had to look fabulous, and we would never want to disappoint them now, would we? I think your next-door neighbour will be suitably impressed,' said Liv with a playful expression on her face.

'Not that again! Pack it in, woman!' said Mel, chastising Liv with an eye roll and a sigh before continuing. 'These shoes clearly hate me. I'm already feeling the piercing pain of their disapproval! Come on, let's go downstairs and get our night started. There's a bottle of champagne out there with our name on it.'

The two linked arms and tottered down the corridor to the lift. Liv emerged first and was raucously greeted by wolf whistles from Tony, who spun her round in a twirl. Mel received a suitably bawdy response that made her giggle. The three men all looked incredibly smart in their well-tailored suits and crisp shirts and smelt better than a fragrance counter.

'Right, come on, let's get the show on the road,' said Tony as he ushered everyone out to get in the cab he'd booked.

The entrance to The Metropole was flanked by two grand Christmas trees on either side of the doorway. They were covered in the most delicate twinkly lights and some tasteful decorations. Two rather handsome security men clad in impeccable suits that struggled to contain their muscles stood either side. Tony was once again their intrepid leader and walked ahead with Kev close behind him. Mel, Jeff, and Liv were several steps behind largely because of Mel and Liv's choice of footwear but also because it gave them time to pass lustful comments about the supermodels who were masquerading as doormen. When they had caught up, they found that Kev was already at the bar setting up a tab and Tony was waiting to show them to their booth. When Mel and Liv realised where they'd be sitting for the evening, their eyes lit up like a four-year-old on Christmas morning.

'Oh Tony, I can't believe you got us VIP seats! You are totally bloody brilliant!' said Mel, grabbing him and planting a kiss on his cheek.

CHAPTER THIRTY-TWO

Kev appeared shortly after with a tray of glasses and an ice bucket containing a magnum of champagne.

'This is going to get messy,' said Liv, and all agreed.

While Jeff set about filling glasses, Mel went to get a closer look at the stage. It was a grand affair with the now familiar Metropole logo taking pride of place above the centre of the stage. The heavy velvet curtains were a deep crimson adorned with the logo tastefully embroidered in gold. Lost in her thoughts, she saw a vision of her grandmother, Liz, standing up there singing as a young woman. *What an experience that must have been and what nerve she must have had to do it,* Mel thought. She pictured her there with Maurice and the rest of the band behind her, almost as though she was transported back in time.

'You must be Mel. Well, aren't you a fabulous little thing!' boomed a voice out of nowhere.

Mel spun around to see a tall, handsome, athletic-looking man standing before her. He sported a year-round tan and looked to be somewhere in his mid-fifties. Before Mel could muster a word, she was pulled towards him and kissed on both cheeks. 'Welcome to The Metropole, my darling. It's so nice to meet you. I'm Dennis, and this is my little club. If you're very lucky, you might get to meet my alter-ego, Denise, later.' His cheeky smile revealed his faultless white teeth, which he had almost certainly got for a good price on his last trip to Turkey!

Mel smiled politely, but her wide eyes gave away her confusion. She could hear her mother say, *your face always gives away what you're thinking.* She was right. Mel had to work hard for a poker face.

FINDING A MIRACLE

'Ah, I see that Tony hasn't mentioned me! Which is, I'm guessing, because he wanted it to be a surprise. Well, beautiful, he has mentioned you to me and told me about your nan being a performer here in the past. When I heard your story and what you guys were up to this weekend, I thought it might be a nice idea to show you behind the scenes. So, why don't you grab yourself a glass of that bubbly before that lot drink it all and come with me, darling.'

Mel did as she was told and grabbed a glass of champagne before dashing back to Dennis. There was no time for explanation, and anyway, she assumed that Tony would let everyone know where she had disappeared to. She didn't want to keep her special tour guide, Dennis, waiting.

'Thank you so much, Dennis. I'm not often stuck for words, but this is a total surprise. I'm already in love with this place.'

'You are more than welcome, darling. Drink more bubbles. That'll take the edge off. It's always worked for me anyway. Ha! Come on, let's go,' said Dennis, taking Mel's hand and leading her to a door at the far side of the stage next to the long bar. He led her up a flight of stairs before taking the door on the left. They entered a large room with makeup stations many girls would dream of to the left, and on the right were racks of colourful, sequinned dresses and bejewelled costumes with an array of wigs and headdresses on shelves above. Around the corner, there were rows and rows of shoes in all styles and colours. Mel was suddenly glad she wore heels that night and instantly forgot the

CHAPTER THIRTY-TWO

pain her feet were in. Where there was space on the walls there were photos of Dennis with no end of celebrities. From one glance she spotted him snapped with Elizabeth Taylor, Dame Shirley Bassey, Dame Barbara Windsor, and UK drag royalty Foo Foo Lamar, The Vivienne and Lily Savage. It was starting to sink in just what a big deal Dennis was, as was The Metropole.

'Just think, Mel, you're walking in the footsteps of some real icons. This place is steeped in history and was graced by many an A-lister in the golden age of Hollywood. Frank Sinatra, Judy Garland, Richard Burton, Cary Grant, Charlie Chaplin, Bette Davis…they've *all* been here.'

Mel held tightly onto Dennis's hand as he led her through another door, directly onto the stage. The place was starting to fill up, but Mel hadn't noticed. Lost in her thoughts and dazzled by the stage lighting, she was in her own world. Being here made it feel even more surreal that her nan, her lovely little nan, could have done something so amazing and never uttered a word about it.

'This is nothing short of incredible, Dennis. I feel so privileged to be here, and I can't thank you enough.' A wave of emotion washed over Mel, and Dennis sensed it. Instinctively, he wrapped his arms around her and held her tight. The crowd noticed, and there were a few whistles from the regulars. Dennis laughed and said to her, 'Let's give them something to gossip about, shall we?'

'Oh, shut up, you horrible lot, you're only jealous!' he shouted before sweeping Mel up in his arms and carrying her through the stage door. At the other side, he lowered her gently, and they both collapsed into fits of laughter.

She may have only known Dennis for a matter of minutes, but she knew then that he was very much her kind of person.

'Come on, darling, I'm going to introduce you to some of my gorgeous queens.'

Chapter Thirty-Three

Back in her seat at one end of the booth, Mel held out her glass to be refilled and Kev duly obliged. All four of her friends were speaking over each other with questions and comments about Mel's time backstage.

'It was amazing! I can't believe I've stood on the same stage my nan sang on all those years ago. It's incredible. I can't thank you all enough for arranging this, I really can't. This will be up there with one of the best weekends of my life.'

'Don't worry, Kev took some photos, so you have a little memento of the occasion,' said Liv. Her eyes were already sparkly, and Mel loved the happy look on her friend's face. It seemed to Mel that Liv was enjoying herself just as much as she was.

'It's not over yet, Mel. We still have the show to enjoy,' said Jeff. His timing proved spookily accurate as a second later, the lights dimmed a little to let everyone know the show was about to start. Mel looked around the room, filled with expectant faces, eyes glued to the stage in anticipation. There wasn't an empty seat in the place, and there was a tangible vibe of excitement building.

On walked a beautiful, statuesque queen bedecked in a red crystal gown with killer heels to match. Her wig was a work of art and totally elevated her look to a whole new level. Mel had already met 'Scarlet Charlotte' backstage when she was applying her fierce makeup. She was nothing short of stunning, Mel had thought, and she had been incredibly warm and welcoming to her.

'Hello, you gorgeous humans. Welcome to The Metropole. I'm Scarlet Charlotte, but you can call me Lottie the Hottie.'

She paused for a few seconds lapping up the claps of adulation, scanning the room with scrutinising eyes.

'Well, let's keep it real, shall we? *Some* of you are gorgeous, and some of you…hmm, not so much! At least you've all made an effort, though, so well done you.' She clapped her hands slowly whilst giving the most dramatic of eye rolls.

The acid-tongued Scarlet paused to allow laughter to fade a little before delivering a few more perfectly barbed insults. The crowd lapped it up.

'Okay, okay, that's overstating it. More like, you've had a little go, bless your little hearts, and we really do appreciate you trying, we really do. To be honest, looking at the state of some of you, we're just happy you had a wash…'

The next hour and a half went by in a blur of belly laughs and show tunes, aided and abetted by another magnum of champagne. There was an electric atmosphere,

CHAPTER THIRTY-THREE

and the place was awash with the smiling faces of people having a great time. During the mid-show break, they played some high-energy dance music and disco classics the audience sang along to. It got most of the crowd up and dancing wherever they could find space. They remained on their feet and broke out in thunderous applause when the next queen appeared on stage. She looked resplendent in a bejewelled, tightly fitted oyster-coloured gown that was split right to the top of her perfectly toned thigh. *I'd bloody kill for legs like that*, thought Mel along with every other woman in the audience, no doubt.

'Good evening, everyone! I do hope you're having a wonderful time. Yes, it's me, your favourite diva, Dame Denise Diamond, your delectable, delicious darling, here to dazzle and delight. Well, it makes sense to save the best 'til last, doesn't it? I do hope Scarlet tickled your tastebuds and whetted your appetites but left you craving a decadent dessert…Denise-style!'

Denise had the crowd in the palm of her hand, and she owned the stage that she strutted across so gracefully. Mel was mesmerised and couldn't take her eyes off her.

'Now then, I had the pleasure of meeting a gorgeous lady earlier who has travelled all the way from South Wales with her friends to be here tonight. Can we get a spotlight on Mel in the posh seats, please? And you lot in the cheap seats, give her a round of applause if you'd be so kind. Give her and her chums a proper Metropole welcome.'

Mel was suddenly framed in the beam of a startlingly bright light and was the new focus of everyone's attention. She died inside but for once hid it better than she realised as her horror was covered by a nervous laugh. She had not expected *this*, not for a second.

'Wave hello to everybody, Mel…go on, don't be shy, love. She wasn't shy earlier when she was backstage swigging from a bottle of champagne, I can tell you. No sir, there's *nothing* shy about our Mel, is there, darling?'

Mel's four friends all shook their heads in exaggerated agreement and burst into laughter. They *definitely* wouldn't describe her as shy. Mel's nervous laugh quickly turned into a proper laugh despite being completely terrified of what Denise might say next.

'Our gorgeous Mel came here tonight to see the place her dear old nan used to sing at many moons ago. Obviously, I'm outraged she didn't make the trip just for *me*, but I'll let her off this once. Now we all know that Wales is famous for its good singers, don't we, so I think it's only right for Mel to join me on stage for a little duet. What do you lot think about that?'

The crowd erupted to a level of noise not achieved until that very moment. It was only surpassed a second later when Mel collapsed into a heap of giggles, shaking her head and wagging her finger like a metronome. She felt a push from behind as her friends urged her on. When she turned around, she saw a musclebound young man wearing just a bowtie and thong, his arm outstretched, and he was not taking no for an answer. Reluctantly, she put her hand in his, and he led her the long way to the stairs that led backstage. He had clearly been briefed to milk this for all it was worth, and the crowd was clearly enjoying every second of her torturous embarrassment

CHAPTER THIRTY-THREE

and seemed to get louder with every step she took.

Once on stage, Mel was hit with a wall of noise from the crowd below. They cheered and clapped for all they were worth, and none were louder than her lot of 'VIPs' who were loving every second. After a well above average rendition of 'Man, I Feel Like a Woman', Mel was encouraged to take a bow. She blew a kiss to her friends before she was released by her glamorous tormentor and allowed to return to her seat. Once again, she was escorted to her booth by the half-dressed Adonis, but thankfully he took the direct route this time. After making a performance of kissing her hand, he left her to the relative safety of her friends. Relative because Mel had a strong feeling that this had been arranged by Tony, but ultimately Liv would be behind it. *Little sods,* she thought as she settled back to watch the rest of the show.

An hour or so later the queens performed the finale of the evening. The whole crowd joined them in singing, 'I Am What I Am'. It felt like the perfect end to a perfect night. The group sat for a little while to finish their drinks and catch their breath in contented contemplation. Mel took a moment to top up her drink and raise her glass in a silent toast to Alice and Maurice just as Alton had requested.

'The look on your face was a picture, Mel!' Liv beamed with delight. 'You didn't see that coming, did you, love?'

'You were fantastic, Mel. I had no idea you sang that well; you're clearly following in your nan's footsteps. You should do it more often!' said Kev enthusiastically.

'Following her nan's footsteps quite literally,' Jeff said to Kev. 'It must have been really something to sing on the same stage as your nan, Mel.'

'I don't think I have the words, Jeff. I had the best time. What a place and what a night. I can't thank you all enough. You've done me and my little nan proud. She would have absolutely *loved* tonight,' Mel said, smiling at the thought of her nan being towered over by the stunning drag queens.

'She was with you in spirit, Mel, your mam too. There's no way they'd miss out on a night like this!' said Liv.

'You're right, Liv. This would have been right up their street. Especially seeing me being dragged up on stage. I know you were the mastermind behind that, by the way, and I will get you back, madam!'

'Shocked and hurt!' Liv flounced, but her half-smile gave her away. *Guilty as charged,* thought Mel.

'As much as I'd like to be sat here all night, and trust me, I would, we need to make a move. I booked a cab for us earlier, so we didn't get tempted to move on somewhere else and stay out 'til breakfast.'

'Oh Tone, my heart wants to do the four o'clock finish, but my head tells me you're right, it's a good time to head back to the hotel. My feet are screaming to get these shoes off, too. How Denise and her girls do what they do in those heels night after night is beyond me. Did you see that death drop? Amazing!'

CHAPTER THIRTY-THREE

Just before leaving, Mel stopped and turned to take one last look at the stage. It really was magnificent. She had another moment of appreciation for her nan's courage in taking the bold step of moving to London at such a young age to sing on that very stage. It stirred a question in Mel. Was it time she stopped playing it safe and started taking a chance or two herself? She couldn't remember how long it had been since she last took a risk or stepped outside her comfort zone. Even though it hadn't ended well for her nan, it didn't stop her from giving it a go. Maybe it was time for Mel to take a leaf out of her nan's book.

'Thank you, Metropole, and goodnight, Alice Miracle,' Mel whispered with a happy heart.

Chapter Thirty-Four

The platform at London Paddington station was cold and draughty, but thankfully under cover. All five sat in a row, wrapped up in thick coats and scarves and Mel with the addition of a quirky velvet hat. They sat quietly with their hands glued to cardboard cups of steaming tea or coffee. Grateful their train was due to arrive shortly, they would reach their destination, Cardiff Central, at around half past twelve.

'Sunday lunch at the Red Lion, anyone?' asked Kev softly.

They had skipped breakfast that morning after collectively deciding an extra half an hour in bed trumped getting fed.

'That does sound good, Kev,' said Jeff, who rarely turned down a Sunday lunch, particularly at his old pub. 'I'm sure none of us can be bothered cooking when we get back.'

Everyone agreed that being cooked for was a sensible and attractive idea.

'Would anyone mind if we invited my dad to join us? I'm sure he'd love to hear about our trip, and of course

CHAPTER THIRTY-FOUR

being fed would clinch the deal for him. What about your dad, Kev? I'm sure Dougie would be up for it too.' Mel's voice was croaky from the previous night.

Texts were sent to John and Dougie, who responded immediately to accept the invitation. Jeff rang the pub and booked a table for the seven of them for one thirty. It gave them enough time to drop off their cases and walk back to the Red Lion. Their train journey was *considerably* quieter on the way home. Jeff leaned against Tony and drifted off to sleep until he was rudely awakened by his own snore. They were happy, weary travellers, sharing comfortable silence for most of the journey, all thinking about their time in London.

They got off the train in convoy, Kev reaching the platform first. He took the bag and then the hand of each friend that followed him to help them off the train in turn.

'While London was great, and it really *was* great, it's lovely to be home,' said Liv, leaning against the wall as she waited for the minibus to take them on the final part of their journey.

Mel and Kev were the last to get home as the driver had kindly dropped everyone right outside their door and helped with their cases, starting with Jeff and Tony. The arrangement was that they would all head over to the pub as soon as they were ready. Just before Mel and Kev went to relieve themselves of their bags, he told her that he and his dad would wait for her so they could walk over together.

Mel noticed that Cat's car was no longer outside the house and decided to send her a quick text to check on her.

She replied quickly, saying that she was fine before asking if Mel needed anything from the shops as she had gone to Marks and Spencer at Culverhouse Cross. Mel asked Cat to pick up some bread and milk and then invited her for lunch, knowing they could easily squeeze in another person. Cat declined, thanking her and saying she would see her later instead.

True to his word, Kev was standing with Dougie, waiting for her outside.

'Hello, my gorgeous wee girl, did you have a good time in the Big Smoke?'

Mel gave Dougie a big cwtch and a kiss on the cheek.

'Oh, Dougie, it was *amazing*! Come on, let's get out of the cold and we can tell you all about it.' Mel linked her arm in Dougie's, and they set off.

As the three walked into the pub, they spotted John straight away, who was propping up the bar with Liv, Jeff, and Tony.

'Our table's ready so we can go straight through,' said Jeff.

John let the others go ahead and waited for Mel so he could give her a cwtch.

'How's my favourite daughter doing? I can't wait to hear all about your trip, Mellie. Did you take any photos?'

'I'm absolutely knackered, Pops, but it was worth it. I loved *every* second of it. I didn't take many photos, but I think Kev took quite a few.'

CHAPTER THIRTY-FOUR

Over lunch, the group reminisced about the trip, making sure that John, in particular, got every last detail. They waxed lyrical about *The Mousetrap* and their meeting with Alton and Morgan, leaving nothing out. Kev showed Dougie and John the photos he had taken at The Metropole, and both commented on what an amazing time it looked like they all had. Neither failed to notice Denise's cracking pair of legs.

'I can't believe it, Mel. I can't believe that you've not just stood on the same stage as Lizzie, but to have sung there too is off the chart, love. I've seen the photos, so I know it happened, but it's just unbelievable! Absolutely incredible.'

'I think I can help you there, John. We have photos, yes, but we also have your darling daughter live in action!' Liv fished in her pocket for her mobile and pressed play on the last video, with the whole table declaring Liv a genius for having filmed it. All bar Mel asked Liv to send it on to them after they had taken their turn to watch it. Mel, however, was far too mortified for words.

'I think you did a great job, love. I'm proud of you. It must have taken a lot of bottle to get up there and do that, fair play to you,' said John.

'You're right. It did take bottle, John. Approximately three-quarters of a bottle of champagne to be precise,' said Jeff, laughing at his own joke and setting off the rest of the table in the process.

'I hope you lot realise I will get you back. When you least expect it, I will strike!' said Mel huskily, shaking her head and laughing in despair. 'Can you imagine if Alton was here right now? He would get on with you two like a house on fire,' she said to her dad and Dougie.

'Well, why don't you invite them up in the new year, him and his lads? He sounds like quite the character, and I'd love to meet him,' said John.

'Great idea! Maybe January? It's such a miserable month and having them visit would give us something to look forward to,' Mel said, looking at her friends, who added their approval to the suggestion.

The weekend was starting to catch up with Mel, and she decided it was time to head home.

'Attention, please, you lot! I just want to say a final thanks to you all for a brilliant weekend. I've had the best time, I really have. On top of that, we've uncovered a lot of answers on the case of the Mysterious Alice Miracle. I could not have wished for a better bunch of friends to be on the investigation with me. In fact, I couldn't wish for a better bunch of friends, full stop. I love you all but don't think for a second you're off the hook for setting me up with Denise, especially you, Liv! I hate to be a party pooper, but after that roast, I'm in need of a nap on the settee this afternoon. I'm sorry, but I'm going to have to leave you to it.'

The group all thought a nap sounded like a great idea and so all decided it was a good time to head home. The whole gang walked back to Harlech Close together, except for John, who had parked his car at the rear of the pub. When they arrived at the close, they gave quick cwtches

CHAPTER THIRTY-FOUR

and kisses goodbye as they were all eager to get out of the cold. There was no doubting that their energy levels had decreased as the day progressed, and they hadn't exactly been Tigger-like to start with.

Dougie went in the house before Kev, who had told his dad he would be in soon and asked him to put the kettle on.

'Kev, thanks for everything,' Mel said when it was just the two of them. 'I know that the whole weekend was largely arranged by you and Tony and I'm so grateful. I've had a great time, and I'm really glad you were there to share it with me.'

'No need to thank me, Mel. I had a great time, too. I've not laughed like that in ages. And seeing how happy it made you was the cherry on top.'

'Well, thank you, anyway. Let's get in before we freeze. See you soon?' said Mel, a question in her voice.

'Definitely. I was thinking of sending a message to the group to suggest a trip to the cinema on Wednesday evening if you fancy it.'

'Sounds good to me. Wednesday it is.'

As Mel opened her front door, she was met by the most wonderful smells coming from her kitchen. She wandered in to find a floury Cat putting the finishing touches to some baking. At first glance there appeared to be a loaf cake, chocolate brownies, and some kind of tart.

'Well, this is all looking and smelling rather good! I'm glad I decided to skip dessert at the pub.' Mel smiled and gave her friend a big cwtch. Cat held her arms out stiffly, hoping to avoid covering Mel in cake mixture.

'I thought I'd surprise you as a little thank you for all you've done. Least I could do, pet. Now, why don't you sit down in the lounge while I pop the kettle on and make you a cuppa? I'm looking forward to hearing about your trip.'

'Cakes *and* tea. I'm so close to proposing to you right now!' said Mel, trying to look serious. 'Anyway, never mind my trip, how are things with Mike?'

'I've done a lot of thinking these past couple of days, Mel. Mike rang last night, so we spoke for a little while. He told me that he had told Clare that I now know about Samantha. Clare was pleased, apparently, and she and Mike will be telling Samantha that he's her dad sooner than planned. Originally, it was to be sometime in the new year, but it's going to be before Christmas now instead. It all feels a bit soon and rushed to me, but it's different for Mike as he's known about this for longer. I think he feels he needs to make up for all the Christmases he's missed out on with her, too.' Cat sighed and paused before continuing.

'Like you said the other day, it all boils down to whether I love him enough. I do, and I need to give it a go. So that's where my head's at. I've not said anything to Mike yet, I want to sleep on it to make sure. I don't want to make him promises I can't keep, and I definitely don't want to be introduced to Samantha until I'm as certain as

CHAPTER THIRTY-FOUR

I can be about things; it wouldn't be fair to her. It may not work out, but I want to try. Mike said he'd like for me to meet Clare whenever I'm ready. He's doing his absolute best to reassure me, Mel.'

'That's positive, Cat. And whatever happens, you're going to be just fine. Just take it one day at a time and see how you feel. For what it's worth, I think you're making a great decision,' Mel said warmly. 'Now, where's that cake and cuppa you promised me, Mary Berry?'

CHAPTER THIRTY-FIVE

At just after five the next day, Cat joined Mel in her group room to help her wrap the presents for the carers' Christmas party. Janet came in shortly after, clutching a precariously balanced tower of Christmas cards.

'Hello, ladies,' purred Janet, unintentionally seductively. 'I'm sorry I can't stay too long tonight. I only have an hour and then I need to leave. I have a list of our carers' names. Would you like me to write out their Christmas cards?'

Mel had always admired Janet's handwriting so felt this was the perfect job for her.

'Great idea, Janet. Thank you, my love. Cat, will you pop some music on for us, please, darling?'

Cat chose one of the relaxing new-age CDs that Mel often used as background music in her groups. She didn't think anyone was in the mood for Christmas music despite the task at hand. Mel looked tired, Janet looked focused, and Cat wasn't particularly feeling any Christmas spirit just yet. The conversation was sparse as all three were concentrating on card writing, label writing, wrapping gifts, and sticking bows on presents to make them look

CHAPTER THIRTY-FIVE

pretty. Janet stayed on a few minutes extra as she was so close to finishing her job of writing out the cards, and she didn't want to leave the task incomplete. With the last card written, she quickly put on her coat and grabbed her bag.

'Thank you, Janet, you're an angel,' said Mel, reminding herself that she would be getting the largest bottle of Baileys available as a thank you for all her help.

'Yes, thanks so much, Janet.' Cat beamed a smile at her.

'You are more than welcome, girls; I just wish I could stay longer.' Janet was about to continue but was interrupted by Colin walking into the room.

'Something I said, or is my aftershave not to your liking, Janet?' said Col with a playful smile.

'Nothing like that at all, just mum duties. Besides, you always smell edible, Colin. Doesn't he, girls?' said Janet in her typically straightforward style.

Mel and Cat agreed enthusiastically, which made Col blush a little and regret his attempt at humour. He hadn't been expecting the compliment, so the joke had backfired on him slightly. The three said goodnight to Janet as she dashed off in a hurry.

'Good to see you, Col. Thanks for coming to help,' said Mel.

'No worries, Mel. I'd have been here sooner, but I needed to nip to my mam's after work. Right, what do you want me to do?' asked Colin, rolling up his sleeves.

Mel directed him to a pile of presents on the table behind him and handed him some scissors and sticky tape. They had made good progress in the last hour or so, and Mel was pleased with their efforts.

'How are things with you, Cat? I didn't text over the weekend in case you were busy. I didn't want to intrude,' said Col gingerly.

Cat filled him in on the latest developments with Mike and explained that she was still at Mel's for the time being. Mel excused herself to make tea and coffee for them all.

'I'm so pleased that things seem to be working out for you, Cat. Great news. I guess this means I need to close the Lisa profile then?'

Cat paused for a moment. 'Do you think you could keep her profile active for a little while longer? Just in case.'

'Course I will. I'm assuming you don't need me to go to the gym now you have your answers. I'll probably need it after Christmas, though,' he said, patting his stomach.

'No, I don't, and thanks again for doing that for me. You've been amazing.'

'Don't be daft; that's what friends are for.' Colin squeezed Cat's arm.

Mel kicked the door open as her hands were full.

'Tea for you, Cat, and coffee for you, Col. Another hour and I think we will have this nailed,' she announced.

CHAPTER THIRTY-FIVE

The hour flew by, and Mel had been right; most of the parcels were wrapped. The rest she could finish off between group sessions. For now, she put everything away and tidied up after them.

'You two are legends, thank you! Cat did some fabulous baking yesterday if you fancy coming back to mine for a wonderfully calorific tea, Col. I can't promise you'll get your five a day, but there is apple in the tart at least.'

'Normally that would have been a yes, but I have to go to Tesco as one of my mates is calling round later. I'm gutted I'm missing out on cake, though! Have a nice evening, and I'll see you both tomorrow.' He was halfway through the door before he'd even finished putting his coat on.

'Right, Cat. Let's get going too,' said Mel, making a start of gathering her things.

'You know what, Mel. I think I might come back to yours, pack up my stuff, and go back to the flat if that's okay?'

'Of course, love, no problem at all. Though I'm shocked you want to pass up apple tart and custard with a side helping of *Love Actually*. As much as I loved Alan Rickman, I will *never* forgive him for cheating on Emma Thompson. The scene with Rick from *The Walking Dead* holding up those cards to Keira Knightley, though… gets me every time.' Mel put her hand on her heart for dramatic effect.

'Chick flicks? Really? You're not usually one for those. What's going on?' said a puzzled Cat.

'It's the Christmas effect, love. In December, anything goes! Come on, let's get you back to mine and packed. I've got a date with Hugh Grant you're keeping me from.'

Chapter Thirty-Six

The moment the credits started rolling, Mel woke. A stone-cold, half-eaten bowl of apple tart and custard on the coffee table was the final damning piece of evidence that she had been guilty of nodding off and had missed nearly all the film. Despite it not even being ten o'clock, it felt like way past her bedtime, so she waved her white flag, deposited the bowl in the sink, and went directly to bed. Within five minutes she was once again in the land of dreams.

It had paid off having such an early night because the following morning Mel felt great. She had finally shaken of the remains of her London hangover. As she had woken before the alarm, she had plenty of time to get herself ready for work, tidy the kitchen that she had neglected the previous night, and even make some toast for breakfast. On her way to work, inspired by seeing all the decorations on the high street, Mel decided to put her Christmas tree up that evening. With less than two weeks to go, it seemed like good timing.

That day, she only saw Colin in passing as he'd booked a half day's leave for the afternoon. Cat had been out and about most of the day doing some activities with her young carers, so they only shared a few minutes together, too. She had briefly updated Mel on how things had gone the previous night. Mel felt things sounded hopeful for Cat and Mike from what she had heard.

Before leaving work for the day, Mel sent Liv a text.

Hey, trouble, how are you doing? Up to much tonight? xx

Well, my response depends entirely on what you're working up to suggesting, my darling! xx

Nothing particularly exciting, so get your excuse in ready. I'm going to put my Christmas tree up tonight and wondered if you fancied coming over while I'm doing it. xx

Want me to bring some food? xx

Yes. It's always yes to that question! I'll be home in half an hour. See you soon xx

Liv arrived shortly after Mel got home. She took a container of homemade chilli to the kitchen to be reheated later before following Mel upstairs. Liv stood at the bottom of the loft ladder, waiting to be passed down the dismantled Christmas tree and boxes of decorations.

'Bloody hell, woman, you just about decapitated me!' said Liv, adding a little poetic licence. In her defence, Mel had let go of the box unexpectedly, and it had landed reasonably forcefully.

'Sorry, love, it slipped! Just a couple more boxes and we're done.'

CHAPTER THIRTY-SIX

Within an hour, Liv was in the kitchen pouring drinks and serving up their dinner while Mel put the finishing touches to the tree. She invited Liv to do the honours of flicking the switch to turn on the tree lights as a reward for her help. Mel's fingers were tightly crossed, hoping they still worked, and was relieved when she saw them in all their glory reflecting off a myriad of silver baubles and bows. The tree looked gorgeous, like something in a high-end department store. Mel had collected some beautiful decorations over the years and was thrilled with the result.

They decided to eat in the kitchen but went to sit in the lounge once they'd finished to enjoy the fruits of their labour. Mel lit a few candles and brought in the wine bottle to top up their glasses. She and Liv sat there chatting about the weekend and what a wonderful time they'd had. The conversation drifted towards the subject of Christmas.

'So, what are your plans this year, Liv?'

'Jeff and Tony have invited me to have dinner with them. I'll call to see my auntie in the morning first, though, to drop prezzies off. What about you? I'm assuming you're having John over for Christmas dinner.'

'Yes, you and I both know he'd disown me if I didn't! You'd have been very welcome, of course, like last year. I'm thinking of inviting Dougie and Kev. I'm going to mention it tomorrow night. Dougie was with us last year, and as Kev is apparently not the best cook, they may fancy coming here.'

'Oh yes. It's cinema night tomorrow, isn't it? I can't make it; I've already got readings booked in. I think Kev will bite your hand off for the invitation and not just because you're the best mash and roast potato maker in the village either,' teased Liv.

'Oh, behave yourself, woman! Speaking of Jeff and Tony, did they mention New Year's Eve to you? They were talking about either booking a table at the Red Lion or doing something at theirs. I blame the booze for not remembering if we ever came to a decision on it!'

'That does sound vaguely familiar. I'll drop them a text later and update you. I didn't half enjoy the weekend, you know, Mel. It got me thinking we should do that kind of thing more often.'

Mel nodded in agreement. 'I had the best time, too, and it also got me thinking. Going to The Metropole made me realise just how brave my nan was and how closed off I've become to doing new things. I've got myself into a comfortable rut. Contentment is great, but it doesn't give you moments that make your heart beat faster or take your breath away, does it? Perhaps that's what I wanted before, but now I'm wondering if I'm selling myself short. There should be more to life, surely, and I'm thinking that maybe I should take the odd risk here and there. It's so easy to not take a chance for fear of failure, but how limiting and miserable is that? It's been so long since I did something for the first time, and that needs to change,' Mel said, her voice filled with determination.

'I hear you, and I can see why our trip has inspired you. Maybe we need to make a New Year's resolution to

CHAPTER THIRTY-SIX

shake things up a bit? Life's too bloody short to settle for contentment alone. On that profound note, I'm going to have to make a move. I've got a few readings booked in for first thing in the morning, and I need an early night.'

'I think that sounds like a good idea, Liv. Not all resolutions have to be about limiting our alcohol and calorie intake, joining the gym, and all that kind of stuff. We can choose to add sparkle and adventures to our list. I'm going to give this some thought,' said Mel as she helped Liv on with her coat.

Mel closed her front door after Liv gave her a wave from her own. Before going to bed, Mel decided to drop her dad a text. Sitting in her lounge lit by the Christmas tree lights had made her realise that she was a little behind with the planning of everything this year. Other than having bought a few cards, she'd done nothing, which was unlike her.

Hey Pops, how are you doing? Quick question for you. I was thinking of inviting Dougie in for Christmas dinner with us again this year. As Kev is home, I thought it might be nice to include him too. Is that okay with you? xx

Hiya love. Of course it's okay. You know me, the more the merrier! I've already got a bottle of single malt for Dougie's Christmas present. Any idea what I could buy Kev? xx

Good call on the whisky for Dougie. I'm sure he'll be happy with that. As for Kev, well I'm sure he won't be expecting anything, but I know you wouldn't leave him out. I'll do some subtle fishing and let you know. xx

Thanks, love. Oh, just to let you know, I've bought the Christmas crackers as usual so no need for you to buy any. And don't worry, they are silver to match your decorations. Night-night, Mellie Adelie xx

Thanks for getting the (right coloured) crackers! Night-night, Dad xx

Deciding that an early night was in order, Mel turned off the Christmas tree lights and went to bed. It took a little while for her to fall asleep as she reflected on the conversation she had just had with Liv. *Time to make a few changes,* she told herself.

CHAPTER THIRTY-SEVEN

Mel was pleased at just how much she had been able to pack into her sixty-minute lunch break. She had managed to go to Lloyd's butchers on the high street to order her Christmas meat and then to the bakery to place an order for bread, mince pies, and her dad's favourite apple sponge cake for Christmas Day. It felt good to get a few essentials organised. While she was at the bakery, she picked up some of their delicious homemade vegetable soup for her lunch, and then shopped online for some Christmas gifts as she ate. She chose a trendy beanie hat for Colin; a perfume giftset, a pair of silver earrings and a tarot book for Liv; clothes and books for her dad; chocolates, shortbread biscuits, and socks for Dougie; a Christmas hamper of goodies for Cat and Mike; and a similar hamper for Jeff and Tony. Kevin was more difficult to buy for, so she ended up getting him a scarf, gloves, and some cufflinks. Her shopping was interrupted by a message from the WhatsApp group.

Hi Kev. I'm afraid we won't be able to make the cinema tonight. Jeff's not been well with a stomach bug. We've been up most of the night. Apologies but we will make up for it another night soon. Lots of love, me and the not-so-brave patient xxx

FINDING A MIRACLE

A wave of disappointment hit Mel. She'd been looking forward to a Christmas film and a bite to eat. With Liv not being able to make it either she assumed Kev would cancel too. Her phone buzzed again.

Hi Tony. Sorry to hear that Jeff's not well. Liv can't make it either so we will arrange to do something another time. Looks like it's just you and me then, Mel, if you're still up for it. K xx

Hi all. Sorry to hear you're not feeling well, Jeff. A shame it's a lower turnout than expected, but I'm still happy to go tonight, Kev. See you later, M xxx

Great, I'll give you a knock about seven. K xx

Unusually for Mel, she had managed to get out of work on time. Although it was just a midweek cinema night, and she didn't have to get mega dressed up, she still wanted to look nice. After she got in from the short drive home, she looked through her wardrobe and picked out a nice top in slate grey and black jeans. As her outfit was understated, she went for a bold red lip and large silver hoop earrings and a cross-body bag to complete her look. She topped up her perfume before going downstairs, then turned on the Christmas tree lights and sat in the lounge as she waited for Kev to arrive. Her mind drifted and was lost in memories from their trip to London.

The sudden ring of the doorbell brought Mel back to the real world with a bang. She quickly put on her coat, grabbed her hat, scarf, gloves, and bag and hurried to the door.

CHAPTER THIRTY-SEVEN

'Good evening, Mel,' said Kev before bending down to kiss her cheek.

'Good evening yourself, Kev,' said Mel, smiling.

'Come on, let's get going, shall we?'

He opened the car door for her and closed it behind her after she was safely settled within.

'It's the first time I've been in your new car. It's lovely.'

'The first of many times if you behave yourself,' teased Kev.

'Cheeky bugger! When am I not well-behaved?' she retorted in fake indignation.

'No comment!' said Kev with a chuckle before swiftly changing the subject. 'I booked a table at The Telegraph. Hope that's okay with you?'

'Ooh, nice choice, Kev. I haven't been there in a little while. It was one of the first pubs we went to as teenagers when it was The Cork and Candle. Do you remember? I felt so grown up going there for a cider and blackcurrant. I think I'll stay clear of that particular drink tonight, though!' She grimaced, remembering the time she had overindulged as a teenager and put herself off that particular drink for life.

In what felt like no time at all, Kev was turning into the car park to the left of the pub. Once seated with drinks in front of them, they ordered their meals. Both decided to skip starters and go straight to a main course. Kev ordered a steak and ale pie with mashed potato and vegetables, and Mel went for roast chicken served with Mediterranean vegetables.

'So, how was your day, Kev?'

'I had a good day, thanks. It's such a treat having some time off. I'm feeling a bit proud of myself, actually, Mel. I did some Christmas shopping today and managed to get quite a bit done. Although, I've just realised I forgot to order wrapping paper, so that's a job for tomorrow, then. It will be with us in no time, eh.'

'You're not wrong. While we're on the subject of Christmas, I don't know if you've already made plans for Christmas Day, but you and your dad would be very welcome to join us. Your dad was with me, my dad, and Liv for it last year. Of course, if you already have plans, I completely understand. Liv has clearly had a better offer and will be having dinner with Jeff and Tony. I don't blame her; they will do everything on a much grander scale!'

'Ah Mel, that's a lovely offer, thank you. With Christmas being just over a week away, there's really not enough time to polish my cooking skills, is there?' Kev chuckled. 'We'd love to come if your dad doesn't mind us joining you.'

'That's great. I've already checked with him, and he's more than happy. His first question was what he should buy you for Christmas. He's already got your dad something. I told him I would do some fishing, but I think it's easier to ask you outright. Just don't tell my dad!'

'Bless him, he's a legend! He doesn't need to do that, but I'd be happy with anything, Mel. My dad is going to be so relieved we're coming to you!'

CHAPTER THIRTY-SEVEN

'Oh no! You're not doing that to me, you need to give me some clues! How about you text me in the morning with a list of your favourite things, and then he can take his pick? It's still sort of a surprise that way.'

'I thought you were going to start singing then. *Raindrops on roses and whiskers on kittens, these are a few of my favourite things,*' sang Kev, barely hitting the notes.

Mel laughed and held up her hand defensively for him to stop singing.

Their chat was interrupted briefly as their meals arrived and then they picked up where they left off. The conversation flowed naturally and barely without pause for the duration.

Kev checked his watch. 'There's no mad rush, but we will need to leave in about twenty minutes. I'm sorry we probably don't have time for dessert. Our tickets are for the nine o'clock showing of *Last Christmas* at Chapter Arts. If we get there a little earlier, we can grab a bag of Pick 'n' Mix for our pudding before we go in.'

'I like the way you think, Kev. You're a man after my own heart,' replied Mel with a smile.

Neither had realised the film was set in Covent Garden and they nudged each other excitedly every time they recognised parts of the location. Mel had a lovely night with Kev, and she had to admit to herself that maybe she wasn't *that* sorry the others hadn't been able to join them after all.

Chapter Thirty-Eight

Mel was at the centre early as it was finally the day of the carers' Christmas party. As the past week had gone by in a blur of Christmas shopping for her loved ones and getting organised for the party, she was grateful that she, Cat, and Col had decided for their night at Merola's the previous evening to be neither boozy nor late. It was so nice to have a much more relaxed and fun evening with them both. The time they had spent together for the past few weeks was more like briefings for a top-secret spy mission and about as far from enjoyable as you could get. There had been only the briefest mention of Mike at the start of the night when Col had asked Cat how things were at home. Cat's response had been that things were going okay; Mike was making a huge effort, and she was just seeing how things went. The first proper introduction between Mike and his daughter, Samantha, was due to happen the next day. While Cat was nervous about it, Mike was losing sleep. He was worried that it would go badly and that Samantha may be resentful towards him. He was also anxious about the impact it might have on things with Cat, of course. The conversation moved on swiftly after that and drifted into a chat about work, weekend plans, Christmas, and New Year's Eve. Before leaving they finalised what each of their roles would be

CHAPTER THIRTY-EIGHT

for the carers' party the next day as both Col and Cat had volunteered to lend a hand.

Just before Mel left to take the first load of presents over to the Red Lion, she popped in to see Janet. As she wasn't at her desk, Mel decided to leave the gift-wrapped bottle of Baileys and a Christmas card on her desk as she had a lot to do. Four trips later and all the presents were at the pub ready for her dad to play Santa. Mel had carefully separated them into three piles: gifts suitable for males, females, and those that would be universally popular. She hoped that this system would be good enough to avoid any disappointment on Christmas morning. Checking the time, she thought it wise to make sure her dad was on his way, so gave him a quick call. He answered within three rings.

'Ho, ho, ho! Is that Santa's little helper calling me?' asked John, doing one of the worst Santa impersonations Mel had ever heard. It was closer to Long John Silver than the chubby man in red. She had little choice but to play along.

'Yes, this is elf number one, ringing to check if Santa has remembered to be at the Red Lion for twelve o'clock.' That was a sentence she'd never imagined coming out of her mouth.

'Have no fear, my favourite little helper, I will be there with bells on! Rudolph and the gang have been fed, watered, and are raring to go. See you soon, just leaving Lapland.'

'Great, see you soon then, Santa. Safe travels from Lapland!' Mel shook her head and laughed. Every year she needed to 'persuade' him yet every year he seemed to get more into it. The previous year he was bandying around terms like 'method actor' and 'role motivation'. This year, she would put money on him talking about getting an agent or something equally ridiculous.

As she ended the call, she saw Cat struggling through the heavy doors and sprinted off to help her. Laden with boxes of mince pies, Cat was glad to see Mel coming to her rescue. She plonked them on one of the tables that were already set up and covered in festive confetti. Some of the food had started to arrive from downstairs, courtesy of the kitchen staff. Cat took off her coat and bag and immediately started arranging savoury food on one table and sweet on the other. Col turned up next carrying a huge and rather beautiful-looking Christmas cake, which had been donated by the bakery along with the mince pies. The cake took pride of place in the centre of the desserts.

'This looks great, Mel. I'll take some photos in a bit, like last year.'

'You're a gem, thanks, Col. I know my dad will want some in his Santa outfit too.'

'I'm glad he's coming, Mel; he was the star of the show last year.' Col laughed, remembering John's ham performance.

On cue, Santa turned up.

'Merry Christmas! Merry Christmas! Ho! Ho! Ho!'

CHAPTER THIRTY-EIGHT

'None of the carers are here yet, Dad, you can drop the act and relax for a bit,' said Mel.

'Righto, love. Get us a cuppa, will you? I'm parched and I am, after all, a man of great influence and can make sure you're on the nice list if you do.' The beard did not hide John's cheeky smile and the little round glasses didn't mask the twinkle in his eye, either.

'Hey there, young man, make sure you get my good side when you're taking photos. I don't want to have to put you on my naughty list.'

The party went fantastically well. There wasn't an empty seat, and all agreed it was the best one yet. It made Mel's heart happy seeing her carers being spoilt for a change. They put in so much hard work throughout the year, looking after their loved ones, so it was great to see them enjoying themselves. Seeing all the smiling faces and hearing the laughter and singing made all the planning and hard work worthwhile. Mel beamed as she looked around the room. Her dad had encouraged everyone to get up and have a dance after they were suitably fed and watered and had been given their presents. Of course he joined in, as did Mel, Cat, and Col. By four o'clock the party had come to an end. Quite a few of the attendees continued their celebrations in the bar downstairs as Mel, together with Santa's other little helpers, set about tidying up. By half past four, the room was back to a semblance of order. Cat and Col had already taken some of the leftover goodies back to the centre for the rest of the team to enjoy. Mel made sure that her dad had a goodie bag to take away too as it was well deserved.

Back at the centre, Mel caught up with Colin before he left for the Christmas holidays. He had some annual leave to use and was going to be off until the new year. He and a couple of friends had managed to get a good deal on a last-minute mini break to Chamonix. He was going to try his hand at snowboarding.

'I'm glad I caught you before you jet off, Col. Thanks so much for today and in general for just being you. I've got you a little something. Open it before you go on your trip; it might come in handy.'

'Oh Mel, you didn't need to do that. Thank you, though.' Col gave Mel a kiss on the cheek and a big cwtch.

'Have the best time, Col, you deserve it. I look forward to hearing all about it when you get back, love,' said Mel.

A few minutes later, Col was in his coat and ready to go, wishing everyone a happy Christmas before leaving the centre for the last time that year.

When Mel got to her desk, she saw there were a couple of presents left for her. Before she could even check the tags to see who they were from, there was a knock on her door. It was Cat, clutching a card and a half-open present. Mel saw that it was the same wrapping paper as one of the gifts on her desk.

'I've had a present from Col,' said Cat, grinning.

'Yeah, me too, but unlike you, I haven't opened mine!'

'I know, I know. I'm terrible,' she said, looking suitably guilty.

CHAPTER THIRTY-EIGHT

'You are!' Mel said in mock despair. 'So, what did he get you then?'

'I had a lovely card and a gorgeous champagne glass filled with truffles and a little bottle of bubbly. It's a fab present but listen to what he wrote on the card.' Cat read aloud the message from Colin.

To Cat, raise your glass to the coming year. I hope it's full of love, happiness, and many adventures. Love Col xx

'Ah, he's got such a way with words, hasn't he? Most people just stick to *Happy Christmas, Love from*. But not Col.'

'He really has. He puts me to shame! Well, I'd better go, Mel. I just wanted to wish you a happy Christmas before I head home.'

Mel gave her a long cwtch. 'Thank you, Cat. I hope you and Mike have a fabulous time.'

After Cat left, Mel sat at her desk for a moment or two to gather her thoughts. She put her gifts into a bag and decided to open the card she got from Colin.

To Mel,

For the memories you're about to make in your next chapter. Grab the moments that take your breath away and keep shining bright.

Much love,

Col

xx

Great advice, thought Mel, feeling inspired and determined to make the next year her best yet.

Chapter Thirty-Nine

Christmas Eve had always been one of Mel's favourite days of the year. There was something special about the feeling of anticipation it had that put her in a great mood. For the past few years, she and Liv had done their last-minute food shopping together, and this year was no different. Mel completed her outfit with a festive red beret and made her way to the door. As she opened it, she was not just met by a blast of frosty air but also Dylan, her regular delivery man, wearing a Santa hat.

'Morning, Mel, I've got a couple of parcels for you. Be careful; one of them has *Fragile* written on it.'

'That's good timing, Dyl; I was just on my way out to the shops.'

Mel took the parcels from him and quickly put them under her Christmas tree. As all her online shopping had already arrived, she could only assume these were presents. Mel called after him to thank him and wish him and his family a merry Christmas, but he was already on his way to make his next delivery. Even if she had wanted to, there was no time to open the gifts now or she would be late for Liv. *Speak of the devil,* thought Mel as she saw Liv trotting down the close towards her.

'Bloody hell, girl, it's colder than a witch's you-know-what today. And I should know!'

'You're not wrong, Liv. Happy Christmas Eve, darling.'

'Happy Christmas Eve to you too,' said Liv as she gave her friend a forceful cwtch. 'Come on, let's get the shopping done and then maybe get a bit of brunch somewhere, shall we?'

They linked arms and headed out of Harlech Close, Mel in full agreement with Liv's suggestion. Within a couple of hours, they had picked up what they needed to make their Christmas perfect. Both had been wise enough to get an online shopping order delivery for most of their wants and needs, so their shopping that morning hadn't been too stressful. Having picked up some last-minute indulgences, they dropped them off at home and, within a few minutes, were back out. They decided to go to The Soup Kitchen, which was at the far end of the high street. It was bustling, and everyone was in a good mood, it seemed. Both Mel and Liv felt the tingling fizz of Christmas spirit all around them as they strolled through the village.

When they got to The Soup Kitchen, they managed to get a table for two in the window overlooking the high street. They were lucky that a couple had literally just left because the place was full. Looking through the menu was a task at that place because everything was *so* good. Mel decided it was close enough to lunchtime to order a bowl of their cream of winter vegetable soup, and Liv followed suit. It was hardly any time at all before they were dipping warm, crusty homemade bread into the best soup they

CHAPTER THIRTY-NINE

had eaten in a while. They chatted about all sorts before Liv asked how the cinema night had gone with Kev the previous week.

'I had a great time, Liv. I hadn't seen *Last Christmas* before, so didn't realise it was filmed in Covent Garden. It was like being back there!'

'No holding hands in the back row then?' said Liv disappointedly. 'That bloody Kev needs a nudge. I think he still thinks it would be a no if he asked you out, just like when we were teenagers.'

Mel paused while she mulled over what Liv had just said.

'What makes you think that Kev is even thinking of asking me out? I've seen no sign of him being interested in anything romantic with us.'

'Well, he's not shouting it from the rooftops, but I think there are signs he's interested.'

'Such as?' Mel said with one eyebrow raised.

'Taking the lead in the online search for Alton, buying you stationery, taking you out to dinner to thank you for making him a bowl of soup, doing most of the organising for the London trip, taking tonnes of photos of you on the stage at The Metropole. Do I need to go on? Shall I mention how he looks at you and how he doesn't really take his eyes off you, for that matter?'

'I can't say I've noticed his undivided attention, Liv. Kev's a thoughtful guy, and he got wrapped up in the mystery about my nan, that's all. We are friends, we enjoy each other's company, but that's as far as it goes. Kev doesn't see me as anything more than the woman next door, I'm sure. Now, don't go getting carried away when I say this, but everything that's happened these past few weeks has got me thinking. I've been happily single for the past three years, as you know, but I'm starting to feel more open to being in a relationship.'

'Isn't that interesting?' said Liv with a playful smile.

'What is?' asked Mel.

'You just said that Kev only sees you as his friend from next door. You didn't say that's how *you* see *him*. I'm taking that as you not only being open to a relationship but a relationship with Kev. Why don't we see what the cards say about this, eh?'

Before Mel had a chance to say no and stop her, Liv was already rooting around her bag. Besides, she felt a little lost for words. She couldn't really argue with what Liv had said. If she was being completely honest with herself, there was a big part of her that wished what Liv had said about Kev being interested was true.

'You have tarot cards with you?'

'Of course I do! I always carry a mini deck in my bag for emergencies,' Liv said with a wink.

She handed the deck to Mel, who did as she was told and shuffled them until she was satisfied.

'You know I'm only doing this to humour you and

CHAPTER THIRTY-NINE

shut you up, don't you? This is just for a quiet life and no more,' said Mel, trying to hide the fact she really was intrigued to discover if romance was on the cards for them. Literally.

'What was it Shakespeare said about the lady protesting too much? Just shuffle the cards and ask the sodding question, will you!'

'Tell me about my future with Kev,' Mel asked the cards as she shuffled. She chose a card and handed it to Liv face down. Liv turned it over, and Mel was taken aback to see the card she had chosen was one of the happiest and most heartwarming cards in the deck. The Ten of Cups. Mel's smile lit up her face as she looked from the card to her friend across the table and back to the card again. The scene was idyllic. A man and a woman with arms around each other with two children happily playing nearby. The couple were looking at their home, which was framed by a rainbow, their free arms aloft as they felt gratitude for all the good fortune in their lives.

'I think we have our answer, don't we? This is the happy-ever-after card! All we need is for Kev to pluck up some courage and ask you out. I've known you long enough and well enough to know *you* wouldn't ask him.'

'I wouldn't do that with anyone, let alone, Kev. I'd be too scared that he'd say no, and I'd ruin our friendship.'

'And I'm guessing that's *exactly* what he's thinking,' said Liv. 'So, he just needs a little encouragement, that's all.'

'My nan always said, "What's meant for you won't pass you by". She was right about most things, so if Kev and I are meant to be more than friends, it will happen, and if not, it won't.'

Feeling that she'd said more than enough already, Mel swiftly changed the subject.

After their brunch, Mel and Liv wandered back down the high street and headed to their respective homes. With the shopping all put away and the log burner roaring, Mel was finally able to relax on the sofa with a cuppa. *Time to recharge the batteries,* she thought. The next day would be busy, but she was very much looking forward to it.

Chapter Forty

With the vast array of vegetables all washed, chopped, and prepped ready to go and the turkey crown and pork already in the oven, Mel set about laying the table. By the time she had finished, it looked beautiful and was only missing the crackers that her dad was bringing over. She would light the candles on the centrepiece just before Kev and Dougie were due at two o'clock. After lighting the fire and switching on the Christmas lights, Mel took her dad's presents from under the tree and put them on the sofa next to where he normally liked to sit. The usual routine for Mel and her dad was to open their presents from each other on Christmas morning before having their dinner and then settling down to some afternoon board games and maybe watching a festive film in the evening. Mel had enough time for a quick cuppa and slice of toast before she needed to get ready. Painting her nails the night before had been a great idea, she decided as she poured hot water into a mug to make her tea. As she ate her breakfast, Mel realised just how much she was looking forward to the day, and Kev being there was definitely a factor in that. With that thought in mind, she went to get herself ready.

A little while later, Mel took one last check in the mirror before she went downstairs. She was pleased with the new dress she had bought. The emerald-green colour suited her and seemed to bring out the green of her eyes. An extra spray of her signature scent and she was ready to go downstairs.

When John arrived, arms filled with presents, the house sprang to life as it usually did when he walked through the door. Thankfully, he had not worn his Santa costume and had also discarded the pirate accent. Instead, he wore a red Christmas jumper that sported the words *Up to Snow Good* on the front.

'Happy Christmas, Dad. Loving the jumper!' said Mel before wrapping her arms around him in a big cwtch.

'Happy Christmas, Mellie! Glad you like it. I just hope it doesn't mean I'm on the naughty list next year. I don't want to be tipping Santa off that I'm not always a saint,' said John with a mischievous twinkle in his eye.

He put the presents for Kev and Dougie under the tree and handed the crackers he had bought to Mel. She duly went and put four on the table, which now looked complete. As she checked the back of the box, she saw that they contained racing penguins and reindeer and came complete with a racetrack inside the box. Mel hadn't a clue what he would pick this year, but in true John style, she knew these would likely be fun.

They swapped their presents, and both agreed they had been very spoilt and had luckily made it to the 'nice list' for another year. John had given Mel a John Lewis

CHAPTER FORTY

voucher as her main present, together with a candle, bubble bath, chocolates, and a bottle of wine. He always made sure she had something to unwrap on the big day. Vouchers were great, but nothing beat opening gifts on Christmas morning, he'd always thought. John opened his presents from Mel, and as usual, she had spoilt him rotten. He had two shirts and two cardigans, as well as socks, slippers, and a dressing gown all from his favourite shop, Marks & Spencer. Mel had also bought him a shower gel gift set, chocolates, and a good bottle of whisky.

Once all their presents had been opened, both declaring how grateful and blessed they were, Mel tidied away all the torn wrapping paper and put the vegetables on to cook. She and her dad sat in the lounge with a glass each of buck's fizz, reminiscing about Christmases that had passed when her mother was alive. Anne had been a huge fan of Christmas and had always done her best to make it magical. For them both, this time of year had its poignant moments as well as happy ones. And as John rightly pointed out, they were not alone; it was the same for nearly every family in the land. Nobody escaped losing someone they loved, and Christmastime was often a stark reminder of that. Rather than thinking about their losses, they focused on the fun times they'd shared and the happy memories they kept safely tucked away in their hearts.

There were about fifteen minutes before Kev and Dougie were due and Mel decided a small glass of wine would be a good idea. She was organised and everything was cooked and kept warm ready for their arrival.

'Let's have a bit of music on, shall we, Mellie Adelie?'

'Great minds think alike; I was just thinking the exact same thing,' she replied as she found the Christmas playlist on her phone and hooked it up to her speakers via Bluetooth.

Just as Mel had lit the candles on the table and was about to reward herself with another sip of wine, the doorbell rang.

'*Siiiiilent night, hooooly night. All is calm. All is bright...*'

'I will pay you to stop! Enough! Now get in or the neighbours will be complaining,' Mel said with a huge smile on her face.

'Merry Christmas, my wee gorgeous girl,' said Dougie, holding up some mistletoe and standing with his lips pursed.

'Merry Christmas, Dougie, my darling,' Mel replied before planting a kiss on his cheek. 'Get yourself in the warm; we're in the kitchen.'

'Happy Christmas, Mel! You look lovely,' said Kev before leaning down to kiss her on the cheek.

'Happy Christmas, Kev! Ah thank you. Come on in, love. I hope you're hungry.'

In the kitchen, John was carving meat and stopped briefly to welcome their guests. Under Mel's instruction, Kev poured the champagne. She told them all to sit down and then brought dish after dish of piping hot vegetables and side dishes to the table, and her guests happily set about filling their plates. There were approving noises as

CHAPTER FORTY

steaming dishes of pigs in blankets, stuffing, red cabbage, and roasted carrots arrived, and far less enthusiasm for the sprouts even though they had been cooked with bacon and chestnuts in a failed attempt to make them more appealing. John reminded Mel the Yorkshire puddings were still in the oven and she rescued them just in time. If Mel hadn't done Yorkshires, her dad and Dougie wouldn't have let her forget it until the following Christmas. With crackers pulled, paper crowns on heads, and jokes told, they all tucked in.

To Mel's relief, Christmas dinner couldn't have gone better. All four agreed it was the best roast they'd had in a long time. Not wanting to leave the table just yet, they decided it was the perfect time to race penguins and reindeer. Kev helped Mel clear a space on the table for the racetrack and put the leftovers in containers. John and Dougie started without them and were already competitive, trying to psych the other out like heavyweight boxers before a title fight. Mel and Kev giggled as they listened to their dads talking up their particular penguin or reindeer.

As Mel and Kev sat down, the game reached its climax. John had won by a small margin, and Dougie protested strongly that he had been robbed because John had cheated. John was outraged and demanded another game, but this time with the four of them. He had kept a penguin for his very own little Adelie and handed Kev a reindeer. All four wound up their mechanical racers and let the battle commence. Once again, John won, followed closely by Mel. Dougie sulkily blamed the unfair weight disadvantage and aerodynamic inefficiency of his reindeer for his losses.

FINDING A MIRACLE

'There's only one thing for it. Snakes and Ladders! I'll show you lot who's boss,' said Dougie.

Mel went and fetched the same box of Snakes and Ladders she had played with as a child and set it up on the table. After Dougie had lost the fourth game in a row, he decided he was ready for dessert instead. Mel brought another bottle of wine to the table as well as dessert options after warming up the Christmas pudding and the mince pies. It seemed that dessert tapas was the order of the day as nobody was able to decide on just one thing despite being rather full after their dinner. As Mel looked around the table, she couldn't help but notice how happy they all looked, and it filled her heart with joy.

CHAPTER FORTY-ONE

Full to bursting after his delicious meal, John suggested it was time to open presents in the lounge. There was lots of tearing of wrapping paper and happy noises from them all. Dougie was thrilled with his bottle of single malt from John and his socks, chocolates, and slippers from Mel. Kev gave John a bottle of brandy, and Dougie gave him a bottle of whisky. John had been given some help from Mel when it came to Kev's present. She gave him a couple of options, and he went with a good bottle of red wine. Mel didn't pick anything from the list Kev had given her for her dad. Wanting to surprise him instead, she'd bought him a scarf and gloves as he had mentioned how cold it was on more than one occasion, a pair of cufflinks to wear at his next job, and a giftpack of special coffees as she'd noticed in Tuttons just how much he appreciated good coffee. Dougie had given Mel a gift voucher and a box of chocolates as he did every year with the usual apology for not having a clue what to buy for a woman that wasn't his wife. Kev decided to play it safe and bought a couple of things he knew Mel liked because he had seen them in her home. She was thrilled to receive a Neom candle and a large gift set from Neal's Yard. His final gift to her was her favourite, though. Kev had framed one of the photographs he had taken of her on stage at The

Metropole. She was touched by how thoughtful a gesture that was, so she put her hand on his arm when she thanked him and let it linger there a few moments.

All suitably pleased and grateful for what they had been given, they'd just sat back and settled down for the afternoon when John noticed something.

'Hey, little one. You've still got something under the tree.'

'Oh yeah! I'd forgotten about those. They arrived yesterday. I was in a rush to get out, so I just left them there. I'm not even sure they're presents, to be honest.'

'Only one way to find out. Get opening!'

Following her dad's orders, Mel retrieved the boxes from under the tree. She opened the first one carefully, brushing aside the polystyrene chips that kept the mystery item safe. There was another box inside. It was sturdy and plain and gave away no clues about what it contained. Mel lifted the lid and inside was two glasses – champagne saucers, to be precise. Etched on the glass was a very familiar logo in the shape of a diamond with an *M* in the centre. Clearly, it was from The Metropole, but who had sent it? She put the glasses on the table to keep them safe before returning her attention to the large box. After a little more sifting, she found an envelope with her name on it. Inside, there was a card that had a retro photograph of The Metropole on the front. It had clearly been taken on a night around Christmas, as there was a decorated tree outside and snow on the ground as well as in the air. She opened the card.

CHAPTER FORTY-ONE

Dear Mel,

I remembered about these glasses after your visit a little while ago. They are from a collection we found in the cellar last year. They date to around the time your nan was here, and I thought you might like to raise a glass to her at Christmas or New Year with someone special. Hope you like them and that you come back and see us soon!!

Love,

Dennis

xxx

Touched by Dennis's thoughtful and generous gesture, Mel couldn't help but think about the great people she'd met and the good things that had happened since she started looking into her nan's secret past. *Nothing short of a miracle, Nan,* thought Mel as she raised her eyes to the heavens and smiled.

'Well, now, isn't that lovely of him?' said John.

'It really is. He must have asked Tony for my address. I will be sure to get in touch to thank him in the next few days,' Mel said, her eyes fixed on the beautiful gift Dennis had sent.

'I think you must have made a great impression on him, Mel. For him to think of doing that on the run-up to what has to be the busiest time of year for him is incredible. Whatever's in the next box has some act to follow!' said John with a chuckle.

Mel turned her attention to the last box. All eyes were on her. The items were all wrapped in tissue paper, which Mel set about removing carefully. First to come out of the box was a selection of postcard-style promotional photographs that she instantly recognised.

'This must be from Alton!' she said excitedly.

Mel already had some of the photographs, but a couple were new to her. She passed them to Kev first after looking at them as he was sitting next to her. In turn, Kev passed them to John, then Dougie. The next item to come out of the box was another set of photographs. The first was of Maurice sitting in the dressing room backstage at The Metropole. He was in a chair and looking over his right shoulder to face the camera. It was as though someone had called him and taken a candid snap. It was good to see a more natural photo of him. He really was a handsome man. Next was a photograph of Lizzie with Maurice and a few other people in the background. It must have been taken at Christmas or on New Year's Eve, judging by the streamers and party hats. Both Liz and Maurice were looking at each other, a glass of champagne in their hands. The look they shared was so meaningful and the epitome of two people in love. The next was a similar pose, but Liz was laughing in this one, her head tilted backwards just as Mel remembered it when her nan belly laughed. This photo made Mel feel happy and emotional at the same time. It was lovely seeing her nan having such a great time, but she missed that laugh. She missed that woman. Mel traced her finger over the photo before passing it to Kev. The next photo was of the whole group on stage at The Metropole. Liz's dress was the same as the other photos,

CHAPTER FORTY-ONE

so Mel guessed it was the same night. The streamers rather gave it away, too. The final photo stopped Mel in her tracks. It looked almost as though it had been taken from Lizzie's own eyes. Her nan was sitting in the *very* place she had sat in when she was chatting with Scarlet Charlotte backstage at The Metropole. Liz was looking into the fabulous Hollywood-style mirror with lights on its border, and the photograph had captured her reflection perfectly. She held a large powder puff in her left hand, and the expression on her face was soft and almost seductive. In an instant, Mel realised that it had been Maurice who had taken it and that look had been for him.

'These photos of our Liz are beautiful, Mel,' said John. His face gave away the fondness he felt for her.

'Mel! Did you notice the champagne glasses? They're the ones that Dennis sent you. Look,' said Kev excitedly as he passed the photo back to Mel.

'Wow! So they are! I can't believe I didn't spot that. That makes them even *more* special now. I think I'll get copies of these photos for Dennis and send them on to him.'

'Let's go one better. Let's take another trip to The Metropole and hand deliver them,' suggested Kev.

'Now *that* is a *way* better idea!' said Mel, smiling at the thought of another trip with her friends.

The final item in the box was a fragile-looking newspaper cutting. The paper had become yellow and brittle. It had a photograph at the top of a large, imposing man standing next to her nan, both smiling broadly for the camera.

'It's a newspaper article and my nan's photo is on it.'

'Read it out, Mel!' said John, almost impatiently.

'Okay, keep your hat on,' said Mel, laughing at her dad's enthusiastic response.

Reginald Newman, pictured above, has secured a new star act at the famous Metropole in London's West End. He proudly announced he had secured the considerable talent a matter of weeks ago. 'I am thrilled to introduce the enchanting Alice Miracle to you all. She is the latest talent to grace the stage at The Metropole. Her voice is beyond compare, and we feel extremely lucky to have her join us. Luck being the operative word as I discovered her quite by accident. I happened to hear her sing in the garden of a hotel I stayed at in North Wales. I was captivated and hired her immediately.'

When Mr Newman was asked about the name 'Alice Miracle', he explained where it came from.

'I asked this young lady her name, and she said Liz, but I mistook it for Alice, being unfamiliar with her accent. We laughed about it, but I decided there and then she was to be known as Alice. The 'Miracle' part came from the way I discovered her. Finding her was like finding a miracle.'

'Wow! So *that's* how she got that name!' exclaimed Mel.

'I've got to say, Mel, as good as you lot are in this detective work, I didn't think you'd ever find out how she got that stage name,' said John.

CHAPTER FORTY-ONE

'Me neither. And we also now have a photo of the formidable Reginald, too,' said Mel as she put the article gently back in the box. As she did so she noticed there was a card inside the box addressed to her. She opened the envelope and read the card aloud.

My Dearest Mel,

I do hope you like the photos enclosed. They show our loved ones together, and I wanted to share that with you.

I am so looking forward to seeing you and your friends again soon. I suspect we both have more to share.

Have the most magical Christmas and a blessed New Year.

With love,

Alton

X

I'm looking forward to seeing you again too, thought Mel warmly. She felt an inexplicable bond with Alton and she couldn't wait for his visit.

After all the presents were put into tidy piles and the wrapping debris cleared, they all settled down for some late afternoon festive viewing. Mel, who was sitting on the sofa next to Kev, felt happy. Her dad sat on the chair next to her, chuckling away to a rerun of *Gavin and Stacey*. Dougie was in the chair next to Kev.

'How about a Baileys coffee, little one?' asked John. 'I could murder a hot drink.'

'Great idea, Pops. I'll go and do it now. Fancy a mince pie with that?' Mel asked.

'Bloody hell no, I'm stuffed to the rafters. Seriously, I couldn't eat another thing. The way I feel right now, I'm not sure I'll manage breakfast!' said John, patting his stomach. 'Oh, go on then, you've twisted my arm. I'll just have the one; it's a shame to waste them. Maybe we could crack open the Quality Street and the After Eights as well.'

Mel smiled and shook her head. Where food was concerned, her dad was like the child in the Bisto advert from the eighties. *The way to that man's heart was through his stomach for sure*, thought Mel.

'I'll give you a hand,' offered Kev, following Mel into the kitchen.

Mel poured milk into a pan and onto the stove to boil. Kev filled the kettle and flicked on the switch. Mel handed him the new bottle of Baileys to open while she put some mince pies on a plate and into the microwave for a minute.

'Thanks so much for having us for dinner today, Mel. I'm having the best Christmas I could have hoped for, and not just because you're a fabulous cook.'

'I'm having a great day, too, and I'm so glad you both joined us.' Looking directly into Kev's eyes, she wasn't sure if it was the wine or finding out more about her nan, but Mel felt a bit brave. Her look was intentionally meaningful, and she knew Kev had noticed.

CHAPTER FORTY-ONE

'Hey, you two, *Elf* is about to start after the adverts, so hurry up,' shouted Dougie from the lounge, interrupting the moment.

They did as they were told and rushed to make the drinks so as not to miss the start with Kev playing waiter, darting between the lounge and kitchen. Alcohol-laced coffee and mince pies all around, apart from Mel, who had a hot chocolate instead. Despite them all having seen it several times before, there were plenty bursts of laughter throughout the film that disturbed Dougie when he sporadically dozed off. Of course, he denied he had been asleep despite the low and suspiciously snore-like rumbling sounds coming from his direction. Kev had put a blanket over his dad's legs, and he remained blissfully unaware.

The end of the film came at the right time for John and Dougie to make a move home. Kev made the excuse of wanting to take some presents home so he could make sure Dougie got in safely.

'Well, my wee darling, you pulled out all the stops today. I think this year has been the best yet,' said Dougie before giving Mel a big cwtch. 'Thank you for looking after us so well, love.'

'I've loved every second, Dougie, and you're always welcome here, you know that.'

'John, you cheating old bugger. I'd like to say it's been a pleasure spending Christmas with you again, but I'm an honest man. I had hoped to spend it with Joanna Lumley, so you were a bit of a letdown.' Dougie held out his hand to his old friend, who naturally feigned offence. They both wished each other a nice night before Dougie left with Kev. As Kev hadn't said goodnight, Mel assumed he would pop back in once his dad was in and settled.

'What a lovely day we've all had thanks to you, Mel. Thank you for everything, love. You put so much effort into making sure we're well-fed and well-looked-after. Your mam and nan would be so proud of you,' said John, wrapping his arm around her shoulder.

'Ah, thanks, Dad. It's been my pleasure. I've had a great day, too,' she said before planting a kiss on his cheek. 'I'm going to walk over to your house with you. I can help you carry some of your presents.'

John was about to protest but was cut off by Kev, who had just reappeared.

'Mind if I tag along? I could do with stretching my legs and walking off some of the mountain of food I've eaten today.'

Mel answered for them both and said he was most welcome to join them. All bundled up with scarves and hats, they stepped into the frosty air. It was a clear night, and the stars seemed particularly sparkly, as did the pavements that looked like they'd been sprinkled with glitter. After a fifteen-or-so-minute walk that was far from rushed, they arrived at John's door. They followed in behind him and put his presents on his kitchen table. After making sure he was settled, Mel gave her dad a final kiss, and Kev shook his hand before bringing him in for a one-armed man-cwtch.

CHAPTER FORTY-ONE

'Take care going home, you two, and thanks again for a lovely day,' said John, waving at them until they were out of sight.

Kev offered Mel his arm as they made their way home through the empty streets.

'Snow! Look!' said Mel excitedly, her voice about two octaves above its usual pitch.

'Oh wow! You're right, it's *almost* a white Christmas!' exclaimed Kev.

For the rest of their walk back to the close, the most delicate, tiny flakes of snow silently drifted down. Mel couldn't have wished for or scripted a more perfect end to the day if she'd tried.

'One more Baileys?' suggested Mel as they arrived back at Harlech Clos

Chapter Forty-Two

When Mel woke, she looked at her phone not just to check what time it was but what *day* it was. Twixmas, that hazy period of confusion between Christmas and New Year, was a strange time when nothing seemed quite normal. The past few days had been great, though, and Mel certainly wasn't complaining. She had spent a lot of time with Kev and Liv, separately and collectively. They had partaken in a couple of walks in the hope of not seizing up completely, but the majority of time was spent on the sofa watching festive films or playing board games in their onesies. They had lived every second of the eat, drink, and be merry philosophy and had a thoroughly good time doing it. Jeff and Tony were doing the rounds visiting family and friends so had been absent for a few days. Today Kev was taking Dougie to visit some relatives. Liv had gone to Cardiff to have a look around the shops. Mel decided to take full advantage of her time alone and caught up on the chores that had been largely overlooked for the past four or five days. She went to the high street to pick up some groceries, enjoying being out in the fresh air and sunshine. It felt odd being on her own after such an intense period of socialising. After picking up a mixture of essentials and treats, she went back home to do some boring but required tasks like laundry and

CHAPTER FORTY-TWO

cleaning. It didn't take too long, and soon enough she was sitting at her kitchen table with a cuppa, wondering what to do with the rest of her day. The following evening was New Year's Eve, and she was meeting Kev, Liv, Jeff, and Tony at the Red Lion for the night. Jeff had booked a table, which was fortunate as the event was now sold out. Mel decided she would go and get her dress ready and choose her accessories just as soon as she had finished her tea. That thought was put on hold as she heard her mobile sing out 'Dusted' by Belly. She often changed the ringtone on her phone, and this track never failed to make her toes tap. It was Cat.

'Hello, my lovely. Happy New Year's Eve, Eve to you! How are you and how was Christmas?' said Mel.

'Happy New Year's Eve, Eve to you too, pet. Things have been quite canny, to be honest. Christmas was quiet but nice, just me and Mike. We haven't done a lot. It's been Baltic out there, so I've been glued to my settee and hot water bottle.'

'We've only gone out a couple of times to stretch our legs too. It's so bloody hard getting out of your pyjamas, isn't it? Is Mike with you, love?'

'No, he's out. It's his second meet-up with his daughter, Samantha. He was absolutely petrified the first time, but he seems more excited than scared today.'

'How are you feeling about it all now, darling?' asked Mel gingerly.

'Not so bad today, but it did feel weird the first time. Mike going to see his ex and the child they share was never going to be an easy thing for me exactly, was it? I got through it, and that's as much as I can say about it. Mike has done well to not go on about it too much, and I'm trying my best to support him. I think only time will tell how we go from here.'

'One step at a time, that's all you can do, love. What are your plans for tomorrow?'

'Hang on a second. When you mentioned going for a walk, you said "we". Has Liv moved into my room already, or is there something I've missed?'

'Ha-ha, no, Liv is still living at number four. It doesn't seem like you need "your" room now, though. I have seen Liv a few times, but I've been spending a lot of time with my next-door neighbour too. Liv seems to think he has a little soft spot for me. I'm not so sure. He's had a few opportunities but never made a move. It's probably all in Liv's imagination.'

'It sounds like you might be disappointed that he's not asked you out. I have to say, pet, it's quite the age gap between you and Dougie but you can't help who you fall for, eh?'

Mel nearly spat out the last mouthful of her tea, and it sparked off a mixture of coughing and laughing.

'Don't be so bloody daft! Dougie's old enough to be my dad,' said Mel, regaining her composure. 'I meant his son, Kev.'

'*Oh*, I'm kinda pleased about that! That it's not Dougie, I mean.' The relief in Cat's laugh was obvious and

CHAPTER FORTY-TWO

made Mel laugh too. 'Didn't Kev move to New Zealand? I didn't realise he was home for Christmas.'

'Close, it was Australia. He isn't back for Christmas; he's back for good. He's looking for work next month and house hunting soon after. He wants to be around for his dad.'

'If Liv is right, then maybe before long he'll want to stick around for more than just his dad.'

'Anyway, what are you and Mike doing tomorrow?' asked Mel, wanting to change the subject and feeling aware that she'd probably said too much.

'It'll be a quiet one tomorrow because I bought Mike tickets to see some bands at an all-day event on New Year's Day. On the subject of tickets, thanks so much for the Amy Wadge ticket. I think that may be my favourite Christmas present this year! What are you up to tomorrow, pet?'

'It will be a noisy alcohol-fuelled night at the Red Lion then back to Jeff and Tony's for an after-party. My poor liver!' Mel groaned.

'Sounds good to me! Have a great time, Mel, and thanks again for being there for me these past few weeks and well…always, really! Happy New Year, pet. I hope it's a canny one.'

'Happy New Year to you, too, Cat. I hope it's your best yet.'

Chapter Forty-Three

The party at the Red Lion was already in full swing by the time they all got there at just after eight o'clock. The music met them on the pavement before they'd even set foot inside. Tonight was a little different from their usual nights there; it was table service only. The owner's daughter, Kirsty, came straight over and informed them she would be looking after them. It took three attempts for her to be heard above an eighties classic played at full volume and the spontaneously erupting racket coming from the table next to them who were enthusiastically playing a drinking game. Feeling the need to catch up quickly to match the mood of the rest of the pub, they ordered a round of double gin and tonics and a couple of bottles of Prosecco to kick things off.

Drinks flowed all night thanks to the lovely Kirsty, and it wasn't long before the five were up and dancing. The DJ didn't miss a beat and kept the crowd on the dancefloor and in the palm of his hand. He played iconic tunes from some of the finest artists of the era. Mel was having a great time, soaking up the atmosphere of everyone enjoying themselves, singing along to the soundtrack of their youth, and dancing as though nobody was watching. Jeff unleashed his signature move, the robot, as the DJ

CHAPTER FORTY-THREE

played 'Don't Go' by Yazoo. Meanwhile, a horrified Tony turned his back on the love of his life and danced with Liv instead, choosing to totally ignore his soulmate and the passive-aggressive pleas from Alison Moyet.

Despite all having had a blast, by the time midnight was fast approaching all five were looking forward to heading to Jeff and Tony's for a more relaxing end to their night. They ordered a final bottle of Prosecco to toast the new year. Mel took photos on her phone and the four obliged her with a variety of daft poses. One of the revellers from the next table snapped a couple of shots of all five of them together. The volume got turned down a notch or two as the DJ requested that someone open the back door of the pub as well as the large double doors at the front. As was the tradition in their village, at the stroke of midnight the front and back doors of every house and bar should be open, one to see out the old year and the other to welcome in the new.

'Okay, everybody, charge your glasses and get ready to kiss someone you love or someone you like. Failing that, come up here and kiss me instead! We hope you've had a great night here with us tonight. We've loved having you; you've been brilliant, absolutely brilliant. Now, let's welcome in the new year Red Lion-style, shall we? Ten... nine...eight...seven...six...five...four...three...two... one...Happy New Year! Happy New Year, everybody!'

Kev went straight to Mel and kissed her on the cheek. He barely had enough time to wish her a Happy New Year before being grabbed by Jeff, who gave him an enthusiastic cwtch. All five went from one to the other in turn. All around them, the explosive sound of party poppers erupting and balloons being burst just added to the happy, retro vibe of the night. The opening bars of 'Auld Lang Syne' started and on cue, all five crossed arms, joined hands, and started singing along with everyone else in the pub. While being vigorously shaken by Liv to her left and Jeff to her right, Mel absorbed every second. Kev barely took his eyes off her and this time she did notice.

As they stepped out into the frosty night air, all struggled to speak without squeaking a little. A fabulous night of singing, laughing, and shouting to be heard over the music had clearly taken its toll. The five of them linked arms and attempted to recreate the famous film scene where Dorothy decided that she and her friends were off to see the wizard. It gave Mel the giggles which in turn set the rest of them off. By the time they got to Jeff and Tony's, they were struggling for breath and wiping away tears without knowing exactly what had started it.

They almost fell through the door at Jeff and Tony's. Their place looked dazzling, bedecked in the most tasteful, sparkly Christmas decorations. Tony went to put some music on as he had already compiled a playlist especially. Jeff was in the large open-plan kitchen popping a bottle of something fizzy. He busily filled glasses while Tony took coats and popped them on hooks by the front door.

'Come on, you lot, don't be shy. Grab a glass and get yourself a plate. The buffet is open!' said Jeff with a flourish, waving his arm in the direction of a dining table laden with food and almost knocking over the first empty bottle of the night in the process. He and Tony did a few

CHAPTER FORTY-THREE

relays between the fridge and the island in the centre of the kitchen to bring out the chilled goodies.

'I bloody love you two. This looks amazing. Thanks, both,' said Liv, her two hands forming a heart.

'We love you too, Liv. We were saying earlier just how lucky we are to know such amazing people. Here's to lifelong friendships and many more magical adventures together!' Jeff raised his glass to the group, who joined in toasting and celebrating each other.

'Speaking of magical adventures, there's something I want to tell you all. This is the first time we've all been together since Christmas, and I wanted to tell you in person. I had two surprise packages arrive on Christmas Eve. The first was from Dennis at The Metropole. He sent me two beautiful champagne saucers with the Metropole logo on it. They're antiques and were in use when my nan was there. The second parcel was from Alton, and it contained mainly postcards and photographs that I'll show you the next time we meet. There was also a cutting from a newspaper containing an interview with Reginald Newman about my nan's appointment at The Metropole. In it he explains why she's called Alice Miracle.'

There were gasps from Liv, Jeff, and Tony.

'You. Are. Kidding!' said Liv dramatically.

'So…tell us everything!' said Jeff.

'Apparently, when Reginald met Liz, he misheard what she said her name was because of her accent. He thought she said "Alice". The "Miracle" part was him thinking it was miraculous that he discovered her quite by accident as she was singing to herself in the garden of a hotel she worked at. He just happened to be staying there and after hearing her voice he hired her on the spot!'

'That's amazing, Mel. I never thought we'd find that piece of the puzzle,' said Tony.

'Thanks to Alton, we have. To Alton!' Kev raised his glass and was joined by the other four. 'Actually, I don't want to just toast Alton. I want to say thank you to you all for the way you've welcomed me into your little gang. I wasn't sure what life here would be like after being away for so long and you all have made it fantastic. It's like I never went away, but better. I knew that coming home was the right thing for me to do for my dad, but now I know it was the right thing to do for me too. The past few weeks have been brilliant and I'm looking forward to seeing what we get up to this year. So, I wanted to thank you all for taking me under your wing, but especially to you, Mel. From the first day I arrived back you've been amazing.'

Kev paused, raised his glass, and toasted his friends, the Miss Marple wannabes, but his eyes were firmly fixed on only one of them.

After a few more drinks and snacks they decided that their beds were calling. Jeff and Tony set about making doggy bags for each of them, so they didn't have to worry about making brunch the next day. As they left Jeff and Tony's, the three took a left so that Mel and Kev could walk Liv to her door. They waited until she was safely inside before carrying on towards Mel's house.

CHAPTER FORTY-THREE

'I know it's late, but do you fancy one more drink?'

'Of course, Mel. Lead the way.'

Once inside, Mel told Kev to make himself comfortable in the lounge and he happily obliged. There were still some glowing embers in the log burner, and it cast some slow-moving flashes of warm amber light around the room. Mel walked in with a half bottle of champagne and passed it to Kev to open it while she went back to the kitchen to fetch the glasses she had been sent by Dennis. He had suggested that she use them to welcome in the new year with someone special and she had thought that to be an excellent idea. Kev had popped the cork from the champagne and put it on the mantlepiece as Mel walked in with the glasses. Kev poured a glass for Mel and handed it to her before filling his own glass.

'What a night.' Kev stretched out his long legs in front of him. 'In fact, what an amazing Christmas overall. Without you, it wouldn't have been anything as good. Thank you for making it so special, Mel,' he said, quickly followed by 'Cheers' as he and Mel clinked glasses.

'You're not the only one who's had a good time. I've really enjoyed it, and you've played a large part in that too. Whether it's been drinking champagne and dancing in Covent Garden or watching Christmas films here, it's all been…magical.'

'I have a confession to make, Mel,' said Kev, his face now more serious as he looked at her. 'The more time I've spent with you, the more I've realised I have feelings for you. I mean romantic feelings,' he said awkwardly. 'The night we went to the cinema I hoped I'd find the courage to say something or even kiss you, but I bottled it. I was afraid you might not feel the same and I would ruin a friendship. By telling you this I hope I haven't done that. I can blame it on the champagne, and we can forget I ever said anything.'

'What makes you think I'd want you to forget you said it?' said Mel, looking into Kev's eyes and holding his gaze. All the thoughts she'd had recently about taking chances in life came crashing down around her. Some things were worth taking a chance on. Some *people* were worth taking a chance on.

'Does that mean I can take you out on a date?' he asked with a shy smile.

'We've made some lovely memories these past few weeks and I'd like to make some more. I'd love to go out on a date with you, Kev.'

Kev leaned down and kissed Mel gently on the lips. There had been many times over the years that they had both wanted this to happen and now finally it had, and it had been worth the wait. As she lay her head on Kev's chest, wrapped up in his arms, she thought, *I'm ready for my own North Star.*

ACKNOWLEDGEMENTS

Hello, lovely reader! I'd like to start by saying thank you so very much for choosing to read my debut novel. It genuinely means the world to me. I hope you enjoyed sharing Mel's journey and becoming part of her gang for a little while.

Finding A Miracle was inspired by, but not based on, my own family history research which I began back in October 2020. Like Mel, I was lucky enough to discover some colourful characters concealed among my ancestors too. I unearthed a Tiller Girl, a playwright, an author, a silent movie actor, a theatre manager, a bank robber, and even a Star Wars stuntman! It was quite a surprise to find out that members of my family had trod the boards of the magnificent Lyceum Theatre in London. Finding out about them and their lives was, without doubt, one of the best things I've ever done. I shall be forever grateful to the family I wish I could have met and those who helped me discover them, especially Denise and Tracey.

On the subject of gratitude, I would like to say thank you to some people, if I may. Firstly, my fabulous developmental editor Katie Seaman, whose suggestions and encouragement were invaluable. To my copy editor, Julia King, for expertly guiding me and making sure my i's were dotted, and my t's were crossed.

My love and appreciation to my early proofreaders, particularly Bambi and Janette, whose wonderfully detailed feedback and gentle bullying for the next chapter spurred me on no end! To my amazing cousin Denise, who read my book in a day - thank you for everything, Marpsy. My love and thanks to Kitty for your seal of approval - always yours, my FF.

I've been so lucky to have been supported and inspired by many friends, family and loved ones who regularly asked for updates on how the book was going. My love and thanks to Andrea, Julie, Sproutie, Ami, Ali, Mark, Eleri, Becca, Colin, Clare, Kirsty, Claire, Lydia, Jeff, Sam, Sue, Jo, Simon and Dave. It can be a pretty isolating experience writing a book and so I appreciate you for encouraging me and having the belief I would finish it, particularly on the (many) days I doubted myself!

A special mention to two fabulous women who are no longer with us. My lovely Nan, who regularly read to me and made up bedtime stories for me as a child. Liv, your light shines on yaya sister.

When I think of those who supported me in life, without question, the first person that comes to mind is my late mother. Her unconditional love lives on in everything I do, and I miss her every day. I hope wherever she is, I've made her proud.

Love to my Dad for his unwavering faith in me, no matter what I do. Finding his biological family was the catalyst for my ancestor research. He's also the inspiration for John - but don't tell him, it's a secret!

Finally, my biggest thank you goes to Stu. My husband, my rock, my missing jigsaw piece, and my absolute best friend. Without you, nothing would be as good or as much fun. You truly are my North Star.

Thanks again, lovely reader for taking a chance on my book. I am so grateful you did. If you would like to leave a review online somewhere, that would be brilliant. Reviews are so important, especially for new authors. Thank you in advance!

I'm on social media, so don't be shy; I'm always up for a chat.

Until next time…

Love, love, love,

Deb

Printed in Great Britain
by Amazon